OATH
OF
FIRE

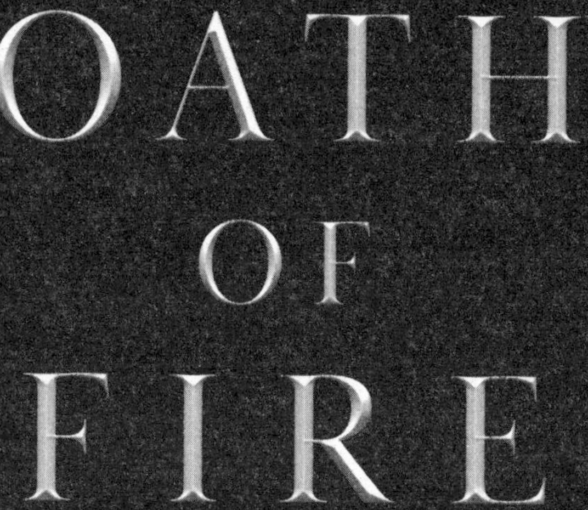

K ARSENAULT
RIVERA

FOREVER

NEW YORK BOSTON

Forever
Hachette Book Group
1290 Avenue of the Americas, New York, NY 10104
read-forever.com
@readforeverpub

First Edition: August 2024

Library of Congress Cataloging-in-Publication Data

Names: Rivera, K Arsenault, author.
Title: Oath of fire / K Arsenault Rivera.
Description: First edition. | New York : Forever, 2024.
Identifiers: LCCN 2023056635 | ISBN 9781538756720 (trade paperback) | ISBN 9781538756737 (ebook)
Subjects: LCGFT: Fantasy fiction. | Lesbian fiction. | Novels.
Classification: LCC PS3618.I8465 O28 2024 | DDC 813/.6—dc23 /eng/20231228
LC record available at https://lccn.loc.gov/2023056635

ISBNs: 9781538756720 (trade paperback), 9781538756737 (ebook)

Printed in the United States of America

CW

10 9 8 7 6 5 4 3 2 1

For the other sapphics who spent too much time reading Greek myths as children

Chapter One

If flames shot down from the sky and anchored themselves in the streets of New York City, Psyche couldn't imagine it would get any hotter. So far as she was concerned, her morning transfer at Herald Square meant running across the molten surface of Venus. But she—brave, curious Psyche—perseveres. At the end of this trip, there are people who need her.

The train, when it arrives, offers her little in the way of comfort. The AC inside is on full blast—but there are dozens packed shoulder to shoulder in the confines of the car. She hardly has room to breathe.

It reminds her of Calhoun's rat city experiments, which generally found that urban areas were inclined to be awful and degenerate by nature. But to Psyche that couldn't be more wrong. However bad morning trains can be, there are always good things to see, too. People giving up their seats for others who need them. Students talking about their classes and their vibrant lives. A woman shouting on the phone is trying to plan a meetup for her mother's birthday, but her siblings can't hear her over the din of the crowd. Psyche catches sight of a couple snuggled up together in last night's rumpled cocktail dresses, and she suppresses a pang of longing.

Yes, there are beautiful things in cities. Things worth protecting.

The walk uptown only makes it clearer to her. Despite the heat there are drummers out beating a rhythm for everyone to enjoy, the clatter of change in their upturned drum cases the only interruption. A runner jogs along the street with his great big Shiba running after him. Construction workers huddle and gossip.

Of course, the runner nearly bowls her over and the construction workers catcall her, but... there's always good and bad. And after five years of living here, she's prepared to accept the city's flaws along with its benefits. A half decade can endear you to a place.

Humming along to the Kacey Musgraves song playing in her earbuds, Psyche checks her phone. Fifteen emails—mostly spammy notifications from this or that site, but there are a couple of session cancellations and reschedules. There always are. She tries not to think of them as lost money but as opportunities to catch up on her work for other clients. Maybe she can watch a little of that *Jujutsu Kaisen* show Alex is always talking about; she seems to project a lot of her problems onto the characters.

But emails aren't the only thing to tend to. She's got well over a hundred notifications from her other followers, too. Mostly comments on her last Instagram posts.

Lovelovelove this layout! Where did you get those stickers? What markers are those?

Your handwritinggggg! It's giving Victorian diary!

Any tea on Laura and Mike?

👀 It's been like two months since you had a date girl what is going ON?

Your hands are as beautiful as ever. My first wife had hands just like this. Long, slender fingers. She used to massage…

Psyche winces. Most of the time her followers were nice people who liked looking at her planners or commenting on her selfies. But sometimes they were…weird. Parasocial relationships allowed people enough of a disconnect to imagine they could say anything at all to her, and they often did. Her older sister, Laura, was a professional influencer—but every other photo she posted included her husband, Mike. She did it to keep the creeps away.

The best Psyche could do was keep her face out of it unless she was posting with her cat. Yet that didn't do much to stave them off. Every day her mentions are flooded with thirsty suitors of all kinds, shooting their shots.

Maybe she should just get rid of her account.

No, no, she can't—for every one thirsty comment, there are three people who enjoy the advice she posts, or her live AMAs. She can't just abandon her regulars. No matter how annoying everyone else can be.

But for now she tucks her phone back into her pocket and

opens the door to the office. There, behind the reception desk, is Jiyoung. But something's off. Instead of her usual bright smile, she offers Psyche only a curt nod.

"Morning," Psyche says. She picks up a Hi-Chew from Jiyoung's candy bowl. Something about them always leaves her feeling better than if she'd grabbed a Kit Kat. "Rough night?"

"Uh." Jiyoung's rapid typing stops. "No, uh. Streamed some movies, you know the deal. Pretty regular."

"What'd you watch?" Psyche asks.

There—Jiyoung's sly smile returns. After glancing to make sure Dr. Kaminsky isn't around to hear, she leans forward. "*Requiescat.*"

Psyche hops in excitement. "No way. That's out already? How's Miss Flo?"

"She's awesome. It's like *Lady Macbeth* meets *Hereditary*. And don't even get me started on Paul Mescal, he's so good in this, and—"

"Don't spoil it!" Psyche says, waving an eager hand. "Bondi made me promise we'd watch it together after my *Crystal Dragon* raid this week and if I cheat, she's gonna kill me."

Jiyoung waggles her eyebrows. "Bondi, huh? This a date?"

"No, nothing like that. She's my best friend," Psyche says. She leaves out that she and Bondi have never actually met in real life. "Anyway, let's talk more about it next week."

The glee that had come into Jiyoung's face flickers and there's a tremor in her voice. "Yeah. Next week. See you, Psy."

There's a certain tingle at the back of Psyche's head—one she often felt as a child. Whenever Laura had chucked Cid's toys out the window, or whenever Cid had thrown Laura's expensive sweaters into the washer to shrink them, she'd feel it. Whenever her father received a new post and they needed to move again—she'd get that tingle and know before he told them. And when her mother got sick, well...

But it couldn't be anything too bad, right? Five whole years in New York this week, and one year working for Dr. Kaminsky. Sure, it's hot now, but it'd be nice and cool when she gets out at night. She brought a salad with her favorite homemade vinaigrette for lunch; she has a movie to look forward to. Everything is going to be all right.

Everything is stable.

She says it over and over as she boards the elevator: *Everything is going to be okay.*

Photos of Psyche's Maine coon, Latte, decorate her cubicle. Potted plants lend it some semblance of life. She read somewhere that you think better if you have plants around you. The truth of that remains to be seen, but they do make her feel better, and that counts for a lot.

Yet the moment her butt touches the cushion, her phone rings. A jolt of shame runs through her. Psyche looks around the room one more time. No witnesses. Probably just a client, right...?

The caller ID says otherwise. Dr. Kaminsky? That guy never comes in before noon. Psyche always comes in around eight so she can leave an hour early.

There it is again: that awful tingling in the back of her head. He wants to fire her, doesn't he? Like her last couple of bosses. Maybe he couldn't stand her. She hadn't bothered to explain the two-year gap in her résumé when he hired her, and her grades never really recovered after all the hospital stuff. Plenty of other therapists were way more qualified, and maybe he'd known that the whole time, maybe the only reason he'd hired her at all was that he was Mike's dad, which technically made him her…what do you call your brother-in-law's dad, anyway?

No, no. She's catastrophizing.

Psyche takes a breath. Maybe he's in for a good reason. What's a good reason to be in so early? Maybe he and Mike are meeting up later and that's why he wants to be done with work sooner. Wouldn't that be nice? A little father-son trip through the city to do whatever rich people do with their time.

Hold on to that idea. Let it become the truth, and let the disaster slip away. Psyche takes two breaths and picks up the phone.

"Good morning, Dr. Kaminsky! I hope—"

"Can you come to my office please, Ms. Dimitriou? We need to talk."

Oh.

Oh fuck.

The tips of her fingers go cold. She swallows. "Of course," she says. It's all she can bring herself to say without her voice cracking. She doesn't even bother saying goodbye; she just hangs up and stands.

Deep breaths. Deep breaths. He might have caught her peeking. Maybe it's a small reprimand? Maybe…

God, this sort of thing never happened to Laura. Even Cid just stayed home playing games all day to make money. Why's she always the one who messes things up?

Every step toward Dr. Kaminsky's office is filled with more dread than the last. By the time she turns the doorknob, it's a wonder she has any strength left at all.

Dr. James Kaminsky sits behind his desk. The tailored suit and slicked-back gray hair don't exactly scream therapist—but then again he doesn't spend much time in the office. Still, the photos and awards on the wall speak to a long and successful career. In one, placed right on his desk, the good doctor poses with his son Mike and Laura on their wedding day.

Psyche's in that photo. The full version, anyway. In the one on Dr. Kaminsky's desk, she's been cropped out.

Not that she noticed or anything.

Dr. Kaminsky gestures for her to sit without so much as a good morning wave. "We have a lot to discuss."

"So early?" Psyche says. To her shame she can't keep her anxiety from reaching her voice. "Did something happen with a patient?"

"You could say that." He hits the intercom button on his phone. "Jiyoung, could you send Kate into my office?"

Jiyoung says she's already on the way.

Which is bad, because Kate's the practice's lawyer.

At that moment Psyche wants nothing more than to sink through the floor. Where would she end up if she did? The finance firm the floor beneath them, probably. She's never liked finance bros, but maybe she could hide out there for a while. Find a spacious broom closet and disappear. Turn off her phone and just... not exist.

But life so rarely allows for miracles; Psyche's least of all. Kate comes in only a couple of seconds later with two coffees in hand. She sets one on Dr. Kaminsky's desk. He picks it up and takes a sip, nods, then sets the cup back down.

"Ms. Dimitriou," Dr. Kaminsky starts. "You've been with us nearly a year now, haven't you?"

"A year and two days," Psyche corrects.

"Right. About a year. And prior to that you worked for..."

"Six practices in three years," Kate reads from a folder.

The urge to argue, to point out that some of those times she got fired were really unfair, is strong. She swallows it down. Psyche's well aware of how it looks.

"That's right," she says. "I'm grateful you've put so much faith in me. I feel like I'm really starting to flourish here."

"We're happy to hear that," he says. "Your sister's always spoken very highly of you. Your... crisis management skills, especially."

She's shocked to hear that Laura's acknowledged her skills at all. She squeezes her fidgeting hands and breaks eye contact.

"I, um. I've had a lot of practice," Psyche says.

People don't like to hear about what that kind of practice entailed. They don't ever like to hear about that.

"That's why we're so puzzled about this turn of events. It isn't like you, and it's certainly not like the woman we heard so much about," says Kaminsky. He gestures to Kate.

"Ms. Dimitriou," Kate says, keeping her voice so gentle

that the knife of anxiety is all Psyche feels, "we received a complaint three days ago. Due to its severity, we took a little time to investigate the claims behind it, and we've found them to have merit."

"A complaint?" Psyche says. "I . . . About me?"

"I'm afraid so. Does the name Alex Lot ring any bells?"

No. Oh, no. Psyche bites the inside of her mouth to keep from throwing up. Alex is one of her favorite clients. What could possibly be the problem?

"Yes," she says. "We have an appointment later today, actually. She's made a lot of progress. I mean, her panic attacks are down to maybe once a week, and I think she'll be ready to come out soon—"

"It's about that," says Kate. From the folder, she pulls a small stack of white papers, stapled together, and hands them over.

Emails, Psyche realizes. The ones between her and Alex's parents discussing her transition. They've known for a long time, even though Alex hasn't felt comfortable enough to tell them. Part of the reason they signed her up for therapy here. They wanted to make sure she was in a healthy place. Planning a family getaway where they could safely talk about Alex's feelings on the matter and let her know how much they cared, asking for resources . . .

"I don't understand," she says. "What's the matter? Alex's parents are really supportive of her—"

"But Alex didn't tell her parents, did she?" Kate says.

Silence in the room.

Like weeds, responses grow in Psyche's head. *It's more*

complicated than that, she thinks, or *I didn't exactly tell them.* But what's the right thing to say? Her heart's hammering so hard she can't hear herself think.

"I... I understand that it looks like I violated Alex's confidence," she says. "But I'm telling you that I didn't. I never told them anything about our sessions. I just wanted to provide them with the resources they needed and requested."

Kaminsky frowns. He takes a breath. "Psyche, if you were Alex and you read those emails, what would you think?"

Once more she looks them over.

> Hi Mr. Lot,
>
> I'd be happy to help facilitate a discussion with Alex about all this once she's comfortable. Your daughter's very bright...

"I'd be... I'd be happy, I think? A little surprised, but happy to know my parents wanted to talk with me," she says. "Isn't that what everyone wants? People around them who care?"

"Some people," says Kate, "value their privacy more than that. And Alex happens to be one of them."

She hands over another sheet. On it: a screen cap of a review from their practice's web page of testimonials, along with an email. Both are from Alex and say nearly the same thing.

> How do you live with yourselves knowing you employ a transphobic therapist? Psyche Dimitriou outed me to my family before I was ready to talk with them.

Two sentences—each an arrowhead in Psyche's chest. The fields of the dead are not colder than the chill that overcomes her.

"Alex sent us the emails. She seems to have seen them on her mother's iPad, which was still synced when one came in. As you can see, the comment's already gotten a fair bit of attention."

The screen cap shows the review has hundreds of upvotes and a comment thread dozens of posts long. Psyche doesn't even want to imagine what's inside that.

"In this life, sometimes we have to make difficult decisions. Do I think you meant to cause any trouble? No. But it does look bad for us. Catastrophically bad. Our clients pay us what they do because of our outstanding discretion."

Kaminsky's right. His firm's clients are mostly rich folks and their teens. Psyche works primarily with the smaller clientele of kids who wouldn't be able to afford this care if not for city grants and assistance programs.

Every day she's come to work proud to be helping people who need her.

She might not have that anymore.

Alex really posted that, didn't she? God, she must be hurting. If Psyche could just explain...

The words come. The inevitable words, the scissors that sever the thread of her fate. Knowing what they will be does not lessen their hurt.

"We're going to have to let you go."

Chapter Two

Few things in life are as pure, as unadulterated, as natural as a cat's affectionate disregard. When Psyche returns home—all her posters and photos and files in a plain cardboard box—her cat does not bound up to the door to greet her. Oh no. Latte has more important things to do. Staring daggers at the birds perched on the fire escape, for instance.

Psyche sets her box down on her kitchen counter. Tomorrow she'll sort through them and figure out what she wants to keep—but today it's all too painful. God, she's going to have to send so many emails. Reschedule things for her clients. Make sure they're in good hands.

And that's if anyone wants to hear from her again now that Alex's post is all over the internet.

Psyche groans. Thoughts swirl faster and faster, catching her in a vortex of shame and guilt.

What is she going to do?

Psyche scoops up Latte from her perch. Outside, the birds

scatter. Only a single dove remains. Pale brown, with white tips, and a stare as intense as the one Latte has for it in turn.

She tries to hold her cat tight.

But a cat will always have ideas of its own—and Latte scampers out of her grip to stand once more at the window.

Loneliness is not new to Psyche. Far from it. Loneliness has stalked her all her life. While her sisters fought and Psyche had to mediate, it watched and waited for her. In the hospital she felt it at her side when her mother slept. And now?

In the time she's lived in New York she's had company only twice. One of those was a visit from Laura.

It was the unbearable weight of loneliness's regard that compelled her to adopt a cat. And it isn't as if she doesn't have any friends. Her *Crystal Dragon Knight XIV* raid group meets every other night, pretty much. Whenever they aren't beating up enemies in the game, they're usually hanging out on one of their chat servers, streaming movies, or playing party games. It's fun. When she's with her internet friends, she doesn't have to worry about what they think of her. She isn't Psyche, Laura's little sister, or Psyche, Cid's older sister.

She's just Psyche.

A jobless, lonely Psyche—but Psyche nonetheless.

She doesn't bother with any of the "productive" things one might do for their grief. Journaling is no comfort when she knows full well what she feels about this already; there's no use talking it out with Latte when Latte doesn't want to pay attention.

Instead she picks up a glass of the mead Laura sent her, heats up some day-old halal food, and sits in front of her computer. With her phone chucked halfway across the room, she won't get any social media notifications—only the messages from her raid group.

And there are plenty of those.

Scrolling through the group chat makes it easier to forget her situation. So she won't have a job tomorrow—there will still be things the group needs her to do in game. Materials to gather, quests to run.

She can still help here without hurting anyone.

So she does. She logs in. Whom to play today? She has two characters leveled up: a gothy, pale dragoon straight out of *Castlevania*, and a cute little black mage with a big hat and bigger damage numbers. Does she want to face off with a big spear and do flips, or does she want to blow things up...?

Taking a sip of the mead, Psyche picks the mage.

She only makes it a few in-game feet before she gets a call that brings a smile to her salt-streaked face.

"If it isn't my favorite little ankle breaker. How's it going?"

Bondi's voice comes through in a thick Australian drawl. Psyche's best friend is awake at four in the morning just as she always is. Bondi's chronic insomnia and Psyche's inability to put a game down once she's started it mean they've spent an awful lot of time together. She's the only one who knows Psyche's real name in the whole group. Bondi's character, an eight-foot-tall elf built like a linebacker, has always loomed over Psyche's black mage.

"There's no way you're that tall in real life," Psyche says—not for the first time.

Bondi scoffs. "Why don't you try me? The drop bears will tear you apart before you have any chance of reaching me. They're vicious creatures, Psy. Do you have any idea how many people die to drop bears every year?"

"You tell me every time it comes up," Psyche says.

"And you never believe me! Would a wilderness guide lie, Psyche? Would she go on the internet and tell *lies* to her *mates*?"

Despite herself and despite the situation, Psyche finds herself laughing.

But there is a strange quality to laughter—the catharsis it brings does not care whether the tears you cry are from joy or sorrow. As Psyche laughs alone in her room, with her only company thousands of miles away, the tears that come are less about the joke and more about what she's lost. Laughter breaks into sobs, her strength leaving her like threads pulled from a doll's seams. Soon she's crumpled over the desk.

"Psyche? What's wrong, love?"

Everything, Psyche wants to say. Her job's gone. Her reputation's in tatters. Laura's probably going to call to ask what happened and berate her for fucking things up...

"Uuuuugh."

"Shit, that bad?" says Bondi. Psyche hears her shuffling in her room on the other end of the globe. "If I've got to track someone down, I will."

"Google my name right now, Bon," Psyche whimpers. "I think it's spread past just the therapy review sites now."

A moment's pause, the clatter of keycaps.

"Oh, Psy..."

"I know."

"What happened? You're not...what was all that about?"

"Alex is one of my clients. Her parents brought her in because they found a bunch of girls' clothes and makeup in her room, and they thought she might be having some issues with her gender. They wanted her to have someone to talk with about it. I mean, they're good people."

Bondi's big elf sinks down to hug Psyche's little witch.

"We kept in touch about Alex, just like I would with any client's supportive parents. I tried not to give too much away, but they already knew, Bon, so what point was there? I wanted to help them make things easier at home for her, and..."

Psyche sighs.

"She saw an email she wasn't meant to see about her and her dysphoria, and she was very upset about it. Which—well, I understand. Really I do. I mean, if it were me, then I could...I could understand, you know, being..."

Bondi's elf pats Psyche's witch on the head. In so doing the elf's hands clip through the hat, making the whole thing a little absurd.

"Psy. You don't have to go making excuses. It's okay to feel hurt."

"Not when there's a kid who's even more hurt," Psyche mumbles. "God. What am I gonna do, Bon? I fucked everything up again, and now Laura's gonna have to clean up after me, and the thought of picking up my phone makes me sick."

"Well, don't pick up your phone, then," Bondi says. "That's

the first step. Posting's the mind-killer, and it isn't going to make your situation any better."

Psyche groans.

There's a certain tone Bondi's voice takes sometimes—maybe she's leaning more into her headset—that makes it feel like she's throwing an arm around you.

"I'm serious. Let me into your Insta and I'll look after it today. Any mess comes in and I'll get rid of it. Whenever you're ready, it'll be cleaner than Blinky Bill's reputation."

Honestly, it isn't a bad idea. Psyche doesn't want to imagine what her notifications are like at this point, let alone how they're going to be for the rest of the day. And who else would she trust to do something like this but Bondi?

Control what you can, right?

Psyche lets her in.

For a little while they don't talk about it. Instead Bondi takes her to the city's hardest jumping puzzle—a series of platforms and overhangs with a treasure at the end. Navigating it requires dexterity and good reflexes; falling at any point means you have to start the whole thing over.

Two hours later Psyche's little witch has fallen well over a hundred times. Frustration and banter have distracted her from the outside world.

"You've got it this time," Bondi says. "I believe. C'mon, c'mon..."

Psyche bites her lip in focus. Only two more jumps...

"Hop... Turn, turn, turn!"

Her witch leaps, turning midway through to latch on to a floating platform and pull herself up.

"Holy shit," Psyche says. "I think this is it."

"Gotta be," Bondi agrees. "Now wait for the vine to swing back annnnnd—!"

No one could be upset watching a tiny big-hatted witch swing through the air above magical cannons on a flowering vine. And so when Psyche finally lands on the platform with the treasure chest, she not only cheers, but stands up, lifts Latte in the air, and shouts.

"There's my little shit," Bondi says. Her elf starts to dance. "Got a treat for you even better than that. You know how you've been single for—"

"Are you seriously trying to wingman me right now?" Psyche says. The absurdity of it makes her laugh. "I told you, dating is weird for me. When people find out who I'm related to—"

"Right, whatever, but check out this DM. When it comes to guys, isn't this exactly your type?"

Bondi starts sharing her screen—which is more like *their* screen, since she's on Pysche's account. The picture that comes along shuts Psyche up. Who the *fuck* could pull off an outfit like that? Ruffles and lace, in this day and age? He should look like a Renaissance fair performer, but the sculpted collarbone and sharp, refined jaw belong in a museum. A carnival-style mask conceals most of his features save for his coiffed mess of dyed-white curls. Oh, he could look like anything under there, it's true, but it takes a certain level of confidence to wear all this. And if nothing else, his lithe body, strong forearms, and elegant hands were certainly…

"How can I even tell if he's my type when he's wearing a mask?" Psyche asks.

"Are you fucking kidding me? He looks *just* like your dragoon, Psy."

Psyche flushes. Bondi's not wrong…

"He's a catfish," she counters, flushing yet more.

"I don't know, he seems legit. There's a ton of videos on his page and they all have the same guy. Or at least the same mask and the same voice. They're at these super-exclusive-looking parties."

Links follow. Psyche tabs out of her game and clicks through with eagerness. There he is, the mysterious masked man, draping himself across what looks to be a throne. A fog conceals the background, though there are two figures gyrating on either side of him. Something about their movements raises the hair at the back of her neck. It's as if she's seeing an old movie on a high-frame-rate television—it looks unnatural. Yet there's no filter listed on the video. An unfamiliar stringed instrument compels her to keep her attention on the screen, to look straight at the man on the throne.

He laughs, breezy and brash, and claps his hands.

All at once the fog blows away, revealing a speakeasy. She'd be sure that it's some kind of effect…except the hanging flower baskets behind him continue to sway in the aftermath of the sudden breeze.

And without the fog, she can get a good look at the dancers.

There are certain kinds of beauty that beggar the imagination—beauty that should not exist. To grasp a full moon's grace is to become one of the moon's own children, lost to society. Divers below the surface of the fathomless sea find themselves drawn deeper and deeper, until the air is forced from their lungs.

That is the beauty of these dancers, masked though they may be. Sitting on her sofa swathed in blankets, Psyche cannot help but stare at the curves of their bodies, the hard lines of their muscles, and the silk cords of sinew. Her perception of their gender changing every time she looks on them anew. Nature itself would stare in naked envy.

Psyche's lips part.

"This... is your invitation," says the man. What a voice—like a bell, clearing away her anxiety as he'd cleared the fog. "If you're seeing this, then you've caught our interest. Join us tonight—you'll never forget our company."

The video loops. Five, six times she watches it. What would it be like to be there with them? Oh, how shabby she'd feel in comparison, but it wouldn't be about her. To sit on that man's lap, to feel the dancers press against them from either side...

It's only Bondi's voice that breaks the spell. "I know, right?"

Psyche forces herself to close out of the video. "That wasn't even addressed to me."

"But this was."

Another video follows—the same man, the same outfit, the same bar.

"Dearest Psy, soother of souls, we are in dire need of you," says the man. She's a little ashamed at how thrilled she is to hear her nickname in that voice. "Our spirits are wounded, our hearts misshapen. My friend Eros's, most of all. But make no mistake—you are also in dire need of us. This recent… mishap has left you unmoored. Let us shelter you. For a single night, we offer peerless refuge and entertainment. Will you heed the call of those farthest removed from your world? We are eager to know."

Her hands tremble. What is this? This sort of thing doesn't happen anymore. Not outside of reality shows and weird stunts. Not to *her*. Laura, sure, or even Cid and her rabid fighting game fan base, but… a person like that, interested in her cute little self-CBT and stationery videos?

"He's got you real fucked up, huh?" comes the throaty, sleepless voice from the other end of the world.

She stops herself to take a breath. "There's no way this is anything but a scam. It's the only thing that makes sense. Maybe they dub these for lots of people, maybe they're reaching out to everyone in New York—"

"He seemed pretty specific to me," Bondi says. "What's the harm in asking for a few more details? As long as you don't sign away your credit card number, there's nothing he can do to you through a screen. And he sounds so hot, doesn't he?"

Latte stares at Psyche from her cat tower. It is the face of a cat who understands that her owner is about to sin. "He does," Psyche admits. "But, come on—a friend named Eros?"

"You're a therapist named Psyche," Bondi says. "I thought you were joking at first, too, but here we are."

Psyche picks up Latte and begins to pace. The bird outside continues watching them.

It could be nothing. It could be a scam. She runs through the list in her head. Cons: She has no idea who this guy is or what he wants. There's no way to know whether the video is genuine since it could have been pulled from someone else's account and dubbed. This might be a freaky thing. Pro: The man is hot. Very hot. He wanted help for a friend. She's good at helping friends, or at least she thinks she is. Her evening's free. And he wanted to talk with *her*, not one of her sisters.

Psyche holds up Latte. "Should I message the weird hot guy?" she asks.

Latte crawls onto her shoulder. It's as good an endorsement as a cat is likely to give.

"I mean, obviously," Bondi says. "Also, they're not ax murderers. A friend of a friend went to one of these. I saw her listed as a mutual follower of this guy, so I asked her about it. Said it was the wildest thing she'd ever seen, but everyone was suuuper strict about their rules."

"What are their rules?" Psyche says. "Do I have to get my leather corset out or something?"

"It wouldn't hurt," Bondi says. "But I don't know, she wouldn't give me the details. She sounded pretty jealous when I asked her about it. Apparently you only ever get one invitation."

A single invitation. A single chance. When Bondi put it that way—well, it didn't sound so bad. Plus if her friend had enjoyed herself, then...

"All right, I'm in. But you'll have to help me pick my outfit."

Chapter Three

This is the kinda place you wear the fanciest outfit you've got," Bondi had told her. "But like. One you don't mind getting *filthy*."

Well, Psyche has plenty of fancy outfits, thanks to Laura's couture addiction and tendency to send Psyche anything she considers "outdated."

Most of it Psyche sells at consignment shops for extra money. But some pieces she clings to, the ones that make her feel as put-together as her older sister and as confident as her younger. The chic neutral-tone turtlenecks, wool coats, and pastel blazers are her favorites.

But she can't wear her sister's calm and collected clothes to what will be, by all accounts, a total fucking rager.

Psyche grabs her stepstool.

Up on the top shelf of her closet—dusty and musty from ill-use—is a clothbound box filled with things she bought herself. When she opens it in her lap, she's hit with the syrupy-sweet smell of her old perfume: cherries, chocolate, vanilla. It still clings to the neatly folded dresses within. Bold geometric patterns in dazzling colors stand out. Part of the reason she boxed them up like this is to keep her closet looking harmonious for social media pics. The other part, well…

She picks up the first of the dresses. Gold cuts through verdant green like an arrow across a field. Radiant lines lend her curves more softness by their juxtaposition. Formfitting and sleek, it sometimes rode dangerously high when she danced. And she liked that risk.

Would she like it now? When she accepted the invitation, her new "friend" Zephyr told her to wear something that makes her feel magical.

She tries it on.

A familiar fear starts as she pulls on her stockings, as she fluffs her hair, as she lines her eyes and lips. Staring into the mirror, she sees flickers of the girls she used to comfort in nightclub bathrooms, of her one-night stands, of the person she was when last she wore any of this.

Long nights in nameless bars. Deep friendships made on stoops with people she'd never see again. Lips on hers, smiles in the dark, teeth against skin.

Can she still be that person?

The dress fits.

Just after midnight, she steps out of her Uber onto a dark East Village street strewn with trash. A wrought-iron gate stands before her, imposing, along with a crumbling art deco ceiling overhead. But thanks to Zephyr's instructions, she easily handles the lock and slips through, being sure to latch the doors again behind her.

Zephyr told her to look out for the "dancing torches," which hadn't made sense at the time. But now she sees them.

Before her is a small garden, or what might pass for one to a pyromaniac; the flowers are all flickering flame. New blossoms bloom and fall to the fiery earth in seconds.

She laughs, a little nervous. The fire garden is the brightest thing about this place. The buildings around her are all sided in black. There are no windows and only one door, at the far end of the space. Beside that there are wrought-iron benches too hot to sit on, cracked cement floors, and a ceiling that hangs like a threat.

Blood whooshes through her ears. She looks around the courtyard again and thinks, *Is this worth it?*

But just as the thought occurs to her, wind caresses her cheek. It is not the grimy-hot wind that so often tears through the streets at night, musty and damp. It is the wind that tousles flowers like a lover's hair, the wind that presses your clothes close to your body, the wind that laughs.

"Is that a new dress?"

The voice comes from everywhere and nowhere. Psyche spins around, her hands close to her chest, but sees only a shimmering haze of heat.

"It's, um, an older one actually…" she says. "Zephyr?"

"The very same," answers the wind. "Tell me, Psyche. Do you come here willingly?"

"I wouldn't be here otherwise, would I?"

The wind rises and falls, a silent laugh.

"We have our ways. Most of them are old-fashioned," says the wind. "The others you'll meet tonight don't even know what the internet *is*, you understand. But the rules are very clear—you have to be here willingly."

Another gust, another flicker of the flames, and she sees Zephyr standing before her. Did he come through a trapdoor? Was the breeze some kind of diversion? She's not sure—but the second she sees him, she knows she's in way over her head.

Firelight brings out the burnished copper of his skin. A leather mask conceals most of his face—but the grin he wears is equal parts wicked and warm. As she turns to face him, he bows, the feather on his hat bobbing along after.

"You must forgive my poor manners. It's a pleasure to meet you in person, young Psyche."

Psyche swallows and tries to mimic the motion as best she can. Video game characters always look so cool doing this sort of thing, but it's hard not to feel like a fool doing it yourself.

"It's a pleasure to meet you, too, uh, Zephyr," she says. "So this is the right place?"

He offers her an arm. "It is *almost* the right place. You will need me to go the rest of the way," he says. Next he offers her a smile. "As long as you still want to go, of course. Should you wish to remain in your own realm, you need only say the word. We are not *monsters*."

She'd shared her location with Laura, and Bondi had assured Psyche this party would be safe. Until that moment the word *monster* hadn't entered her mind. But when someone says they aren't a thing…

"Uh. I mean. I haven't done this in forever," Psyche says. "Partying, you know? And I'm still not sure why exactly you invited me, of all people. My videos aren't about…"

He takes her fingertips in his cool hand, then brushes his lips against her knuckles. She can't help noticing how soft they feel against her skin, or the thrill that runs through her.

"You have thousands of admirers," he says. "Is it so difficult to believe that we've grown enchanted with you, too? Did you not say that we should place our faith in others when they praise us?"

"Well, yes, but…"

"Have no fear. We will keep you safe."

"How do I know this isn't one big scam?" she challenged.

"A *scam*?" he says. His laugh is like the wind through the trees. "Do you think us so pedestrian? No. We do not *scam*. It would be against our nature."

That only raises more questions! Psyche can't stop herself from speaking them the second they come into her head: "What do you mean, against your nature? Why exactly am I here?"

Once more, Zephyr offers his arm. "Come with me," he says, "and I will answer all that lies within my Domain."

She realizes, looking at him, that she cannot see his eyes. The mask conceals them.

But…she admits, she is curious.

Psyche takes his arm. She expects that he will smell of

fantastical things like gunpowder or sea spray. Lavender and rosemary greet her instead—a scent that makes her think of meadows in the early afternoon, not fire gardens in the middle of the night. Still, it suits him somehow, this man who guides her toward the golden door at the other side of the courtyard. She can imagine herself in that meadow.

Though, where do you even find a meadow in New York City?

"There are rules," he says to her. "Which you must heed with care. Much like your boundaries. Shall I tell you ours and then you share yours?"

"I'm listening," Psyche says. In truth she's a little relieved.

On the other side, she can hear laughter and music. The ground trembles; the bass in there is strong enough to rattle the air in her lungs. As the current song comes to a close, there is a moment's silence.

She thinks she hears a moan.

Oh. Is this... *that* kind of party?

Zephyr snakes an arm around her shoulder.

"First, you will take nothing except that which you are offered," he says. "But you can have your choice of anything offered to you."

"The offerings," Psyche starts. The woman moans again, and she has to fight to keep her train of thought. "D-do you mean food?"

"Among other things," Zephyr says. When the woman continues, louder, he smirks. His teeth look sharp in the flickering light. "Rest assured, nothing will be forced on you. We are very, very strict on that point. We make offerings; we do not insist."

Offerings. Sure. What if he offers...?

Focus, Psyche. She nods. The woman on the other side of the door is driven to greater heights. A crowd cheers for her—*More, more, more.*

"Second, you will not wander alone among us. Either Eros or I must accompany you at all times."

The music returns. Psyche's breath catches in her throat, her mind already starting to wander. That woman sounded so...

"The third rule is the most important," Zephyr says. He leans toward her, his fingertip beneath her chin. "I will need your...how would you put it...undivided attention."

Psyche has many, many questions. "You have it," she says.

"You may not lie to us," he says. "You must mean everything that you say."

Oh, she can think of a few things she wants to say, and she means every single one of them. "Right," she says, licking her lips.

Zephyr nods, smiling. "I must hear you agree. They're very particular, in there, about consent."

"I agree," Psyche says. "That all sounds, ah, reasonable."

"It gladdens my heart to hear that," says Zephyr. He clears a curl from Psyche's face. "And you? What are your boundaries?"

"B-boundaries?"

"If it is more helpful to speak in terms of...traffic lights, is that the word?"

He's quoting her own video back at her again. One of the more popular ones adapted the red/yellow/green system favored by the kink community to broader social boundaries. Some of her fans weren't comfortable communicating hard boundaries, so starting with softer ones and working their way up helped.

"All right," she says. She pauses, forces herself to focus, to think. "Well…I'm here to help your friend, right?"

"Is that your *primary* wish?" says Zephyr.

What she wishes is quite out of the question if she wants to get any work done.

"If I'm here to help your friend, then there won't be any flirting," she says. "With anyone. Especially not you."

Zephyr chuckles. She tries, very hard, not to notice how sculpted his chest is as it rises and falls. "Do you find me so distracting? I was told the masks would help."

"Not when you sound like that," Psyche fires back. Another breath. "I'd like a private space, too, if possible. Discussing things in public never goes well. Is this…are we going to someone's house?"

"Something like that," says Zephyr. "A private space can be provided for you. I suspect Eros will insist, as a matter of fact."

"Why's that?" It strikes her that she does not know much about her prospective client. In ideal circumstances they would have had a proper getting-to-know-you meeting.

"She detests these gatherings," he says. "But obligation compels her to come. I should warn you that she will be miserable when you meet her, but you mustn't hold it against her."

"Unfortunate circumstances don't excuse someone for being rude," Psyche says, "but I'll try my best to be understanding."

"You are the same as you are in your videos," Zephyr says, and for this Psyche is unprepared. He continues as she flushes red. "It is not always the case with our guests, you understand. Most wear unseen masks and shed them the moment they lay eyes on us. They want fame or fortune. But I can tell you're not here for that."

She could use a little more fortune. Latte likes expensive cat food. But it hasn't occurred to her to ask for payment until now.

"I like helping people," she says. The drums threaten to drown out her whispering, like they had the moans. She thinks of the woman on the other side of the door again.

"Then by all means," says Zephyr. "Let us survey the helpless."

He opens the door.

Light fills Psyche's world. Yet this is no guiding beacon through the fog, no signal in the starless night. This is a dazzling, blazing inferno. Only flames lie ahead, dancing and beautiful. Her eyes well up beholding this strange new world; sweat coats her brow. And though she knows that to walk into a burning room is to walk into death itself, an arm around her waist has sealed her fate.

Fire has so long fascinated humanity, and for good reason, but these are no normal flames. Within them are silhouettes giving themselves over to dance. Dozens of them. Limbs undulate and entwine, laughter meets her ears, she smells ecstasy and pleasure.

A world of living flame.

Really, it should frighten her.

But she's come this far. How could she live with herself if she went home now? Lying there in her bed knowing she could have seen something extraordinary, witnessed something extraordinary, *been* someone extraordinary. How could she live without knowing?

Zephyr pulls her in.

Crimson and vermillion, carmine and amber, the flames lick at her skin. There is no pain, no burning—only the embrace of heat and a dizzying rush of energy. Everything tingles. Breathing leaves her giddy with delight. Were it not for the weight of Zephyr's arm, she might have floated away on all this hot air.

"Remember this, Psyche," he says to her. His voice is rich as his lips brush her ear. Her pulse quickens in her veins. "Few see this world."

But how could she forget it? This feeling as the flames tease her lips, the lusty thrill of something wanting to come in. She laughs. How long has it been since someone held her the way the flames are holding her? They pour into her and she allows them in, her eyes widening, her heart pounding, her throat threatening to close around this new visitor—

And when she opens her eyes, she sees everything anew.

Psyche went to her fair share of clubs when she was younger. She's never seen one like this. There is a dance floor, yes, and people are pressed tight against one another within it, but there is also a banquet table with otherworldly fruit.

And people lying on that table where there should be plates. A man bites into fleshy red fruit and squeezes the sticky juice onto a grinning woman.

The flames now confine themselves to the walls and ceiling—rippling veils to serve as a backdrop to debauchery. A shining chandelier sways like a drunkard; two women are draped across it, tipping glasses of wine to their lips. Silk banners with dancers entangled trail beneath, their lithe bodies like smoke curling from the fires below. They, too, are laughing.

Masks are the only consistency—but why bother with the masks when they're naked otherwise?

Golden chain mail draped over bronze skin cannot hide the hardened nipples of a writhing woman. Is she the one Psyche heard? She's certainly loud enough. The man rolling his hips against hers wears only a single sash of silk across his sculpted body. Beneath the moaning woman lies another reveler, their lips pressed against her neck, holding the middle woman's legs apart for him.

How she stares at them, this trio. Heat courses through her—but everything here is hot, everything an ode to flame. These three are no exception. The sweat slicking his body as he picks up the woman's leg and hikes it over his shoulder, their braying moans and laughter, the fire of their gazes.

Oh.

They're looking at her. The masks conceal their eyes—like Zephyr's—but that doesn't change anything. They're staring at her as she stared at them. The teeth they bare when they smile…Is it the light that makes them look so sharp?

"Zephyr, she's adorable," says the person on the bottom. They lick the woman's neck but keep looking straight at Psyche.

"I l-love—*oh!*—your little outfit," says the woman. Her tongue lolls out of her mouth with every thrust. She rakes her nails down the man's back, and he grunts, driving himself deeper into her.

"Care to join us?" he asks.

Psyche has never felt more overdressed. She has never felt more out of place. And she has never, in her entire life, wanted to be anywhere more than sandwiched by the three of them. Four, maybe, if Zephyr joins in, too. The person on the bottom doesn't have anyone attending to their needs, after all, and isn't that what she's here to do? Psyche cannot take her eyes from the joining of their bodies, from the glistening wet. What do they taste like, these three?

She swallows. "I—I have...work...to do," she stammers. But she does not take her eyes off them. The woman's lips are so thick and soft. To kiss her would be to sink into a cloud. What she wouldn't give to...

But the woman laughs, and her partner beneath her, too. "More for us, then," says the bottom.

The man grunts. Oh, he's close, she can see it in the way he's tensing, the strain of him as he grabs the settee with both hands and...

"You can't take in the sights if you've refused their company," says Zephyr in her ear. A tug at her elbow follows. Though she longs to linger, the hairs on the back of her neck tell her that breaking rules here would be...very ill-advised.

He leads her through the crowd. They pass serving girls on their knees for proper ladies, chins already slick. Dancers call to her in voices lovely and tempting, praising her bravery, fawning on her. Yet they do not touch her. When Zephyr walks her across the dance floor, revelers part to keep away.

But their eyes are on her. And she can hear their calls, the gossip, the whispers.

"Wouldn't it be fun to unwrap her?"

"I wonder how many I could get out of her..."

"She's a little meek for a human, isn't she?"

It isn't just lust that sets her heart hammering. Is this real? If this is a dream, it's on the verge of tumbling into a nightmare, and she hates how much it thrills her to be in a place like this. To be in danger.

She clutches Zephyr's arm. "What are you?"

"A friend," he says. "Or else I would have left you to the others."

A woman licks her fingers and grins at her. Psyche's breath hitches. "And what are *they*?"

"Desperate for you," Zephyr says. "Your restraint is *very* admirable; you know, most people would have given in by now."

"Where is your friend?" she asks him, for she is not sure how much longer she can put up with this—the eyes, the tongues, the places she'd rather be.

"Not far," says Zephyr. He points up ahead, to the wall. Here is the greatest blaze of them all—a roaring, smokeless bonfire, around which tumblers leap. "We'll find her there."

Psyche narrows her eyes. Who among them is Eros? Is she

one of the dancers? No, Zephyr said she hated these parties. Perhaps she's the woman tossing oil onto the fire? Or…

"Zephyr! My *oldest* and *most loyal* companion. What an unexpected delight to have you visit our court!"

A pale man in a tentacled mask grips Zephyr's shoulder. Where his fingertips brush Psyche's skin on the other side, they leave a slick trail. She shudders, but he doesn't notice, pulling Zephyr closer.

"How long has it been, hmm? Ten court cycles? More?" says the newcomer. "You've found yourself a new plaything, but that hardly helps me keeping track of the time."

"I'm not—" Psyche starts.

Zephyr digs an elbow into her ribs. "We can address our business another time, Glaucus."

Glaucus tilts his head. Though she cannot see his eyes, there is something of a scowl to his mouth. Needlelike teeth complement his mottled, moist skin. " 'When next we meet,' was the phrasing, was it not? Well, here we are. Meeting. You owe me."

The music around them picks up. Psyche's heart creeps up into her throat. Zephyr's breathing catches; his hand has gone cold. Glaucus frightens him. She can't let her friend feel like he's alone, no matter how afraid he is. Or how sharp Glaucus's teeth might be.

"Zephyr's a little busy," she says, taking a step forward. "I don't see the harm in waiting another five minutes. It'll still be within the same meeting, won't it?"

Glaucus sneers. What she took to be a thick belt uncoils

from his waist and reaches toward her, tentacles puckering. Zephyr shoves her out of the way before they can make contact. He tears her dress in the process—but when Psyche spots the smoke coming from the melting skin of his forearm, she realizes it's a small price to pay for her life.

"Go!" Zephyr shouts. "Don't stop until you find Eros!"

Psyche kicks off her heels and bolts toward the great bonfire at the other end of the room, driven by survival instinct alone. What use is trying to help when Glaucus can *melt* her?

Eyes bore into her again. Fanged mouths whisper; clawed fingers point. Amid the naked and the masked, she's a housecat among tigers. Drumbeats drown out the screams and the fighting that now spread among the revelers—but she knows that if she looks over her shoulder, she will see it. She knows.

Don't say anything you don't mean. Accept only that which you want. Stay with Zephyr, or stay with Eros.

How can these things keep her safe? They didn't keep Zephyr safe. Maybe Eros can help, if only Psyche can find her, but she doesn't know what to look for, and she worries that if she stops to ask…

If she stops to ask, she might never make it to the fire.

For beautiful women are offering her cups of sweet wine, their bodies soft and inviting, their lips shaped for savoring. Men are reaching for her hand. There are wicked grins, and sharp teeth, and all of them are coming for her.

Can't they see what's happening to Zephyr? Don't they know the danger he's in?

"Can't you help him?!" She screams to be heard over the music. No one answers. There are only hands and hunger.

She runs.

The great bonfire looms at the top of a staircase full of revelers. Four of them link arms across the entrance to the stairs. Psyche skids to a halt.

"Please, you have to let me go," she pleads. "Zephyr's in trouble—"

"What do you offer?" asks one—an androgynous figure with a beaked mask.

"I shouldn't have to offer anything. He's your friend, isn't he?" she shouts. Behind her, the others are closing ranks. A small circle of breathing room is all she has.

"He is a guest. He has drawn blood," says a woman in a serpent mask. "His compact is broken."

"He's—he's defending himself," Psyche stammers. "Glaucus attacked him first. Zephyr didn't mean to hurt anyone."

Strong arms hook around her from behind. She drives her foot into her captor's instep, but she might as well be stomping on stone. He does not move.

"His compact," repeats Snake, "is broken. You are no longer under his protection."

The drums, the flames, the dizziness. So hard to think, so hard to know what to do. Desperate, she kicks at the snake, only for Beak to catch her legs. Soon Beak and the man behind her lift her up like an offering.

"Her Majesty requires sacrifice," says Snake. "It will be an honor to feel her teeth against your flesh."

In that moment, Psyche thinks of many things.

Her sisters, and what they will make of all this when they hear. If they hear. In true-crime podcasts, the victim's family often has to cajole police into investigating disappearances. Laura would probably offer some ridiculous reward and talk about how close she is to her little sister—despite turning down all Psyche's offers to meet for coffee.

People will blame her for coming to a weird party like this, won't they? They'll say it's her fault she died.

And maybe it will be.

She hopes someone will look after her cat.

And she wonders if, once it's over, she'll get to see her mother again.

Up the stairs, one by one, her pallbearers sway from side to side. Overhead curtains of fire unfurl. The great bonfire roars and roars. It sounds something like laughter—or perhaps that's coming from the people carrying her. How amusing they seem to find this. How amusing they find her.

Psyche screams.

A bolt of golden light shoots down from the ceiling. When it hits the stairs, it explodes into scintillating fire, billowing out, swallowing those who carry her. Psyche closes her eyes—it's too bright to follow what's going on, and it won't matter what she does anyway. She's going to die here.

Arms close around her. This scent reminds her of camping when she was younger—the firewood, Laura's pilfered wine, the honey Cid poured into her morning tea. Despite the howls of the crowd, it brings her a strange peace.

The light against her eyelids fades.

She hears the flap of wings, feels herself rising higher in the air. The howling dies down, fading into the gentle crackle of a campfire. There is no music here, no drums—only a strong heartbeat below a warm breast.

"You should never be alone," says the woman holding her. Rich as velvet, her voice. "It isn't safe for humans."

Psyche opens her eyes.

Certain things are inborn knowledge. A swallow knows the way it must fly when the winds grow cold; a salmon knows it must leap against the currents. Humans like to believe we are above this—but that isn't true. We know that we must form bonds. We long to climb mountains, to discover what lies beyond distant hills. Fire fascinates and frightens us; death compels us to live fruitful lives.

Psyche is no different. She knows these things as well as anyone else. And so too does she recognize the crowned woman holding her tight.

Before her is Eros.

Chapter Four

If this is a dream, Psyche isn't sure she wants to wake.

Where Zephyr had brought her to a flaming ballroom, Eros has taken her to an ancient courtyard straight out of one of her video games. Two cherubs stand back-to-back on a pedestal, water cascading beneath them. Sleek black marble floors give way to a carefully tended garden. The moon shines down onto the gathered flowers. There is a tree near the fountain, a cypress she thinks, shaped and pruned. The air is bright and bracing. There is no burning here, only the smell of the flowers, the flow of the fountain.

And Eros.

Unlike Zephyr, Eros wears a mask that covers her entire face. Gold accentuates its ivory base. Ornate feathers form a crown all the way around her temples, the yellow lending depth to the red of her braided hair. A red arming coat hides much of her skin, though her hands and jaw are firewood brown, and she's strong enough to hold Psyche with no trouble. An intricate golden quiver filled with burning arrows hangs at her hip, though its companion bow is nowhere to be seen. These things alone are enough to enthrall the imagination—and that is before considering Eros's wings.

Eros is held aloft only by flame. And as she sets Psyche down on a carved stone bench, these blazing wings fade into cinders.

The relative silence of the courtyard leaves Psyche's ears ringing. Still, Eros's voice comes through with perfect clarity—a soothing counterpoint to the earlier chaos. "Did he bring you here for me?"

Sense returns to Psyche; she stands, laying a hand on Eros's vambrace. The leather feels as if it's been left to bake in the midday sun. "Never mind why I'm here. Zephyr is in trouble," she says. "There was this... Glaucus? A-and he melted part of Zephyr's arm right off, while I was there, and—"

Eros tilts her head forward. It reminds Psyche of the eagle at the Prospect Park Zoo. You could spend twenty minutes waiting for him to show himself, but when he looked right at you like that, it was all worth it. So it is with Eros—there is a grace and confidence to her that defy explanation. "After everything you've just seen, that's the first thing you're going to say to me?"

Psyche frowns. "My friend's hurt, and you've got fire arrows and wings, so yeah. I'm going to ask you to use them."

A gentle scoff, one that rolls into a laugh. Eros plucks an arrow from her quiver. "A bruised ego is the only real danger for him."

"A bruised ego?" Psyche repeats, her voice shooting up in

anger. "How can you say that about a friend? His arm was fucking *melted*—"

Eros picks up the arrow and drives it through her own palm.

Psyche screams and recoils, but Eros calmly draws the arrow out in one fluid motion. To Psyche's surprise, there's no blood—only what looks like golden ink. "There's no need to worry. Wait a few seconds."

What else is she to do? She waits, too curious about what might happen to yell at her anymore. Sure enough, the wound stitches together before her eyes. A small seam of gold is all that remains.

"It will be the same for him," Eros says. "By the end of the Court Season, there won't even be a mark."

"But doesn't it hurt?" Psyche says.

"Everything hurts, one way or another. Pain isn't anything new for us," Eros says. She lays her quiver on a seat before a glass table. Atop it is a bowl of golden fruit. "We aren't worth your worries. None of us are."

Just what had she gotten herself into here? That fight seemed so serious. Wasn't that real fear in Zephyr's voice? But if they could just heal with no pain, then what was the point of any of it?

Therapists aren't supposed to judge a client when they come in telling them something over-the-top. People have different tolerances, after all. While one person may cope well after losing a family member, another might have great trouble after a simple breakup. Everyone is different.

Psyche has trained herself not to make judgments.

But that's when it comes to . . . well, normal psychological things. All of this is something else. What's she meant to say?

Eros picks up a fruit and draws a square across its top with her thumbnail. Despite her gentle touch, the crown comes right off. The flesh within is a vibrant, fragrant red. "Are you hungry?"

Psyche closes the distance between them. Despite Eros being a good head taller than her, Psyche has no qualms about plucking the fruit from her hand and laying it on the table. Nor does she fear using her arms to cage Eros in against the table. The mask prevents eye contact, but Psyche aims for it anyway, staring into the gleaming carved ivory.

Very pointedly, she does not allow herself to notice how good Eros smells when they're this close together.

"The only thing I'm interested in is knowing more about this place, and about you," she says.

Of course, then her stomach rumbles and ruins all that bravado.

Shadows flicker on the surface of Eros's mask; light shifts beneath it. The taller woman bends until their eyes are level. "We hate liars. I thought Zephyr would have told you that much before he let you traipse through Court."

"I'm not lying," Psyche says. She puffs her cheeks and stifles the urge to put her hands on her hips. "It's the only thing my *brain's* interested in—"

Eros lays a gentle palm on Psyche's throat. It is the lightest touch in the world, a delicate thing, and yet so like a threat. Her thumb lies just below the tip of Psyche's chin, her index finger brushes Psyche's earlobe. It might be a caress. It could be something else.

Either way, one thing is certain: the heat of Eros's skin against hers sends a shiver through Psyche unlike any other. Old men who sit on porches sometimes call their whiskey firewater—but they have no idea what firewater really is. In this moment Psyche can feel it coursing through her, relaxing her limbs, working at the tension she's held so long.

"I can see why he liked you so much. You just can't leave well enough alone, can you?" she says. Something's changed about her voice. Richer and throatier, a voice that compels the mind to wander. "Even after all you've seen, you still dare to lie to me. It's impressive. It's been at least a century since I met anyone this brave."

Brave? Oh, but she isn't brave, just persistent. She wants to say that, but she's afraid that if she opens her mouth, she won't sound brave at all. Not when she's being held like this. Psyche only stares up at the mask. What sculptor had rendered ivory so soft, so plush? If she reached out to touch it, she's sure she'd find…

A sudden shift in gravity shakes her from her thoughts. Eros has scooped her up, as easily as one might scoop up a cat.

"Since you're so determined to get into trouble, I'll explain the position you're in," Eros says. "When you lie to us, you break compact with us. And when you lie to us within our Domains, we gain power over you."

That can't be right. Psyche wriggles her legs, tries to kick and squirm, but her limbs are too heavy. "You don't have—"

"I do, or else you would have been able to finish that sentence," Eros says. "Now, I don't mean you any harm. But you seem to think that you're dreaming, or that these rules don't apply to you simply because you wish them otherwise. And I need you to understand that isn't the case."

Eros carries her through the hall, up a flight of carved steps. Golden statues stare down at her, their faces contorted by the shadow and flame.

"Where are you taking me?" Psyche asks.

"Somewhere you can rest," Eros says.

"But I don't want to rest," Psyche says. "We only just met, and I'm feeling so nice now. Zeph wanted us to talk, didn't he? We should talk, face-to-face."

It feels a little like her mind is melting, but in a pleasant sort of way—like she's lying out on the beach reading her favorite book, and nothing else matters. How did she get here, again? There's something she's meant to remember, something important. As Eros walks her down another hall, the mask shifts, step by step. What's under it? Maybe that's what she's forgotten. Psyche reaches up. Her fingers brush the ivory—

And Eros gently lays Psyche's hand back down. "There'll be time for talk when you wake."

They pass beneath a proud marble arch. Beyond is a bed the size of Laura's walk-in closet, bedecked in velvet and covered in pillows. On either side are two carved stone nightstands, each bearing another bowl of the same fruit from earlier.

"Deflection is clever, you know, but it won't get you everywhere."

Psyche finds herself laughing. "Carrying women off when they tell you white lies won't get you everywhere, either."

Eros looks down at her. It is foolish to imagine such a placid mask smiling—and yet Psyche thinks it is. "That only applies to humans, and I am very much not human. When *I* carry a woman off, she always enjoys herself."

"That…so?" Psyche mumbles. She curls up in Eros's arms and, soon, on the soft sheets. Eros lays her down so gently Psyche doesn't even notice the transition. "You sound…like a narcissist."

The laugh she hears then is like the roar of a flame to a desperate, cold vagrant. "Never compare me to that man again."

"Delusions," Psyche says, waving a finger in the air, "of grandeur."

Eros pulls a blanket over her.

"A need for admiration," Psyche says. "Or else why would you go around looking like that?"

"The others think I'm reserved, actually," Eros says. She picks up another fruit and splits it open as she had before.

"And last but not least, a lack of empathy," Psyche says. She frowns. From the pleasant fog of her thoughts emerges a memory. She sits up, throws off the sheet. "Wait. You're trying to distract me!"

"Only for a little while. I actually need you aware for this next part," Eros says. She takes a wedge of fruit and pinches it between her forefinger and thumb. "In recognition of your bravery and your strange nature, I've decided to grant your extravagant request. I'll help Zephyr tonight. In exchange, I accept your offer of help. Whatever you meant by it."

"I'm not strange," Psyche says.

"You haven't once mentioned anything odd about my people or their proclivities. I whisked you away to my private Domain, and you never thought to ask where we were, or lobby for your own safety. You did not fall into my arms the moment you saw me. You're very strange," Eros says.

"Well... thank you," she says. "For helping, and for agreeing to be helped. He's very worried about you."

"He tends to be," Eros says. She holds out the fruit. "What's your name?"

Psyche takes the offered slice. Already its juices coat her fingertips. Her mouth waters. A scent somewhere between honey and apple—but with a touch of citrus. Once more, her stomach rumbles. What does it taste like? Well, there's only one way to know. "Psyche," she says, then takes a bite.

Eros chuckles. "In the future, try not to trust people like me when we ask that. Never offer your name without asking theirs in turn."

To bite into a sunbeam and have it illuminate your mouth—that is what it is like to bite into this fruit. A brightness rolls through her, a lovely joy, an understanding. Giddy, she takes another bite. "But I didn't ask for yours."

"Zephyr granted you that which I did not. It's like him to do so," Eros says. Then she reaches for the fruit. Psyche is hesitant to let her have it—but she relents after a firm tug. "We need to see each other again, don't we?"

"If we're going to be working together, yes," Psyche says.

"We could probably set up a Zoom schedule or something, though, if it's hard to get…wherever this is."

That's the most thrilling thing about all this.

"I have no need of your services," Eros answers.

Psyche blinks. "You're not interested in my services? But I thought Zephyr said…"

"He says many things," Eros says. There's a rise in her voice, an amusement.

"He said he can't lie," Psyche says, pointing.

"He can't."

"And you can't, either."

Eros raises her hands. "You've shot true. No, I cannot lie to you. I have no need of your services, Psyche. But I…would like to speak with you again. And for that to happen, you must swear an oath."

"That still doesn't tell me *why*," Psyche presses. "If you don't need my services as a therapist, what are you looking for? I mean, you've got a flaming bow, huge wings, you're superstrong, and you've got—you don't even know what people would pay to live in a place like this. What do you get out of it? Why me?"

A long beat of silence. The masked woman does not move. Marble stares back at Psyche; polished gold reflects her face.

Has Psyche pressed too far? Will this woman—this incredible woman, so unlike anything Psyche's ever known—forsake her? Well. Psyche never could hold on to anything…

"I'm sorry, that was—my sisters always say I never know when to stop bothering people over things—"

"Never deem yourself a bother in my presence," Eros answers, firm as warm steel. "Far from it. You cannot imagine how long it's been since a mortal demanded something pure of me. But if you would like to see me again, as well, then we would need to swear an oath. You have no ties of your own to the Court."

"And this oath would tie me to *you*?" Psyche says. Focusing on the objective facts leaves her free to deal with the subjective ones later. Like this tall, hot, otherworldly being wanting to talk with her.

Eros nods. "Zephyr invited you here as a guest, but you'll need stronger protection to see me regularly. If you haven't noticed, Court is . . . intense. Too intense for most of your kind."

That's one word for it. The images haven't yet settled in Psyche's brain. At this point, she's not sure if they ever will. So much of this night feels dreamy. Eros said she'd show her otherwise, but lying on a bed with a beautiful masked woman eating fruit is still a dream so far as Psyche's concerned. Better than her usual dreams by far, even.

But she has to know.

"What if I refused to swear it?" she asks.

Eros's posture stiffens; in the flicker of a shadow, she is back to a statue's stillness, a coal where she once was a flame. "Then after you rest, you will wake up at home. You can choose to forget all you've seen, if you like, and I'll see it done. You can resume your life."

Psyche forces herself to sit up. She studies that mask—the

noble nose, the eyes large and adoring, and wonders what Eros looks like beneath it.

"What am I swearing to?" she asks.

"Hrm." Eros is still. "You might call it fealty. You will swear that I am a special person, with whom you share certain connections."

"That's cagey, isn't it?"

That laugh again. Oh, how Psyche wants to hear more of that laugh.

"I already told you, company is what's most important to me," Eros says. "In exchange for that—you will want for little, and should trouble find you, I will be there to meet it."

"Even if it's the IRS?"

"The…what did you say you are? You are human, aren't you?"

Now it's Psyche who laughs. Zephyr seemed comfortable with the regular world, but Eros clearly isn't. How she wants to be the one to show Eros more of the human experience.

"Yes, I am human. The IRS is just a government agency no one likes dealing with," Psyche says. "What matters is that I'll swear your oath. Just tell me what I need to do."

Does she detect relief in Eros's shoulders, in the small grunt of affirmation that leaves her? Psyche can't hide a smile. Maybe Eros is only surly at first.

The masked woman reaches near the bed and pulls another flaming arrow, this one with a golden shaft, then lays it on the sheets between them. The flames don't catch—but at this point, Psyche doesn't expect them to.

"Close your eyes," Eros says.

"So you can drive the arrow into my palm, too?" Psyche teases.

"Ah, paranoia. So new to me," Eros says, flat as a board. "The quicker you close your eyes, the quicker I can help Zephyr."

Fair enough. Psyche does as she's told and shuts her eyes. She hears shifting from Eros's side of the bed—the rustle of braids, the snap of a leather strap stretching. Is she taking off the mask? "Oh Flame of Desire, heed my call. Bring life to the lifeless, and death to the deathless. Serve me and be served in turn."

Surely a little glimpse wouldn't hurt. The smallest glimpse. When Laura took her to see *Freddy vs. Jason* as kids, Psyche peeked *all the time*, and no one ever caught her. Of all the unexplained things she's seen tonight, this is the answer she wants the most.

Psyche hears the rush of flame catching. The smell of caramelizing fruit fills the room.

"Bind that which cannot be bound, free that which is already free. Let the flames consume this offering: our love."

"Our *what*?" Psyche blurts.

"I'll thank you not to interrupt," says Eros. "This ritual is very old and serves many purposes. If you wish to be able to enter this realm again, and if you wish to be able to do so without being attacked by my Court, then it is necessary. Otherwise, I can return you to your home before you wake."

"You don't even know where I live," Psyche says. "You didn't say anything about love—"

Before she has time to ask another question, Eros rolls on ahead.

"I'll leave it to you what sort of offering we should make, but you should decide quickly."

"Are you going to tell me what you meant by love first?"

"There are many kinds of love, Psyche. It's how the ritual ties us together. You, unlike most, have not fallen to your knees in adoration..."

"Now *that's* bold."

"I'm a bold woman, on occasion," Eros says. "But the truth remains unchanged. These are the vows we must speak if we are to be bound."

Oh, she's lucky she's so alluring, with that voice. Psyche has plenty of questions. Part of her wonders if this is a bad idea. Is she selling her soul? But even if she is, what does she really have to lose? Only her cat and her internet friends would *really* miss her. Her sisters would probably be happy they didn't have to care about the family fuckup anymore.

And accepting means she would see Eros again.

"What do people normally give?" Psyche asks.

"I think you have some idea," says Eros with a light laugh. "You saw what things are like out there."

As intrigued as she is, Psyche isn't quite ready to let Eros ravish her. But what about a kiss? It was forthright enough not to require any explanation, but also casual enough that they could shrug it off later without hard feelings. Actors kiss all the time. This wouldn't be any different, would it?

Psyche reaches out. Eros's hands find hers—roughened

fingertips and warm palm. How long her fingers seem when Psyche's eyes are closed like this. She wonders... she does not wonder. Cannot.

"We can kiss," she suggests.

"Accepted. Open your mouth," says Eros. She squeezes Psyche's hand.

It is a vulnerable position to open your mouth for someone else. All the more so when you've got your eyes closed. Yet trust seems to be in great demand here, so Psyche does as she's told, holding her mouth open as wide as she can.

"Don't swallow until I tell you to."

Warmth shoots down from her tongue to her center. A kiss. Just a kiss, that's all. Eros wouldn't break an agreement; she said she couldn't.

Heat coats her tongue. Sweetness follows, thick as honey, sliding down her throat, lighting her on the way down. Her stomach tingles as her blood begins to burn. Without thinking, she reaches for Eros's other hand, then her wrist, then pulls her close.

Psyche can't help thinking of the bonfire parties her mother loved. No matter where they were living, every summer they'd find someplace to go light things on fire, invite whoever was around, and turn it into a party. Her family kept it going even after Mom got sick. The first year they'd FaceTimed her; the second year they all gathered around a single lighter in her hospital room. And the third year, well, it'd been small, but they did what they could. It took a while for Psyche to get back into the swing of things.

Until the year Cid dared her to jump over the fire.

It was such a stupid thing to do. The fire was huge, Psyche's hair was long, and everyone was goading her.

Jump, jump, jump.

She hadn't wanted to. She walked, bare feet on the grass, to the fire. It was at least as tall as she was.

Jump, jump, jump!

Walking backward. Taking a breath. Trying to tell herself that her sisters would look after her if she fell. Not quite believing it.

Jump! Jump! Jump!

An impossible moment in the air. Flames surrounding her, licking at her skin, but not hurting her. Smoke at the roof of her mouth, her lungs burning. Exhilaration and delight.

And then, of course, the spike of pain as she broke her ankle landing.

Kissing Eros, holding her, feels just like that jump. Like she's suspended in the air, like the world's warmth has enveloped her, like eternity. All the eyes of her sisters' stupid friends are on her, and they all want what she has, and she knows it. She revels in it. Eros's hand on the back of her head, fingers tangled in her hair, an arm around her waist pulling her close. The two of them are so close that Eros can surely feel the hammer of Psyche's heart—as Psyche can feel Eros's breath hitch. Never in her life has anyone kissed her like this: as if her lover is the sun, and she the breaking dawn.

When at last Eros pulls away from her, Psyche can feel herself beginning to tumble from the heavens. But it doesn't last long. And Psyche is hoping there will be no painful landing.

"Do you swear to heed my warnings, as I swear to keep you from harm?" Eros asks.

"Yes," says Psyche. She tries to pull Eros closer again, but once more her mysterious savior holds her at length.

"And do you swear you shall not behold my face until I permit it?"

To feel as if she is in the center of the sun? "I swear it," she says. "I won't peek."

"Swallow this time," Eros says.

Once more she's taken into the heart of flame, once more she gives herself over to it. Eros's hands wander and Psyche wants them to, needs them to, needs to feel more of this adulation. All that's asked of her is to swallow the flame that she's been given. A small blaze that might burn for ages after this moment—why wouldn't she want to keep a piece of this with her?

She swallows. But in so doing, her tongue skates across a set of pointed teeth.

Eros touches her lips.

"What burns in me shall burn in you," she says. "Air will not carry you, water will not quench you, and the earth will not support you—but for all these you will have me, and the Oath of Fire that binds us."

In the silence that follows, Psyche waits, her heart still pounding. "Is . . . is it done . . . ?"

A whisper of fabric, then a now-familiar hum. "Yes," she says. "How are you feeling?"

Horny is the first word that comes to mind—but the more

Psyche considers her emotions, the more she realizes what the night's taken out of her. Much as she'd like to keep going, she wouldn't have the energy. And Eros has to help Zephyr, anyway.

"Like I should get some sleep," she says with a hazy smile. "But we should talk more in the morning. I... don't understand anything that's happened tonight."

A small laugh. "Rest well, Psyche. You will see me tomorrow."

Later that night, Psyche dreams that she sees Eros again. This time, her mask and armor are splattered with golden paint. The confident grace of her movements is replaced with weariness and resentment. When she rolls into bed next to Psyche, it is not as a proud warrior, but as one who has given all her youth to war.

In the morning, there is a smear of gold on Psyche's cheek.

Chapter Five

Velvet slumber comes for us all. Such is its skill that it happens without our notice.

Wakefulness, on the other hand, delights in making itself known.

So it is that—though Psyche has no memory of falling asleep, and only scant dreams to keep her company—she bolts awake at the sound of her name. From peaceful stillness her heart leaps to a war-drum tattoo, her eyes struggling to take in the brightness of a world she'd briefly left behind. Bleary as she is, it takes her a full ten seconds to realize that she hadn't imagined the call.

In those ten seconds, her first hope is that Eros is with her. A vision comes to her unbidden: lying on those soft, silken sheets, Eros feeding her more of that fruit. But the hope is dashed when she recognizes the fabric against her skin as value-priced cotton instead.

"Psyche. I hope you've a good explanation for this."

That isn't Eros's voice, nor is it Zephyr's. It's not even Bondi's comforting drawl.

Laura sits in Psyche's only good chair. Against the messy background of the apartment, she is a beacon of cleanliness—her suit pressed, her curls tamed straight with serums and heat, her nails polished and identically trimmed. Despite holding Latte in her lap, there is not a trace of cat hair to be seen anywhere on her black blouse. Her makeup is applied with such precision that Psyche wonders, not for the first time, if Laura has some kind of stencil for it. From the huge diamond glittering on her ring finger to the Rolex on her opposite wrist; from her straight brows to her glossy lips; from the tip of her head to the red bottoms of her shoes—there can be no doubt the sort of life Laura enjoys. In this reasonably priced Brooklyn apartment, she is as out of place as a sculpted bronze among Lego constructions.

"Laura," Psyche mumbles. "It's, uh, good to see you."

How is it that, ensconced as she is in so many layers of fabric, she feels so cold? Her groggy mind struggles to figure out what to say or what to think. Why is her sister here now?

Laura draws in a breath. She interlaces her fingers and lays her joined hands on Latte's serene back. It's as if she means to have a board meeting in the middle of Psyche's studio.

"If you need me to find someone for you to speak with again, then you should have told me. We don't want a repeat of five years ago—"

"What?" Psyche says. The mention rankles her. "I'm—it sucks to lose a job, yeah, but I'm fine. I promise I'll be fine. You don't need to call anyone."

Laura hums. She tilts her head just so—only a few degrees,

but that's all you ever get from her these days. Where Cid handled their mother's death by becoming a shut-in, Laura had thrown herself face-first into ambition. She rarely indulged in any kind of emotion. There was plenty to analyze in that decision, and in fact Psyche's spent a great deal of time dwelling on it, but her mind's not up to it right now.

Right now she's getting tenser as the seconds pass.

"Dr. Kaminsky said you took the dismissal badly. It's a terrible situation. You understand he had no choice, don't you? Whatever you meant to accomplish, you violated someone's privacy. Now, I don't hold that against you. I'm not upset with you—"

Psyche can't stand it anymore. The echoes are all too painful. "Why are you here? Did you come just to rub it in?"

Finally—a flinch on that impassive face. "Because my little sister, who always goes on about how much she misses talking with me, hasn't responded to any of my calls in three days."

Psyche's first instinct is to ask Laura what's wrong with her sense of time. But she tamps that down. Your first instinct, she often told her clients, is the reflexive one. It's not the one that always reflects who you really are. So she instead pulls out her phone to double-check the date before she does any shouting.

It really *is* three days later.

Her bed feels as if it will give way beneath her, as if she will tumble out into the endless sea of time. Three days…?

"I thought you were past lost weekends," Laura says. "I thought you understood that after the *last* incident, you need to pick up when I call you."

Why does she have to keep bringing that up? Psyche pinches the bridge of her nose. "I'm sorry, Laura. I just—I don't know how this happened."

"Haven't heard that one before," Laura says.

There it is again: the urge to shout, to argue, to tell Laura that she's wrong in no uncertain terms. But that isn't the right thing to do. Laura came all the way out here to see her. Isn't that worth something? For once she cared enough to come in person. Of course, that might be because she was concerned that Psyche was—

"I didn't mean to worry you," she says. Slow, careful, considered. Their nerves are frayed; more anger won't mend them. "I shouldn't have snapped at you earlier. I just wasn't expecting to wake up and find you here, and I... I'm still a little sore about what happened."

This earns her a brief reprieve. Laura takes a breath of her own, and Psyche lets one out. Any kind of relaxation from Laura is a victory hard won.

"That's what I was calling you about," Laura says. She tucks a strand of hair behind her ear—a ridiculous thing to do given it wasn't out of place to begin with. "I know how much it means to you, being able to help people. I don't want you to lose that."

"I kind of lost it on my own, didn't I?" Psyche says. "It's my own fault."

"Wanting to do nice things for people isn't a fault, Psy. Except when you neglect other things to do it. Your cat was *very* upset when I came in."

Psyche winces. Three days... She always made sure Latte had extra food in case she needed it, but seventy-two hours was stretching it. She'll have to give her some sashimi to make up for it.

"I came here to make sure you were all right, and to let you know that you aren't alone. No matter what. I know I'm not the best at showing it—"

"Latte likes you."

"Latte, hmm? She's a cat of good taste," Laura says. "But I'm serious. You don't have to deal with these things on your own. When you're settled, let me know, and we'll find you something else to do."

Psyche looks down at her hands. She's not sure what to do with them. She's not sure what to do with her feelings either, right now, but her hands feel more approachable. Easier to contemplate the chipped nail of her left ring finger than it is to absorb that this is really happening. When was the last time Laura spoke to her like this? Five years ago, when...

Well, she has good reason to worry. Anyone would. And Psyche wants to accept this all in good faith. She wants to say thank you.

But she doesn't know how to do that without feeling like a burden.

"I...you don't have to..." she starts. But she knows the words are wrong the second they're out of her mouth.

"I want to," Laura says. "Anything you need, anytime you need it. All you have to do is ask."

Asking is the hard part, she wants to say. But she doesn't. It isn't the right thing to say, or the way she really feels about it. Because she is happy that Laura's here—she just doesn't know how to express it. Or to process it, for that matter. It's all been so much lately. Losing her job, the party, and now this.

She's stirred from her thoughts by Latte's purring. The cat has bounded out of Laura's lap and into Psyche's. Psyche holds her tight. The thrum of the purring against her chest drowns out the rest, the weight of the massive cat a reassuring reality among so much that seemed unreal.

"Thank you," she says. Then, lifting her head: "It really does mean a lot to have you here."

A touch of a smirk from Laura. "I'd hope so," she says. Then she looks around the apartment. "Now… it doesn't seem you have much in the way of food, hmm? Get ready and let me take you out to breakfast. You can tell me how, exactly, you *didn't realize* three days had passed."

"I have breakfast stuff," Psyche protests. "There's toast, and honey, and eggs…"

"Psyche, I'm looking at your kitchen right now, and I am not going to eat anything you make in it. We're getting real food."

"Okay. Just let me feed Latte first," Psyche says.

And the moment Psyche goes for the tin of cat food, Latte is already bounding to her altar–slash–feeding bowl.

Few problems exist in this world that cannot be solved with waffles, bacon, and mimosas.

Psyche learned this in all the early morning hours she'd sneak out of her shared bedroom to help her mother in the kitchen. Humming the songs her mother half remembered from her childhood in Cyprus, they would feed the family together. Waffles and bacon, yes—but also grilled Halloumi, hard-boiled eggs, and soft cheese.

Laura must have learned the lesson at some point, too, though Psyche can't remember her ever cooking. And she doesn't need to when she has a private chef preparing their breakfast at the grill. Psyche can't complain when it means she gets such a gorgeous rooftop panorama of the city, though. Against the impossible gleaming backdrop, it's hard to feel anything but awestruck.

"I can't believe you get to see this every day," she says.

Laura hands her a mimosa. "Yes, well. Michael works hard to keep us here."

Does he, though? Psyche's not even sure what her brother-in-law's job actually *is*. So far as she's concerned, he makes money into more money.

"Does it ever feel weird for you?" Psyche says. "I mean, we lived in some nice places growing up, but..."

There's a pause. Laura glances down into the bubbles, tapping her finger against the glass. "Not in the ways you'd expect."

Now, what does she mean by that? What does she think Psyche expects—and what did Laura expect when she married him? At the time she and Psyche weren't speaking much; Psyche was a little surprised she was invited to the wedding at all. She's met Michael maybe twice in the entire decade Laura's been married.

Questions well up inside her. She can't help it. She wants to *know*. She wants to *help*. There's a pang in Laura's voice she's not used to hearing, and if she can just figure out—

"Mrs. Kaminsky, Miss Dimitriou," says the chef. "Pardon the interruption, but breakfast is served."

Seeing the hearty spread before her, any questions drop right out of her mind. Because despite all the wealth and all the trappings, Laura's still requested a Cypriot-style breakfast. Psyche's mouth waters at the sight of the figs and olives, the plump sausages. At the far side of the table are the waffles and bacon she smelled earlier. Her stomach rumbles.

"God. I see god in that platter."

Laura chuckles. "That's why we pay her," she says. "Thank you, Kristina. We can manage from here."

With a nod the chef heads for the elevator. A whole squad would have trouble finishing all the food the chef had made—and it was only the two of them now.

Psyche piles her plate high and pours honey over the lot of it. Laura's much more restrained—she takes the figs, bread, and a bit of the Halloumi, but leaves the meat aside.

The second she starts eating, Psyche can't stop. Flavors come alive across her tongue. Hunger impels her, a puppet master she is helpless to resist. It occurs to her that people who eat this much this fast usually do so as a trauma response, and she doesn't even care. All of it is too delicious and she is so, so hungry.

It isn't until Psyche is licking her fingers clean that she realizes Laura is staring at her. The confusion and judgment on her face are enough to nail Psyche to the spot.

"Did you forget to eat while you were... wherever you were?" Laura asks.

Psyche reaches for a napkin. Green stains the white. "I, uh. I had some fruit?"

"In three days, all you had was fruit." Laura doesn't often use her older sister voice, but when she does, it's well wielded.

"In my defense, it didn't feel like three days," Psyche says. She can't look Laura in the face after her little devouring stunt, so she looks off at the city instead. "I went to this party..."

She pauses, lets it hang in the air, too nervous to see how Laura reacts. When there's no hum of disapproval, Psyche continues.

She tells Laura everything. Mostly everything. Talking about the details of the revelry with her sister feels weird, so she avoids those—but the rest she leaves in.

It surprises her how easily she opens up. She keeps expecting a snide comment, a dismissive wave, but one never comes. More than anything, being *listened* to keeps her going.

"And when I woke up, you were there," Psyche finishes. "So I guess you know the rest of it, huh?"

Her throat's parched from all the talking. She all but chugs her mimosa. Now comes the moment of truth: Will Laura think she's lost it? Extravagant parties, potential sacrifice, a masked woman who captivated Psyche so much that she spent twenty minutes alone talking about her before going on with the story. Psyche had gotten up to a lot of things in her college days—what Laura always called her "sabbatical"—but nothing like this.

She hears the soft rattle of Laura setting her plate down.

"Psyche."

"I know it sounds like I'm having an episode again—" she begins.

"*Psyche.* I believe you," she says. "It isn't the first time I've heard of those *soirees.*"

The gentle breeze might well knock her off the roof, so light does she feel. "Wait, you know about those? I guess Bon said they're exclusive, but...really? No offense, Laura, but you don't really go for...that kinda stuff..."

"I don't. That might be why *I've* never received an invitation," she says. She tips her mimosa to her lips. "Michael, on the other hand, has."

Psyche's heart sinks. "Oh, Laura. Did he...did he go?"

"We discussed the matter thoroughly, as any married couple should," she says. But the way she clears her throat makes it sound less than amicable. "He decided he valued me more than he did the potential connections he'd make."

Oh, it wasn't amicable at *all*, was it? No wonder Psyche had never really talked to the guy. She's got no great want to now. But at least he made the right choice.

"Does that happen a lot for you guys? Disagreements over—"

"We can leave the counseling aside for now, yes?" Laura says. "We need to talk about what you've gotten yourself into. Just how did you get into the Court?"

Psyche doesn't think they should leave that aside when her sister clearly has feelings about the issue, but that's Laura's choice. Psyche will just file it away as something to circle back to. "A guy named Zephyr slid into my DMs."

"That doesn't make any sense. They don't really use technology," says Laura. She pinches her nose.

Psyche frowns. "I don't think he's like the others. He's posted a bunch of videos. Let me show you."

She pulls out her phone, dismissing a swarm of notifications she'd rather not read, and searches for Zephyr's account.

Or tries to.

"The account's been deleted?" she says. "That's weird. Hey, Laura, check if I've been blocked or something."

Double-checking from Laura's account teaches Psyche two important things.

First, though she's proud of her little stationery-and-counseling following on social media, she's a flicker of light in comparison to Laura's sun. Her older sister's carefully curated lifestyle posts have amassed her a veritable army of followers. A familiar wave of envy rolls over Psyche, tamped down only by years of practice. Of course. And Laura probably doesn't even really care about them.

Second, Laura can't find Zephyr's account, either.

"I swear, I saw it," Psyche says. "He sent me my own private clip, and that's how it all started. Maybe he's laying low? I mean, he did get into a fight."

"Don't you have more important things to worry about than some strange beings you just met?" Laura says. From the twitch at her brow, it comes out harsher than she intended. "Sorry. It's just—of all the things you could have gotten involved with, you chose the Courts?"

It's a nervous laugh that leaves Psyche. "They aren't all awful. Eros looked after me the whole time, and she brought me home like she said. With the oath we swore, she couldn't hurt me if she tried, and neither can anyone else."

Laura lines up her utensils on the table as if she hasn't just used them. She does so with tiny little pushes, her touch so light it's a wonder she makes any progress.

"You need to be careful with this," she says.

The flash of sharp teeth, the beating of drums. *The Queen.* Part of her wants to brush off any suggestion of danger and run headfirst into adventure, but...

"If I were you, the next time this Eros visits you, I'd tell her I need time to consider what I'd done. And I'd do all the reading I could about the Wine-Dark Courts."

"I don't think she'd hurt me," Psyche says.

The wind threatens to carry the quiet utterance away from Laura's ears—but cannot manage it. "You can't know that for sure, Psy. And that's the trouble."

Chapter Six

Would Eros hurt her?

How easily she had lifted Psyche, how bright those flaming wings. Eros had driven an arrow through her own palm and suffered no ill effects. Eating unknown fruit and swearing strange oaths...

Why had Zephyr chosen her? Why did Eros claim her? She has so many questions.

Bumping into her fellow straphangers on the subway ride home reminds her of the touch of masked strangers. In the flickering dark between stations, she sees smiling mouths of sharp teeth, reaching hands, Eros's mask.

Being with Eros felt safe. But was that only because of what had come before?

Someone touches her on the shoulder. Her heart catches. *I'll see you again soon.* A heavy touch, a warm touch—

But it is not Eros.

Just a woman looking to get to the door.

Psyche takes an open seat.

Wine-Dark Courts, she types into her phone, and hits enter.

There aren't many results. Plenty for *wine-dark*, a common way to describe the seas in classical poetry. It came up in Psyche's classes back in freshman year. Cultures all over the world had different ways of conceptualizing color. *Wine-dark sea* was a stock phrase to understand the deep blue of the ocean, when the algae is so thick it becomes almost violet.

There's plenty on that.

But the Courts…

This is: Seventh Avenue.

Isn't there a library near here?

She could go home, of course. She could scour the internet and try to learn more about whatever put the fear in Laura's eyes, whatever her husband decided against joining. But Laura said that these people—Courtiers?—don't know much about the internet, and Zephyr had said something similar. What if it's easier to find mention of them somewhere more old-fashioned?

The train hisses to a stop, and she slips through the doors.

Librarians are a gift unto mankind, granted as agents of knowledge.

The librarian that Psyche manages to flag down wears braids decorated with cowrie shells. She's pushing an overstacked cart from one end of the halls to the other, refilling emptied slots as she goes, with the sort of speed born of repetition.

"You look like a woman on a mission," the librarian says. "What can I help you find?"

"I need to learn about the, uh, Wine-Dark Courts...?"

A pause, a hum. In the eternal space between niceties the fear resurfaces. No good, no good. She wishes she had a hat, or...

Or a porcelain mask.

"I think we've got an Elizabethan epic with a name like that," the woman says. "Kind of a deep cut. Guess I was right, huh? It's six aisles down, to the right, fourth shelf from the bottom. Author's Kilman Saren. Lord Kilman Saren."

Psyche thanks her and wanders off. Kilman Saren presents himself right where the librarian said he would. Scarlet letters decorate a rich brown leather tome. *The White-Dove Queene and Her Wine-Dark Court.*

Truth be told, she's never been much for poetry. As a child she was too busy looking after her sisters to get much reading done, so a lot of her imagining came in the form of movies or games they all watched together. When she started college, her reading centered on nonfiction of all kinds. Like anyone else she'd read the classics, but this...

This is a lot.

Bad enough that the language is arcane; she's determined enough to stick it out through that. Antique spellings and grammar have a certain sense to them once you immerse yourself. But something about the sentences themselves twist in her mind. They're constructed more like mazes than anything intelligible. Though each page bears only a scant two stanzas on its yellowed paper, she finds herself having to read them three or four times to glean understanding.

Whoever Lord Saren was, he and Psyche have a lot in common. The poem starts off with Lord Saren himself receiving an invitation to a ball of which he's never heard. His companions advise him that the invitation—written in gold on the glimmering feather of a phoenix—isn't one to be ignored. When he turns up there, he discovers utter debauchery in place of the genteel parties he's used to. His companion—a woman named Melpomene—advises him never to leave her side, take anything unprompted, or lie in the presence of the Court.

There are some differences, though. Saren's got a silver tongue and encyclopedic knowledge of "all the great verses written and ere to be." Instead of partaking of the festivities, he recites poetry to his companion. Word spreads and the Courtiers gather. A brown dove lands on a bough of yew nearby; Saren recites lines even to the bird.

The Courtiers offer him slices of "divine fruit" in exchange for the verses "unknown to the knowing." Saren is leery at first until Melpomene offers him some fruit of her own. Literally, or figuratively? Psyche's not certain, but the result's the same: a five-verse aside about the fruit and its sweet taste, the way it had set him alive, its unnatural color and scent.

Her mouth waters as she reads. This part, at least, she understands. That fruit really was incredible. Is it such a valuable thing that they offer it to him in this way?

Saren goes on. For what he deems a full day and night he stands before the gathered Courtiers and recites all the poetry he can. Stories of knights and princesses, of dragons, of the changing seasons and the beauty of nature all spring from his lips. Whenever he fears his throat might trouble him, he asks for another piece of the fruit.

The Courtiers listen—but they do not remain still. They hunt, they cavort, they do whatever their hearts desire. At one point he recounts in vivid detail watching four of them burn a hind on an altar, then dance around it, inhaling the smoke for sustenance. Sometimes in the throes of their passion they pierce one another with their sharp teeth and lap at the gold that flows from the wounds.

As time wears on he finds himself running out of poems. Desperate and fearful of these clearly inhuman creatures, Saren invents a poem of his own on the spot. The listeners are captivated—until he labels it the work of one of his students. Then the night begins to turn.

Teeth bared. The beating of drums. Psyche hears them in the pounded syllables of the poetry and squeezes her thumb tight to try to soothe herself. With painted, predatory smiles the Courtiers tell him he's broken covenant. Like wolves they close ranks—

Only for the dove to land before him and transform into a flaming woman.

All at once, the Courtiers fall to a knee in reverence. When the woman speaks, Saren is too dazzled to take in her words. How it pains him! It is agony, not reverence, that brings him to his knees, for the woman's voice is too beautiful to comprehend.

He feels an arm around his waist. Someone ties a blindfold over his eyes. Soon, he is aloft, the woman's voice his only reality.

She tells him that she is the Queen of Flame, who has in her time been known by many names, and that she has taken a liking to his poetry. In exchange for the amusement, she has decided to spare him the usual fate of those invited to the Court.

He asks what that is.

She tells him that she would have eaten him.

Psyche snaps the book shut. Outside, the sky is going violet with dusk's approach. Just as she had in the Court, she's lost track of the time. And, perhaps, a little track of reality.

Because she remembered something as she read this—something important.

There had been a brown dove watching her the morning she received the invitation, and a brown dove on her fire escape when she returned.

Had the Queen of Flame been watching her this whole time?

She doesn't bother to put the book away; her hands are shaking too much to be of use, anyway. She tucks them into her pockets as she heads back downstairs. The librarian spots her, but Psyche doesn't stop to acknowledge her. In her echoing footfalls she hears the beating of the drums; in the warm breath of night she feels the touch of the Court.

How long had they been watching her? Had Eros planned all of this? What felt so simple at the time—comfortable, maybe even romantic—now feels sinister.

How can you know she won't hurt you?

Her thoughts swarm. She cannot sort through them, cannot focus, and thus it is natural she walks straight into someone on the way out of the library.

"Sorry," she stammers—but the brick wall of a stranger she's bumped into catches her with an outstretched arm.

"I should be the one apologizing. I tried to return to you sooner, but this world is a strange one for me."

That soothing voice.

Eros.

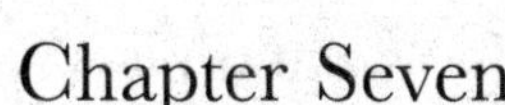

Chapter Seven

What do you do when your centuries-old unknowable maybe partner maybe something else turns up unannounced in the middle of a city street?

You panic.

Psyche tries to keep it low-key, of course. She doesn't want to make a scene. Why run from fate, if this is what fate is?

Because it might eat you. Right.

Yet a small part of her can't help being happy that Eros sought her out.

Eros—dressed in a *Pride and Prejudice*–style burgundy frock coat and high-waisted gold breeches—stares down at her. The mask's eyes do not blink. Psyche wishes that they would. It would make it easier to act normal. How is she supposed to be normal about how incredible Eros looks like this? *No one* should be able to pull this outfit off in this day and age. But Eros looks somehow dreamier than ever.

"E-Eros?" Psyche says. Oh, that's not good, her voice is wavering already. "How did you find me?"

A small sound. Amusement, or concern? Eros tilts her head. "We are Oathsworn. Wherever you wander, I am certain to find you. Is it the delay that troubles you?"

Concern. Okay. The Courtier who can find her anywhere in the world is concerned. That's okay. Psyche swallows, looks around. Prospect Park is still open for a couple of hours. They could get lost in there, maybe sit by the lake and talk, but...

Did she really want to be alone with Eros? Can Psyche trust her?

"Psyche?"

"I'm sorry, there's a lot on my mind," she says. Should she ask Eros for space?

"Whatever troubles you is also my trouble now," Eros says. While the chatter of the people around them is rushed and hurried, Eros is suffused with calm. To look on her is to look on a stone in the center of a roaring flame. "I can soothe you, if you let me."

"With your"—Psyche lowers her voice to a whisper—"powers?"

This time she can be certain it's a laugh she hears behind the mask. That damned laugh. "Yes. In some places, I am known as the loosener of limbs. Though I am uncertain of what people think of me here."

"They probably think you're an eccentric," Psyche says. Truth be told, the powers may already be helping. The longer she spends around Eros, the more her fear melts away. How can she possibly be afraid of someone who shows up dressed like Mr. Darcy? And who does so without having any idea what she's doing, or why it might be weird? There's a charm to it that eats away at her uncertainty.

"Are my fashions out of date?" Eros says. To make matters worse, she sets her hands behind her back as she surveys the crowd. Parade rest. Cid always liked to mimic when their father did it. "Zephyr told me I would blend in perfectly well."

A group of teenagers take stealth photos of Eros as they pass. Psyche knows well the giggle that follows. Before the end of the day Eros is going to be in at least a dozen "only in New York" Instagram posts.

What happens next is pure instinct.

She holds Eros's hand.

If Psyche had thought about it at all, she would have realized it a strange thing to do in the circumstances. Not an hour ago she read a tale all about Eros's... relatives trying to eat people. She'd even witnessed it herself at the party. Wings of fire, skin that repaired itself, golden blood—the woman whose hand she holds could incinerate her in an instant if she wanted.

But Psyche doesn't think about any of that.

She just wants Eros for herself.

"Come on. There's a garden near here."

In all the world there are precious few sights as this: a mortal leading a god down the street, a not-quite couple not quite in love.

People at the garden still stare—but there's more to distract the eye. In the depths of summer, there is plenty of beauty to be found. Hibiscus, which never seemed at home to Psyche in the city; lilies, their petals thick and waxy; the herb garden as fragrant as it is vibrant. Psyche and Eros are not the only couple in attendance nor even the most strangely dressed. As they meander along the path, they encounter a woman in a pink wig and epaulette-embellished coat doing a photo shoot.

"I have no idea what the issue is with my attire," Eros says, spotting her.

"That's a cosplayer. Are you a cosplayer?"

A hum. "You have no way to prove that I'm not."

Psyche laughs. "Oh yeah? Which character are you cosplaying, then?"

The silence that follows isn't uncomfortable. Quite the opposite. Eros's warmth is as light as mulled wine, as precious as polished jewels. Amid the hubbub of the other visitors, she has something private here, something special. It isn't just the company, but its nature. Her own private god.

She cannot see Eros's eyes dart from this plant to that—but she can imagine that she does, and that makes all the difference.

It isn't long before Psyche finds herself narrating things. She's been to the gardens here a few times with clients. Sometimes it helped to move things to a less formal setting to get them to open up. Plus, the garden has all sorts of activities for teens. The cherry blossom festival's particularly popular, and with good reason.

"You have been to this place before," Eros says.

"All the time," Psyche says. "I was supposed to be going again next week, actually, but I can't anymore. I got fired."

A pause. Where Laura's silence is a needle, Eros's is calm and steady, like a column to lean against.

"I can go with you again next week, if you like," she offers. "Though that is a different kind of firing than I think you meant."

What a ridiculous woman. How can she be so soothing? "You wouldn't get bored of seeing a little mortal garden twice in a row?"

"Not if it was with you."

She knows these paths. The winding ones to the pond. The Japanese garden, with its replica shrine.

"Hmm. I believe I've seen something like this before," Eros says.

Which is funny, since she earlier had no idea what the "little squares the youths are holding" were.

Psyche hooks her pinkie through Eros's. There is something in her chest—not quite a flutter, not quite a skipped beat. "Yeah? Have you ever been to Japan?"

"More than you would think," Eros says. "They have a certain fondness for me, since my name became known there. But their Court is at war with ours."

Ah, a thread to tug on! Psyche touches her knuckles to her lips to hide her growing smile. "So there are more Courts than just yours?"

"Hundreds," Eros answers. The mask's eyes remain trained on the small shrine. "Each people have their own Sovereignty, each Sovereignty has Courts."

She wishes she'd brought one of her planners out for taking notes. "So... the Wine-Dark Courts, that's your Sovereignty?"

Eros nods.

"Who rules that? Is it the Queen of Flame…?"

An untrained eye might have missed Eros's flinch—but to Psyche it is as clear as a full-body tremor.

"Suffice it to say the Queen of Flame does not rule everyone. Only my immediate relatives and me," Eros explains.

"I'm sorry—that seems like a difficult subject," Psyche says. "We can leave it for now."

"Thank you," Eros replies.

The two leave that subject, and the shrine, in the shade of summer leaves.

To the greenhouses next. First, the miniature jungle. Eros reaches to ease thick leaves out of the way, and Psyche, with a smirk, has to stay the ethereal visitor's hand.

"You aren't supposed to touch them."

"I see no signs forbidding it," Eros answers. "It's folly to expect someone to read the minds of an unknown Sovereign."

"You can't put up a sign to forbid *every* possible thing someone might try," says Psyche. The leaf, heedless of what she has done for it, smacks against her forehead. Eros hums in amusement but does not help her—which is good, of course. Psyche wouldn't want her to. "I mean, there's no sign saying you can't breakdance, but I'm sure they don't get B-boy crews here on the regular."

As Psyche ducks the leaf, she spots a couple leaning against a railing a short distance away. The woman's eyes are pointed straight at Eros in a devoted, longing stare. A morning-after look. Her partner must have noticed, too, for he wraps an arm around the woman and pulls her close.

When she and Eros walk by, Psyche offers the woman a warm smile. It's not her fault that Eros is so mesmerizing.

But Eros hasn't noticed the attention at all. Her bronze visage remains trained on Psyche alone, even as the colors begin to bloom around them.

"What else is forbidden here, then?" she says. "Since you insist there are unwritten rules and seem to condone them."

"I don't remember seeing any signs with rules in the Court."

"Of course not. Zephyr invited you, and it's Law that he explains what's forbidden."

"And if he didn't?" Psyche asks. "What if I broke a rule he hadn't explained to me?"

"Then he would be dead," Eros answers. The statement comes easily, as if they're discussing video game mechanics and not someone they both know. Someone Eros knows well. What happened in her life to make her so casual about death?

Psyche swallows. The warm greenhouse feels a little colder. "Would... would the others have...?"

"No, the Law would have killed him, and the weight of his broken oaths," says Eros.

Across Psyche's eyelids an image bubbles to the surface of poor Zephyr lying on the ground. Living in the city, Psyche has seen dead pigeons plastered onto the street more than once. Hard to tell they're pigeons at all sometimes, only bits of white feather against the asphalt. You can forget until you see the red.

Would it be the same if Eros broke *her* oaths? Would she be reduced in such a way? Only it would be gold, and not red.

They aren't just talking about video games. They're talking

about real people and real consequences, and all of that is starting to sink in.

Yet as the horror threatens to upend Psyche, Eros keeps talking. "We cannot kill each other. At least, not without concerted efforts… Psyche?"

Before a corpse plant, of all places, they come to a stop. Eros's hand on her shoulder is as warm as it is soft and reassuring. She leans over until they are eye to metal eye, Psyche's skin against Eros's mask.

"Psyche? Have I upset you?"

"I… it's just, uh…"

Square breathing, Psyche. In. Count to four, hold. Count to four, out. Count to four, hold. Ground yourself in the moment.

But the moment feels impossible. Here she is standing with some strange *god* in the middle of a greenhouse. People are staring at them. Someone might have almost died yesterday, but that might have been three days ago, and maybe if Eros tells a lie, she'll die on the spot, who knows?

Somehow it's real.

How can she ground herself in the face of all that? She tries to step forward, tries to keep it going—but she stumbles, and it's only Eros's arm that keeps her from falling.

"Psyche. May I carry you?"

Another impossibility to try to square with reality. She feels as if she's watching someone play her in a game. If she tries, she can see the dialog box coming up below her: Accept—(X) Yes or (O) No?

"Isn't that a little s-sudden?" she stammers. "I mean. I'm—people would stare, wouldn't they?"

"I don't care," Eros answers. "Their opinions are ash light to me. I'm your Oathsworn. I want to help."

But how can she not care...? They're already staring. People will think all kinds of things. They'll wonder what's going on. They'll wonder—

"Why me?" Psyche asks.

"You are braver than the hold your fear has on you," Eros says—with all the force of a fire at the door. "Will you let me help you, or not?"

Something in her shifts then, like the ashes blown away. Something in her burns. No one has spoken to her like this.

Her instincts kick in. Yes, she is sinking—but why not trust the woman with wings to lift her out of it?

"All right," Psyche says. "Please help me."

Before she knows it, right there in the middle of the gardens, Eros scoops her up and strides away.

Eros's pace is quick, yet her grip is steady. When Psyche closes her eyes, she isn't conscious of any movement—only that she is floating near to a fire.

"Eloquence is not among my talents," Eros says. Psyche puts her cheek against Eros's chest, and a pleasant thrum resonates within her. "Please don't expect that of me. Many do, what with all the poetry people have written in my honor, but I never asked for any of that."

"I can't write poetry," Psyche mumbles. The part of her

brain that won't slow down wonders if Eros will be angry with this as soon as she's said it.

"I wouldn't expect it of you, either," says Eros. "Because it isn't your Domain."

Is it the gentle breeze that guides Eros? For the heady scent of roses only grows stronger as they go. The wandering eyes of the others do not seem to trouble her, either. Psyche listens for her heartbeat, hoping it might soothe her. What will Eros's be like? Strong and steady, she imagines, like the soothing breath of a campfire.

She doesn't hear one.

"My kind are simpler, in some ways. Easier to predict," Eros says. "Each Court has within it several Domains. We embody them. All things tied to our Domain lie within our reach and fall within our realm of responsibility. Zephyr's Domain is the West Wind—whenever there's need of him, he must tend to it. That's why he so often visits the other Courts; the Wind goes where it will, and is always welcome."

A piece falls into place. Psyche opens her eyes. Against the clear blue sky, Eros is crowned with gold.

"Yours is..." Her cheeks go hot. How to say it? "It's love, isn't it?"

They come to a stop. Eros sets her down on a bench in the middle of the rose garden. All around them the blossoms sway in the gentle breeze. In one of the aisles, a beautiful young man poses for another man's camera. Their laughter is as sweet as the smell of the flowers.

"No. Love belongs to someone else," Eros answers. She sits

next to Psyche on the bench with a strange formality, then lays an arm across Psyche's shoulder.

"But the words that come from your name all have to do with love," Psyche says. "I mean, those were about you, right? All the stories and stuff?"

A soft sound that might be amusement—or might be a tired sigh. "Yes. What did you think of those stories, Psyche?"

She touches a finger to her chin as she thinks. There weren't many about Eros herself, were there? It's more the name that stuck around. She hums. "I haven't heard much about *you*, if that's what you mean. You're as mysterious as you probably like to be."

"Do you think I like being mysterious?"

"I think you like redirecting," Psyche answers. She leans over and pokes the mask in the nose. "You're trying to distract me from knowing what your Domain is, but I'm not so easily shaken."

Eros's head tilts forward. "You're the one distracting *me*," she says. "My Domain has little to do with the matter. We were discussing you and your fears. Do you often, when presented with the unknown, act like the first woman who ever saw a flame?"

She can't help but laugh—though she does feel a little bad about it. "Look, I..."

"Go on. I'm certain you have an explanation. Philosophers always do," Eros says. She crosses her leg over her knee and perches her head on her free hand. "I make an excellent listener."

Psyche rolls her eyes. "Okay, okay. What were you going to say?"

"My dress was not what upset you earlier, was it?" Eros says. "You were afraid of what I am. That is why you visited that library and why you stiffened when I spoke of broken oaths."

As the camera clicks away and the birds fly overhead, Psyche takes some time to think. How strange it is to be seen without having to explain herself.

But it isn't, is it?

Sitting on the bench, she realizes that. This is something else. A step toward…becoming. But becoming what?

Eros leans closer. "You asked me: Why you? I will tell you. You and your Domain call to mine, like air to fire. So many are called to me—but I have never before felt that pull myself. Part of me is frightened of it. But I think of how brave you were, alone in a world that meant you harm, and I decide: yes, I will enter the world that has so used me, and I will do it for her sake."

Psyche's breath catches in her throat.

"Hurting you is the furthest thing from my mind. And should any of the others get any ideas, rest assured, my arrows will find them if my words cannot sway them. You are safe with me. I swear it. Ask me to leave and I shall. But I would like to learn more of you—and to see more of that bravery."

Psyche holds the god's hand. "So much for lacking eloquence, huh? You made me feel…"

"Ah, you liked it?" Eros says. "So you will not cast me aside?"

"You knew I wouldn't," Psyche teases. She squeezes Eros's hand. "Thank you. I think…I'd like to be brave with you."

Chapter Eight

Sailor Nadeshiko just might be the prettiest blue ink in all the world—pale cerulean with a touch of pink shading around the edges. Laura sent her a bottle last year as a congratulations on keeping a job so long. It isn't particularly hard to get, but it's so pretty that Psyche's always reached for her other inks instead. She didn't want to run out of her favorite.

That ends today.

She refills her favorite fountain pen—a Pilot Custom 74, medium nib—and gets out her priciest imported paper. With Latte draped across her shoulders, she titles it.

Brave Things to Try

She doesn't have to think about the first few. Her pen skates across the page like a dream.

1. *See Eros again*
2. *Try to wield the power of the Courts*
3. *Visit a new Court*

4. *Invite Laura and Mike to dinner without feeling bad*
5. *Hang out with Cid and all her followers on stream*
6. *Kiss Eros again?*

She does have limits to her ambition. As much as she wants to imagine what it'd be like to kiss Eros for real, outside their oath—can it really be considered brave?

No. Kissing isn't brave.

Is it?

"Latte, what do you think?"

The only answer is a meow.

Psyche caps her pen.

Psyche always tells her clients that once they've made a list, it's a lot easier to follow through on it. All you have to do is break items on that list down into smaller tasks. Bit by bit, you'll get to them. And it's very important to put something on there you can cross off easily to start your momentum.

For item two, her sublist is simple.

–*Make an otherworldly creature swear an oath to me*
–*Research Courts. What's it like to live in one?*
–*Ask Eros about her powers*
–*Pick a power to try to wield*
–*Ask if she'll let me (offer knowledge of humans, homemade baklava, seduction???)*

Seeing as the first (and objectively hardest) is already done, that leaves the second. And the second is much easier now that she knows where to start.

Lord Saren.

Wikipedia tells her Lord Saren was fabulously wealthy. He had a whole system of tunnels built beneath his palace to allow him to visit town whenever he liked. Legend has it that he held lavish parties in some of those underground chambers. Some historians suspected these parties were the real, factual basis for the encounters he described in his most notable work.

But Psyche knows better than that.

She looks up his friends, his compatriots. People who knew him. So many people kept diaries back then. With her thankfully still valid credentials, she can access all kinds of databases full of the stuff.

For the next week, she reads more than she has since college, and more difficult material at that. The daily lives of English nobility become her new obsession. Within the pages she searches for any hint of capital-C Courtiers.

There are more than she thought.

That goddamned dove, for one. In her head it's the same one. Saren describes it several times before the day he woke up at 4:00 a.m. to write his story, claiming he'd been dropped back in bed by the Queen's messengers. Like Psyche, Saren noticed it watching him, and remarked on how odd it was for a bird to be so well-behaved.

He noticed it afterward, too—but his attitude had by then changed.

She watches me still. Dare I speak with her...?

He debates it for the rest of his life. Only on his deathbed does he recite for her again—the bird lands on his chest then and coos. His son reports Saren died that very moment.

But Saren is not the only one to have written of Courtiers. His son wrote often of dealings with masked merchants of great wealth, possessing odd accents and a complete lack of social grace.

They offer me raw meat and ask why I slight them by cooking it; they offer saffron, and incense, and finest silk for a pittance.

How is it that no one's realized who they are before now? Spotting them in the pages feels like glimpsing them in the crowd at the party. It's a thrill, a reward, and all the more impetus to continue.

Saren's devotees are her next focus. Both in literary criticism and in the spiritual sense she finds much. The literary critics add more to her backlog. By the end of the week, she's hauled up half a dozen boxes of old books, at least. Some of them are pure reimagined fantasies of what Saren saw—extrapolations with no basis in reality. But some have a touch of realness to them that strikes her with fear.

Mythic beasts hiding beneath the surface of the earth. A woman with serpents for hair who spat venom that ate right through stone. A man cursed to turn everything he touched to gold. Wars fought between different sovereignties, wars that spanned hundreds of years. People stolen away for a day only to return and find a decade had passed.

Just how much of this is true?

The bird watches her as she reads. She has half a mind to ask it. Instead, she adds it to her list.

7. *Chase off the bird that might be a god*

It'll have to wait for another day.

So quickly does the week pass that Psyche notices it only when she nearly misses raid night. A set of pings and calls from her friends draws her away from her latest find. When she signs on, she doesn't do much more than the minimum required of her. Her mind's too busy processing what she's read.

"Psy? You there, mate?" asks Bondi.

"Yeah," she lies. "Totally. You were talking about Blinky Bill again."

A long pause from Bondi—one punctuated by laughs from the others in their group.

"I couldn't care less about that fuckface koala if I tried," Bondi says. Which is also a lie, but not one that Psyche is going to call her out on. Because Bondi sounds upset, and maybe she has reason to be. "Can we chat for sec? Just you and me?"

The others agree. After finishing up the remains of their quest, Psyche and Bondi have their characters walk to a nearby inn together. Then they split up the voice calls.

Bondi doesn't waste any time. "You gotta get that night outta your head."

"It isn't the night I'm thinking about," Psyche says. She lets out a happy sigh. "I feel like I've discovered a whole new area in the game or something. An expansion pack just for me."

The silence from the other end of the line isn't what she expected. She lets it stand only a few seconds; she can't bear more of it. "I'm fine, Bon. Really I am! You were right, it was just what I needed. I've never felt better."

"Psy," she says, "whatever you do, don't try to summon them, all right? It never goes well."

So of course the first thing Psyche does when raid is over is look into how to summon them.

Powers That Be: Summoning Extraterrestrial Beings to Do Your Bidding arrives in the vestibule of her walk-up the next day. The miracles of one-day shipping. For a volume with such outsized ambitions, it's a slim little book, hardly taller than Psyche's phone. A blurry jpeg of a mandala adorns the front—probably lifted off of somebody's Pinterest page—and the title, in yellow, is almost illegible. It really is the shittiest-looking little book in the world.

But she has high hopes for it.

The author, who has chosen to go unnamed lest they be "tracked down by those who wish them ill," alleges that what they outline isn't *really* to be attempted. It's just a thought experiment. Any who would tamper with the Masked Ones are reaching beyond their station.

Remember always that their definition of a word and your definition might be very different. The promises they make to you are not always the promises you make with them.

Psyche writes that down. Not that she has anything to worry about. Eros is the most straightforward person she's ever met, almost painfully so.

Each Mask has a Calling…

Different people use different words, she guesses. She makes a mental note to swap Calling for Domain.

To summon one, it is first necessary to determine the proper Domain, and the things that entice it in our world. Ancient mystics here triumph over the cacophony of our modern, phone-addled…

Psyche rolls her eyes and skips ahead.

Votive offerings are not unlike what a would-be summoner should seek for the purposes of this exercise.

All right. That's easy enough. Though it does lead to a giddy, bizarre question.

Just what is it people have been offering Psyche's Oath-sworn all these years?

Honey. The answer is honey. Preferably local, say all of the old texts, but in New York City there isn't much in the way of local honey. Oh, there's stuff from upstate, sure. But all the ones in the city come with a side of whatever it is that lives in the Gowanus, and who wants to eat that?

Definitely not Eros.

So Psyche picks up a jar of the upstate stuff at the farmers' market, along with a bunch of figs and dates, the best chocolates she can afford, and, for good measure, some incense.

The book advises all kinds of arcane patterns for this sort of thing. Salt circles, designs made of sanctified earth, the whole nine. As much as Psyche appreciates aesthetics and theatrics, she realizes that none of this is meant to appeal to *her*—it's supposed to get Eros to take a day off work and come see her.

Work is what Eros called it. Now what that entailed was left entirely to Psyche's imagination.

"Well, how long will you be away?" Psyche asked her at the gates of the garden the last time they'd spoken.

"As long as I am required to be," Eros answered.

Psyche crossed her arms and pouted. "And if I want to ask you more about where you're from? Or see you?"

"If you have *need* of me," Eros said, "then you may call, and I will answer. But I'm afraid I cannot spend all my hours learning the intricacies of…what did you call it? Increasing your actions per second…?"

Okay, maybe Psyche had gotten a little technical in her discussion of *CDK XIV* mechanics, but Eros had asked her what she did for fun, and what was she supposed to do? Not talk about it at length?

Still, she smiled hearing the stilted way Eros spoke the words. It was like dressing up a cat in people clothes. She tiptoed up and brushed a hand against the mask's cheek.

"APM—actions per minute," answered Psyche. "How many days should I wait before I start to worry?"

"You should never worry about me," said Eros. She plucked a fallen petal from Psyche's hair, then laid it in the smaller woman's palm. "I will do as I have always done. Harm has yet to find me."

How the hell could she say those sorts of things with a straight face? Psyche's heart felt light and warm. It shouldn't be working as well as it was.

"But…how many days?" she ventured.

Eros laughed. "So dogged. In truth, I have trouble with the length of human days. I can promise you that it will not be long, but my work is often…tempestuous, and difficult to predict. Before the change of season."

Of course, that could mean anything, and that had been just what Psyche said to her at the time. Did that mean that they'd see each other again the next day, or in mid-September? There was no way of knowing. And she wanted to know. She wanted to know how long she had to wait before she could feel that way again.

Nothing else seemed to matter as much. Bondi still had the passwords to all of Psyche's social media accounts, but she hadn't thought of them since all this started, not once.

Losing her job was a wound already scarring, a hurt that had brought her where she needed to be. Some doors you could open only with blood.

With Eros she felt invincible. Special. Apart from the rest of the world. When she walked into coffee shops now, it did not matter whether or how people looked at her—what mattered was that she knew something they didn't. Even if someone did recognize her from Alex's post, Psyche had her own secret to share.

She was sworn to a god. And that god was sworn to her.

But that knowledge was burning a hole in her pocket. How was she supposed to wait for more?

Thus, the summoning circle. The books. The wish she writes, in her pale blue ink, on her favorite paper: *Show me the Domain that's keeping you from me.* A wish that feels almost too brave, almost painful.

She crushes the paper, dips it in a bowl of honey, plucks a date to go along with it, and lays both in her mouth.

The last step is the most frightening. The book prefaced it with a four-page admonishment that one should never, ever try it on their own, and that the whole thing was purely theoretical.

> *But a daring mage would do well to consider the element tied to the Mask one wishes to summon, and consume it as best they can.*

She'd considered it long and hard. Not that her determination made action any easier when push came to shove.

Knowing that you had to light something in your mouth on fire is very different from committing to do so. The lighter—a gift from her grandfather—sits warm in her hand as she tries to summon up the courage.

Just a quick light. Just a bit of fire, and it should be enough. Eros said she'd protect her from getting harmed, right? And the oath—it included a line about fire. If Eros really couldn't lie about things like that, then this shouldn't hurt Psyche at all.

But the body remembers what has caused it hurt. The mind can overcome its fears, the heart may forgive all it likes—but the body will remember.

Lucidity comes to her as the honey coats her tongue. This is wild. A couple weeks into whatever this is, and she's lighting herself on fire? What would the Psyche of a month ago think? A psychotic break, or perhaps a manic episode? If she heard a client had behaved like this, she'd be greatly concerned. So why is she doing it?

She could stop.

She could spit all this out, and she could sit on the couch, and she could wait as she's been told to. She could pass the day looking for new jobs or trying to come up with new posts for her accounts. She could even while away the hours on *CDK XIV*, if she wanted, and all would be more normal than this.

But…

And this *but* whispers to her, wraps its arm about her waist and pulls her close—

But if she stops now, she'll never know if the summoning works.

And, the voice continues, *what if she needs to know that for the future? You can't go running into fantastical situations like this one unarmed. You need to learn what you can, don't you?*

Eros wanted her to feel braver, didn't she?

Psyche's eyes land on the fire escape. The bird is there, watching. The Queen of Flame—she's sure of it. And she's sure, too, that the bird is staring at her just as much as she is staring at it. Does it doubt her courage?

Time to prove it wrong.

Psyche sucks in a breath, opens the lighter, and sets fire to her bravery.

Her body tenses in anticipation of the pain. Heat spreads across the delicate surface of her tongue; the taste of honey soon turns to smoke. Her eyes open wide, and when she takes a breath, there is only smoke there to comfort her. She sputters, coughs, whirls backward. Fear overpowers her as she feels the flames burn hot, and—

And . . . stay at a pleasant tickle?

Her hand rises to her mouth. She laughs a giddy, unhinged laugh and falls back onto her couch.

Or tries to.

Because it isn't the soft cushions that meet her—it's the solid muscle of Eros's body.

"What am I going to do with you?"

The laugh only grows. Psyche leans against her savior and tries to stand. Eros instead scoops her up.

"Swallow, then hold your breath," she says. "We're going to my Domain."

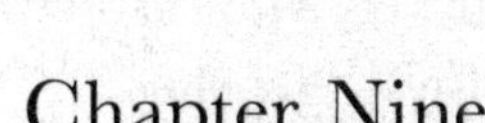

Chapter Nine

A rush of heat, the smell of burning wood, her stomach turning, and then—peace.

Psyche knows before she opens her eyes where they've ended up: the old-fashioned marble mansion from the night they'd met. The eerie quiet and still air can be nowhere else. Eros has once again set them down in the courtyard.

Here in the courts she must be less keen on disguising herself. Her wings are still burning on her back as she tosses her quiver onto the divan.

"What you did was dangerous," Eros says. A cloud passes over the sun; Eros is back in her armor. Once more the eyeless mask stares back at Psyche. "A false move could have summoned another in my place. What would you have done then?"

"Asked for you...?" Psyche mumbles. To her embarrassment, she hadn't considered that possibility at all. "You said that would protect me, right?"

"Yes," Eros says. She lays her hands on Psyche's shoulders.

"But why invite so much danger? All I ask is that you wait until you understand us before you do things like this."

"I'm sorry," Psyche says. How natural it would be to lean against Eros, when they're this close. "It's just—I was starting to worry, and I really wanted to see you again. To be part of all this again."

A rumbling consideration from Eros. Psyche studies her mask. If everything in this place is magical, maybe there's some trick to it. Something that could let her read emotion from marble. "There is never any need to worry about me," says Eros. "Psyche, what fascinates you so much about this place? Why do you not fear it?"

"Oh, I'm afraid of it," Psyche says. A nervous chuckle leaves her as she holds herself tight. "I mean, I almost died the first time."

"But you wished to return."

Psyche hadn't expected this. A nice, fun time in the land of the gods—that's what she'd wanted. Marvels and brilliance beyond imagining. Couldn't they do more of that? But no, Eros is right. This is something they should talk about.

A whisper in the back of her mind: *What if she hates it when you tell her?*

It's worth daring.

"I'm afraid a lot of the time," Psyche says. Steady, steady.

"Would you like to sit?" Eros offers. "I'm told that's helpful."

The stiff, well-meaning offer pops the stitches of her nervousness. Yes, this is a conversation they can have, and one that doesn't have to go badly. Psyche lets Eros guide her to the divan, where she takes a seat. Eros sits at her side.

"There," says Eros. "I'm listening, Psyche. Tell me of your troubles. Let there be no fear between us."

Psyche reaches for Eros's hand. The irony of the position is not lost on her—the therapist on the couch talking to someone else. But maybe this is what she really needed when she did that ritual—to take a second to slow down and talk.

"I didn't have the most stable life growing up. With all the moving, we never had a home for more than a couple years at a time. Didn't help that my sisters hate each other," she says. She waits, but Eros says nothing, only squeezes her hand. "What I'm saying is, I was always expecting the next big change in my life or the next fight. Always on guard. Everything I've ever done, I've done while I was afraid. And for a long time that was it, that was the truth and there was nothing to be done about it."

"And that no longer feels to be the case for you?"

Psyche runs her thumb in lazy circles around Eros's palm. "The night I went to the Court for the first time, I'd lost my job. I thought, 'All this time I've been afraid of the world falling down around me and now it has. So why not?' "

"Few would have made the same choice," Eros says.

"I think you'd be surprised. Humans can be pretty daring," Psyche says. "But it's just... it's like everything about you and this place is dangerous. But I'm never afraid of you. I know I should be."

"It's the wise thing," says Eros. She lifts Psyche's hand to the lips of her mask. "But I am happy to hear you aren't."

"Every time I do something that brings me to you or brings me to this place, I get a little braver, and the things I worry about seem a little smaller," Psyche says. "That's why I wanted to come here again, to see you again. I like the person I feel like I can be when I'm around you."

Therapy is all about showing someone else your goriest wounds and learning how to stitch your flesh back together. It's a vulnerable thing.

Sitting on the divan with a silence growing between them, Psyche wonders what it is Eros will say to all of this.

In the end, there isn't any need for worry.

"Psyche." Eros's voice is firm, but warm.

"Yes?"

"I would like to make you two offers, if you would hear them. To thank you for trusting me."

Psyche looks up at the impassive mask and imagines she sees a smile. "What did you have in mind?"

Eros reaches for the bowl of fruit on the table. She takes a bite, then passes it to Psyche. "First: you needn't complete the full ritual whenever the urge strikes you to visit me. Simply open any door while holding an open flame. If you think of me, you will return to this place when you cross the threshold. Though I caution you not to stay more than an hour of your time. Take a clock with you."

"We have phones for that now," Psyche says, smiling. She takes a bite of the fruit. As it had that night, the fruit awakens all her senses at once. Soothing flames course through her muscles; warmth blossoms in her belly. There's a freeness that comes from this, a languid joy that compels another bite. "Thank you. It means a lot that you'd let me in here."

"This was not a home meant to be so empty," says Eros. Without letting it linger, she continues. "How would you like to feel a fraction of my power? For an instant, no more. I wouldn't want to hurt—"

Psyche sits up, looping her hands around Eros's neck. The god's skin is fever hot to the touch. "You'd really let me do that?"

Eros shifts to cradling her. "If it is something you desire so strongly, and something that lets us understand each other better, then it may be done. I ask only that you listen to what I'd like to tell you, during."

The urge bubbles up inside her all at once: Psyche plants a kiss on the mask's cheek. "Thank you," she says. "And of course I'll listen. I love learning about you."

"Careful," Eros says. With ease she stands, and sets Psyche down. "There is nothing in this world so virulent as love."

What a strange thing to say—and yet said so plainly. Psyche raises a brow as Eros walks behind her. "Isn't that a little dark?"

Eros takes Psyche's hand. Within it she places a small, ornate golden rod, one chased with flaming designs.

"Oh, plenty."

A soft laugh. Eros closes Psyche's fingers around the grip. As sails unfurl from a mast, so too do flames grow from it, shaping the bow Psyche had seen last night. Despite this, it remains as light as ever. Power prickles against Psyche's palm.

"Once stricken, love's sufferers become different people. For some the benefits outweigh the loss of their old selves. For others it consumes them. They carve out pieces of their soul and lay them at the feet of their beloved. And if that beloved should forsake them, they cannot take those pieces back. They are gone. Love is the great transformer."

Eros stands behind her again. She lifts Psyche's bow hand and helps the other into position. Armor presses against Psyche's comfy sweats; Eros's hard body is hard to ignore. So is the absolute comfort of being in her arms.

"If you ask me," Eros continues, "there's no finer weapon. Fill a heart with love, and you can start a war or end it; compel a coward to bravery, or cow the brave. The right stroke of a cheek, the right kiss, can do more to change the world than any sword."

Is it coincidence that she presses her cheek against Psyche as she says this? Eros slips an arrow between Psyche's fingers.

"You wanted to know more about me, and about this place," says Eros. "I'll tell you a little. This place is part of me, and I am part of it. You may think of it as a place within my heart. Here, only my mother can see me, and then only when she deigns to. I have a freedom here I have nowhere else. I need not give in to what my mother asks of me. And someday, if my grandfather allows it, this place will become a Court of its own."

Arrow touches grip. Psyche's breath catches as power hums through her. The closest she'd come to this feeling was toying with prank buzzers as a child, but this is on a different level.

With every beat of her heart she feels bigger, stronger, headier. Yet Eros holds her tight and keeps her from wandering too far afield.

"You asked me what I am," says Eros. She leans closer, turns Psyche around. The blazing tip of the arrow, so like a sun, now points straight at the strangest of the statues: a seashell adorned with flowers, hanging from the far balcony. "I don't believe your people have a word for us. 'Gods' might suit, but it isn't quite right. Within our lands and within the Courts, I have absolute control over my Domain. I can strike any of my fellow Courtiers with passions so consuming they would offer their flesh to escape its grasp. Make no mistake—it isn't happiness I bring them. It is the same with humans. But your kind do ask me for happiness, and I grant what I can, only to watch them mangle it time and again."

Eros draws back their joined hands to caress Psyche's cheek.

"Does it frighten you to know that I've gotten my hands dirty, Psyche? That I've caused wars, broken families? That I am that worst of weapons?"

"You don't frighten me," Psyche says. "You're fascinating. I want to learn more about you. I want to understand...all of this. And I want to help you realize that love doesn't have to be ruinous."

A quiet hum. "I have taken you to a land that is not your own and asked of you a strange oath. I've introduced you to things no human should ever know. After what you've seen of the court—you have no fear?"

"No," Psyche says. "I try my best not to judge people."

What a ridiculous thing to say at a time like this, with a flaming bow and arrow in her hand, in the arms of someone who may or may not be a god. A greeting card given to a queen.

Eros squeezes her tight. And then: "Fire."

This time Psyche does not hesitate—she looses the arrow. What was a small lance of flame erupts into a column that consumes the stone oyster shell, the flowers, and even the balcony above it. Roaring fire rages above. Destruction—so easily wrought that Psyche's hands tremble—lends them warmth.

Eros rests a hand on Psyche's shoulder. Together they watch the flames flicker—red, to gold, to blue, to white.

"How did it feel?" Eros asks her.

"Like holding a world in my hands and then destroying it," Psyche answers. She looks down at her palm—at the grip gone cold. "I...it was..."

"You understand, then," says Eros. "A little of what it's like."

Does she? She's not sure what she understands. Yet Psyche can't deny that something in her feels different after firing that bow. The world feels smaller—more distant.

Eros swaps the grip for the rest of the fruit. "You should finish it," she says. "You'll feel better afterward."

Somewhere in the distance a woman keens. Eros suddenly snaps to attention.

"Is...is someone hurt?" Psyche asks.

"Not yet," Eros says. "But I'm being summoned." Her head drops; she stares down at her hands as Psyche had. Then she grunts. "I'm not certain how long I'm going to be away. It wouldn't be fair of me to keep you waiting—would you like me to return you to your world?"

Fire flickers over Eros's head. The keening grows louder and louder—hearing it sets Psyche's teeth on edge. Just what is Eros being summoned to do?

She wants to go with her. She wants to see. She wants to help. But even she knows she isn't ready—not yet. There's still more to learn.

"You said no lying, right?" Psyche says, little more than a whisper. "Then no, I'd rather stay here. But if you need to return me right now—"

"What I need is more time with you and less with them," Eros says. "You haven't told me what the internet is. But I can't refuse this summoning, and I think it would be best. You've your own life to tend to."

Psyche wraps her arms around Eros. "Then take me back," she says. "But don't be away too long."

A gentle hand on her hair, quite at odds with the power humming in that bow. "I keep my oaths, Psyche."

Chapter Ten

When Psyche returns home, the flames are still crackling in the back of her mind. The great curtain of fire continues shimmering and gleaming. Her fingertips tingle, and her heart hammers; there is a looseness and ease to her limbs that feels almost alien.

She scoops up Latte from her cat-tower perch. She dances across the apartment. She opens the window and sits on the ancient fire escape, surveying the city. And not once does the thought occur to her to check her phone.

No, the other world has her attention.

From her desk she once more fetches her planner and favorite pen. Out on the fire escape, with the twinkling city lights and streetlamps to guide her, she writes what she knows.

She writes, and writes, and writes. Descriptions of what she has seen as best she can remember them. Sketches of Eros's dwelling and of her fearsome mask. As her pen skates across the page, she dares to sketch what she thinks might be under there, too—a private glimpse of the face of her private god. Full lips; long lashes and intense eyes; a high, arched brow.

She draws Eros smirking. She draws her scowling. Psyche's never been a particularly talented artist, but that doesn't stop her now—the fire of imagination has her in its grasp. What would Eros look like sitting across from her at breakfast? Dancing together? They were to see each other again, Eros promised; to ask each other questions.

Psyche has so many questions. One by one she writes them down, sometimes along the lines of the paper and sometimes curling around her imagined drawings. Normally she's so much more organized than this. *Are you doing this to me?* she writes. *Are you making me this disorganized?*

Do you like holding me as much as I like being held? she adds underneath.

She draws, and writes, and she only stops when sleep takes her right there on the fire escape.

Lo, rosy-fingered dawn! Lo, the sun's chariot!

The squawk of a bird wakes her from her slumber. There, on the rusty black banister, is the pale brown dove. Except this time there are two more, one on each side, all staring at her without so much as twitching.

Wait a second. They're awfully close. Did she... she fell asleep on the fire escape?

Cold bites at her skin, and her hands are too numb to be of

much use. Her favorite pen topples from between her fingers and plummets to the damp concrete stories below.

It lands nib first.

"Fuck," Psyche says.

But the doves say nothing.

To avoid dropping her notebook, she tosses it into the apartment ahead of herself. Next she slides in. Flexing her hands to loosen them, she pulls down the window and draws the curtain. As they sway, she catches a glimpse of the doves—still there. Still watching.

Well, she thinks, *let them watch.* Eros isn't here to stop them. Unless...? She pauses, holds her breath. Thinks of campfires and arrows and fruit too sweet to be of this world. She touches her lips and remembers, for a moment, the heat of the kiss they'd shared.

You need only think of it, Eros had said.

But perhaps she is still busy, for this time she does not come.

Psyche does not sigh. Her heart does *not* sink. It would be foolish if it did, really, foolish of her to hang her hopes on something so childish as that. Eros has her own things to take care of. Hadn't she made that clear?

Real bravery is going to have to entail living on her own for a while.

Psyche focuses on her own routine. Watering the plants, rotating the ones that need rotating, and pruning leaves. Feeding Latte comes next. As usual, the sound of a tin opening sends Latte bolting over toward Psyche. Within a minute or two all the food is gone—and Latte returns to staring out the window.

"Feeling like chicken, huh?" Psyche says. Latte lays a palm against the glass.

Hmm. Cats are natural acrobats, but letting her out onto the fire escape feels dangerous. Psyche shakes her head. "You're gonna have to intimidate them from here, buddy. And try harder than you've ever tried, because I'm pretty sure that's a god over there."

Latte meows the meow of the oppressed, the great sufferers of society. Such injustice has never been seen before, and she will be sure Psyche knows it.

Hours pass. The sun sinks below the sky.

Eros does not visit.

Around eight her alarm rings. Her weekly meeting with her gaming group is coming up soon. Psyche puts on her headset. The others greet her, and she greets them. On the character select screen she sees her black mage and dragoon staring back at her.

The thought is there before she knows it: Could she make Eros? Bards are the only characters that get bows. She's never played someone that hasn't been able to fight before, but maybe an Eros avatar can be her own private little thing on the side. Her own way of getting to know someone who doesn't seem to want to be known.

Not tonight, she thinks. But soon.

There's a delightful normalcy to the gaming. Who gets what gear? Who stands where? Which character is the hottest?

(Countess Carlock, obviously. Tall leather corset mommies are unbeatable.)

The cinematic atmosphere of the fight itself never fails to get her blood pumping—the music, the fearsome mage at the center, the mechanics and the way they evolve. For the first three minutes of this encounter, they have to avoid the incoming columns of magic with only a second or so to spare between attacks. The intense focus takes her away from everything else—and when she's fallen into a rhythm, the conversation keeps her there.

"Hey, what do you think High Mage Dellann even does in his free time?" someone asks.

"Probably plays *DDR*," says the raid leader, with absolute certainty. Psyche's always admired Foxglove's lightning-fast reflexes and multitasking ability. As the group's main support, she had to bounce from one to the other and keep them alive—all while navigating the incoming dangers herself. Given that High Mage Dellann is the game's ultimate boss, she's got her work cut out for her tonight. "He looks like a *DDR* nerd."

"He's not wearing *DDR* nerd pants," Psyche says. "There's no straps or anything. They're going to laugh him out of the arcade."

"Goldie, please stop being such a boomer, arcades aren't real anymore," says the party tank.

Psyche laughs. She's...she's not a boomer, is she? "Am I really that old-fashioned?"

"Uh, yeah," is the unanimous reply.

"I'm surprised you know what *DDR* is," says Foxglove. "You're the world's most grandmotherly dragoon."

"I bet when you're done with raid, you knit," says Knucklebone—their tank. "Cute little socks and hats and baby blankets and stuff."

"I wish. I'm a terrible knitter," says Psyche.

"So you do knit," says Foxglove. "That's gotta make you real popular with the ladies."

"Honestly? Knitting is a valuable skill," says Psyche. "If you end up sent back in time, it's a good one to know. As a society we undervalue traditionally feminine skills—"

"Okay, Professor Goldie, but can you maybe focus on not dying right now?"

She can't help but laugh. Yes, there's no pressure to any of this. Old-fashioned, huh? Well, maybe she is. She likes to write things longhand where she can. She likes phone calls over messaging, when it comes down to it, an attitude that has gotten her in trouble with many of her friends. She likes dating in person and she likes reading physical books. Maybe those things do make her a boomer. But she doesn't mind, and she's made a bit of a side hustle out of it besides. People want to live old-fashioned lives sometimes. They want to slow down and get a better look at things; they want physical evidence of the times they've had and the work they've done.

She doesn't point that out to the others, though. She doesn't need to.

Their raid finishes for the night. No items drop for Psyche, but she doesn't mind. She's content to have spent time with friends—and, admittedly, to have done an absolute assload of damage to High Mage Dellann.

Strange. It used to be that this gathering every week was the only time she felt like she had actual power. Watching the numbers tick up over the course of the fight and seeing where she ranked at the end of the raid gave her a sense of satisfaction she got nowhere else. The rest of the world thought of her as soft and meek; here she could be the team's main damage dealer.

The thoughts stay with her long after the others have signed off. She thinks about being a different sort of Psyche, one people didn't know. A braver one. Making her own little Eros avatar to run around this imagined world—one somehow less fanciful than the reality—so that they might spend a bit of time together. And a third thought: What would her friends say if they could see this version of her? Would they like her?

Would her followers? With all the Court research and focus on Eros, she hasn't considered them at all. Her account must be practically dead. With the kind of cozy content Psyche posted, it was important to keep up daily routines. She'd cast all those aside once she got a whiff of the Courts.

But what if she went back to it?

What if they knew she's more than knitting and pens and planners? That she has other hobbies, that she likes doing tons of damage, that her favorite characters are all edgelords and her favorite glamours look so fanciful?

Would they leave her behind if she weren't so much like her sisters?

Psyche drums her fingers on her laptop. Hmm. A lot of people made a fair bit of money streaming themselves playing their games. While Psyche's setup isn't meant for that sort of thing, she can rig it up if she wants. Wouldn't take very long. Bondi might have the log-ins to Psyche's mains, but Psyche does have a streaming account she's never used. That one she kept.

She logs in now. Five thousand followers. More than most people could dream of, but only a fraction of what her sisters have earned. Only the diehards followed her here. Her eyes go to the camera, the ring lights, her outfit.

She can do it.

But whom does she ask about it? Bondi doesn't know much about this sort of thing. She glances over the contacts on her Discord account. Only one jumps out to her.

Her younger sister, the fighting-game celebrity and shut-in. If anyone knew the ins and outs of streaming, it would be Cid.

Would it be weird to ask her for advice, given how little they talk? Cid's internet celebrity is very different from Laura's, or from what Psyche has fallen into herself. Their interests have never quite lined up, either.

But the hesitation lasts only as long as a candle flicker. She's a new Psyche now, one who doesn't mind asking for things she wants.

Cid, she writes, do I have to get on camera if I'm going to stream myself playing something?

Do you like money? comes the answer, quick as anything. Because it's the same answer. Unless you paid for a vtuber rig and never told anyone.

I don't know what a vtuber is.

Lol boomer. It's like an avatar for you while you're streaming, so you can be gremlin mode irl but look like a cute anime girl.

Hmm, there is something appealing to that. Though Psyche doesn't watch much in the way of anime—Japanese role-playing games were always her primary vice. Maybe she could look like a cute JRPG girl? Either way, a matter for another night.

Wait are you about to stream? What are you playing? Can I come? I can have my stream raid yours, you'll have like a bajillion people coming in.

Psyche doesn't know what raiding a stream means, either, but she isn't about to ask. Cid will call her a boomer again.

I'm going to freshen up a little first but yeah. I'll send you the link. Just be cool okay?

I'm cooler than you'll ever be, kiddo.

When it comes to gamers, Cid's probably right. Psyche sends a heart and then gets ready to stream.

Chapter Eleven

When recording videos, Psyche always takes at least an hour to do her makeup and get her outfit ready. Curation's important there; people can never know how many takes you needed to get everything just right. And maybe the same is true for streamers—but right now, Psyche doesn't care as much as usual. Eros stared at her when she was in sweatpants and light concealer. Why should she need to do any more than that now?

Her comfy NYU hoodie, a little primping for her curls, and just the basics for makeup. For a moment she watches herself in the mirror—the mass of dark curls she could never quite tame, the aquiline nose she and her sisters all share. That nose has never suited Psyche the way it does them—on Laura it's proud and noble, and on Cid it gives her a raptor's arrogant look, but it just makes Psyche look classical. Maybe that's why everyone thinks she's such a boomer; it goes all the way back to her face.

She smirks to herself. Next time she visits Eros, she'll just have to ask about it. *Do you think I look old-fashioned?*

Looking at herself in the webcam test feed, she tries to see herself as Eros had. *I want to see you.* The chin that knew Eros's fingers, the mouth she'd kissed, the cheek she'd caressed. It is as if the gold Eros left behind had seeped into her skin and lent it a new luster.

She turns on the camera, the eye of the world; the microphone, that ferrier of voices; the internet, the great crossroads. After a few routine tests, Psyche takes a breath.

She starts the stream.

No one joins at first. The chat window on her second monitor is empty save for Cid's encouraging emoji spam. She is alone with the game's character creator and her thoughts of the woman she's shaping, the woman who might be under the mask. For what seems an eternity, she flits between her options. Rich, dark skin, first of all; a tall frame. The armor can't be helped at this point—everyone starts off the same—and so she addresses the hair next.

A ping catches her attention. She has her first viewer. Is this really PsySaysHi? Then, when she waves: Holy shit, it is you.

"Hey!" Psyche says. "Thanks so much for coming, I'm so happy to have you...BigBootyTieflings!"

God, did they have to have such a silly name to start the night? But, then, maybe it's good to laugh so much. "It's really me, and I'm really here. I just wanted to spend some time playing a game and I thought I'd invite everyone to come."

Damn, cool. You should promote it, though, so people know it's really you.

What a sensible admirer of big butts. "Isn't it cooler if it's a cozy little stealth stream though? I think that makes things more special. So... Tief. What are you up to tonight?"

By the end of ten minutes, they've got a couple hundred people hanging out in the chat. Messages flood in. She doesn't have a special notification set up for those, or a sound, or anything—but she reads them aloud all the same.

"'Happy to see you back on my screen, and this time on my PC instead of just on my phone!' Thank you so much for donating, SliferSky34! It's good to be hanging out with all of you."

"'Show cat!' Oh, I'd love to, but I'm not about to tell Latte what to do," Psyche says. "You know, cats can teach us a lot about boundaries. You can't force them to do anything they don't want to do—not really. Even if you manage to get them into the cute little costume, they're going to take it off the second you're not looking."

There are some flowers so famous that people travel from around the world to watch them bloom once. Psyche feels as if she's become one now—as if she's blossomed in her own private garden and her followers have turned up to admire her. Every message is sunlight against her waxy petals.

Why hasn't she tried streaming before? Well, aside from making planners and stuff. This is pretty wonderful, all told. She isn't doing anything she wouldn't normally do, and since everything's live, there's less pressure to be perfect. The comments on her videos always talk about goals this or serving that, but everyone here seems content to simply share space.

Of course, they ask questions, too.

"'What's it like taking such a long break? Have you been holding up okay?'" she reads. "Honestly? It's kind of... freeing. I missed all of you, don't get me wrong, but I've had some time to myself to think because of all this. Maybe I was taking myself a little too seriously. What do you guys think?"

Chat explodes. She's up to a thousand viewers by now; the followers are pouring in by the second. Messages go by so quickly that she can't follow them. Emoji and reaction faces, mostly, with questions mixed in among them. Psyche feels a pang of regret that she can't read them all aloud, too; everyone should get their chance to ask something. On her second screen, she finds Cid's username and quickly promotes her sister to mod.

You want me to give them the business when it comes to those questions? Cid messages.

It's fine, really. I'm fine.

And it is fine. She's sure of that now, in the weeds of it. Sure, she might have made things weird for a little while after the whole Alex situation, but who cares? All of this is just internet stuff, anyway. It can't reach her. And she has plenty of people who still care about her, plenty of people who turned out for something as impromptu as this.

Psyche stretches. "All right, everybody. For the next twenty minutes I'm going to answer whatever questions come in via superchat. If you can't superchat now that's totally fine—my sister will be picking out fun questions from the regular chat, too. But keep it within reason! I'm not answering anything that'll get me banned."

The first question comes in instantly: QuarterCircleCid is your sister?!?! The perfect parry god?!? Asasdfsfsdfsdfsdfs!

She laughs again, scrolling through the options for walk animations. "Don't tell her that, or her head's going to get even bigger. Yeah, she's my little sister. I guess I've never said that in public?"

The next few questions center around Cid, which is to be expected. Of course people who like gaming streams know QuarterCircleCid. But maybe... maybe they can like Psyche, too?

"Let me answer a few of these at once," she says, scrolling through the notifications. "I don't play fighting games. No one else in our family does, but sometimes I'd drive Cid to the arcade and hang out while she cleaned the place up. It was pretty fun. Most embarrassing thing she's ever done? Hmm. I mean, I don't really think anything she does is embarrassing. Sometimes we find ourselves in embarrassing situations, sure, but I've always been happy to be her sister."

In the back of her mind she *knows* Cid is wriggling under the force of all this attention. Psyche's not about to make her look uncool in front of her followers. In fact...

"I can tell you I used to embarrass *her* all the time, though. Cid's been bigger than me since we were kids, and I've never met an argument I haven't tried to settle. I can't tell you how many times she had to yank me out of trouble because I couldn't leave well enough alone. One time when I messed up my lines for the school play, she beat someone up for laughing at me."

Psyche leaves out that it was the boy Laura had a crush on. That part can remain their own.

" 'Pineapple on pizza? Are you among the chosen or have you forsaken the light?' I'm pro pineapple. People should try new things!"

A war sparks off in the comments; somehow, she watches Cid ban no less than twenty people in under a minute. Perfect parry god indeed! That speed!

"'How long have you been playing *Crystal Dragon Knight XIV*? Favorite class? Favorite expansion?'" Psyche reads. She touches a finger to her lips as she thinks. "Hmm...I think five years or so? Since before the big reconstruction patch. My favorite expansion is *Fall of the Righteous,* winner of game of the year, best soundtrack, and players' choice. And I mostly play dragoon or black mage, but I thought I'd try something different and make a bard."

Another ding as six of the same question come in. Watching the numbers tick up—subscribers, viewers, donations—she wonders why she ever decided focusing on premade content was the way to go. This feels so much cozier, so much easier. Sure there's a lot to keep track of—but if she hires some mods and filters things out, then maybe this could be doable as her regular form of content.

Plus it lets her focus more on her imagined Eros. With the right kind of braids now in place, she starts to shape her character's face. Lips first, then nose, then cheekbones. Some comes from her imagination, and some from the mask Eros is so fond of wearing. The high cheekbones, severe brow, and wide shape of her eyes all come from the mask.

Psyche lets out a happy sigh. Here it's easy to reach out and touch Eros's cheek. The screen beneath her fingertips is just as false as the mask.

"'Have you and Alex squashed the beef? You seem so relaxed. Tbh I wish I could be that unbothered when bad stuff happens to me.' That's kind of you to say, CountMarkoff. Sooner or later we're all going to end up in a situation like this, right? We've all made mistakes before. To tell you the truth, the situation's a complicated one. I wanted to make sure Alex had space to share her side of things. It's more important than mine. Now if Alex wants to talk things out, I'm more than open to that, but at the end of the day, she's entitled to her feelings, and I do owe her an apology. She deserves to make her decision about all this as she likes."

Shouldn't it be more frightening to talk about the client who got her fired? She isn't trembling, not a bit. Maybe she really is a braver Psyche, one who can admit that she's done something wrong.

Back to the character designer as more questions flood in. Voice next—the most crucial part of all. Psyche has her doubts that anyone could match the throaty purr of Eros's voice. *CDK XIV* has only four voice options for two genders, each locked to the gender in question. Not exactly the most progressive game in terms of options. She picks the deepest of the women's voices.

"Heed my orders and victory is assured," her character says. The voice is deep, yes, but that of a strict disciplinarian. However much Eros might hold herself that way, there's a sarcastic tone beneath.

"Let's crush our enemies!" says the second lowest. No, too brash, too energetic... If only she could use the male voices. The highest of them would be perfect for Eros. All she'd have to do is pitch it slightly up. Why are games still locking voices to gender in this day and age?

The next option for women is labeled *seductress.* "You'll *enjoy* bowing to me," she says.

Hmm.

It isn't right. It doesn't sound anything like Eros, not really. Far too high. But hearing that line come from the imagined Eros's mouth is...

Psyche feels her cheeks go hot. She crosses her legs under the desk and hopes no one watching notices the effect that just had on her. Or the effect it continues to have on her as she pitches the voice down as low as it will go.

"Oh, a question from the chat," Psyche says. She clears her throat. "Let's see... BigBootyTieflings thinks I should use the Aurelian Tragicomedy helmet for this character? I don't know that one off the top of my head, let's pull it up together... oh."

Psyche's spine tingles. The Aurelian Tragicomedy helmet is a full-face porcelain mask. How did...?

"Wow, that... is exactly what I was imagining, actually," Psyche says. She can't keep the surprise out of her voice. "You must be some kind of mind reader, Tief."

Five questions follow one after the other, all asking variations of the same thing.

" 'Are you making someone special?' " Psyche reads.

She takes a breath. *Think.* With the camera staring down at her, she can't afford to be quiet for too long. These people are all her friends, aren't they? She can chat with them.

"Maybe a little," Psyche admits. "It's not such a bad thing though, is it?"

Tell us about her!!

New boo? Omg so cute to make her in game.

Psyche I can take care of you better than she ever could, please dm me please notice me.

That one Cid quietly removes from the queue the second it enters. But the implication's clear enough—her viewers are definitely onto her.

"I'm not sure if I'd use the word 'boo,'" Psyche says. "It's all very... new, and I'm not sure how to describe it yet."

GOTTA SECURE THE TALL HOTTIE, PSY comes in.

"I'm going to tell her you all said that," she says with a laugh. And she will, she thinks. "We've only seen each other a couple times so far, but both have been wonderful, honestly. New, and a little frightening, but in a good way. Like skydiving or something."

The last box for character creation is name. Psyche fills in Eros and hits next. The opening cinematic begins to play—Eros wakes up in a strange chamber surrounded on all sides by stars stretching into infinity. A voice calls to her to take up her weapon.

"'What's with the mask, though?'" Psyche reads. "It's a, uh, cultural thing. Let's be respectful of people's closely held beliefs, okay?"

Psyche hits a button; Eros picks up her bow. This section serves as an introduction to her character's abilities—they're all available within this chamber, all the way up to level ninety-nine. You're meant to be sure of the class you've picked by trying them out. Psyche runs through each of the abilities in turn. Her brows narrow. Her focus shifts to the screen itself, to navigation, to gaming.

A notification comes in—another superchat.

"'But if it's really new, then why is she in your apartment right now?'" Her first reaction is to laugh. "Oh, sure, the old made-you-look prank. I guess she's with me in the game."

"I'm with you in person, too," comes a familiar voice. A campfire scent, a hand on her shoulder. "You really do need to be more aware of your surroundings, or you're going to get into trouble. I could be anyone."

The pure shock on Psyche's face will live on as a meme for years after this—her ruddy cheeks, her eyes going small as pinheads, her mouth hanging open.

She swallows. If the chat had exploded before, it is in cinders now, with new reaction faces coming in every second. And plenty of demands for Psyche's expression to be made into one, too. On her other monitor, Cid is keyboard smashing at her about the "weird-looking stranger in my sister's apartment."

In times like this, there's only one thing to do.

"H-hey, guys, I think I'm going to hop off for a little while. Catchyoutomorrowatthesametime!"

Chapter Twelve

Never has anyone closed out of their windows so quickly. The swiftest ships of the sea would envy Psyche's speed. Though not her lack of grace—in doing this she knocks her mouse from the desk and upsets her papers, too.

"You're back," she stammers. Eros is wearing the armor this time. Isn't she hot, all bundled up like that? And there's the matter of the mask again, staring down at her from on high. Like the punishing angels outside of courthouses. "I—I wasn't ready for guests. I haven't even made dinner—"

"There's no need. Your company is meal enough," says Eros. Psyche's all too aware of how small the place is now that Eros is standing in the middle of it. Well, it isn't the first time, but Psyche's mouth had been too on fire then to notice.

"But everything that isn't on camera is a total mess, and—" Psyche starts.

Eros quiets her with a squeeze of the shoulder. "Are *you*… on camera?" she asks.

Better to double-check and be sure than to accidentally

broadcast her supernatural conversations to a couple thousand people, right? Her lock screen—a commission of her dragoon—assures her there's nothing to worry about.

"No, but I was, and you walked right up behind me like you live here," Psyche says.

Eros tilts her head and gives a small laugh, like she finds Psyche amusing. "I think you've been lying to me again," she says.

"What? No. We're not on camera," Psyche says. She points to the screen. "Look—I closed out of everything, and here's my phone. See?"

Eros leans over to study both the phone and the PC. She nods in the manner of sages and wiseasses. "I understand with perfect clarity," she says. "You *were* lying."

"But I wasn't!" Psyche says. She's on her feet before she knows why. "I haven't told you a single lie since you got here—which, by the way! You still haven't explained. Meanwhile there's no dinner here and no cameras, like I said."

Eros chuckles. "We really should get you lessons in dealing with my kind," she says. Then she leans forward. "If I wanted to, I could have eaten you alive for that one. It's very precise business."

Psyche crosses her arms. She does not move, oh no. To move away would be to admit the effect being so close to Eros is having on her. Truth be told, part of the reason she's standing like this is to consciously keep her hands to herself. The temptation to wrap an arm around Eros's waist is strong. *Very* strong.

"You're gaslighting me now," Psyche says. She keeps her eyes trained on the tip of the mask's nose, a place that does not set the mind to wandering. Not very much, anyway. "I told you I haven't lied to you. You keep saying that I have, but you won't tell me when."

That head tilt again—then a turn. Psyche watches Eros explore the apartment. She starts near the plants, walking a long, deliberate line around them.

"I was trying to flatter you," Eros says. "You said that the things that were not on camera were a mess—but you weren't on camera, and you're as charming as ever. Thus, a lie. A small one."

Psyche pouts. All right, so it was a cute reason. "Can you be a little nicer about that sort of thing in the future?"

A pause. An ages-old part of Psyche anticipates an argument and braces for it.

"You're right," Eros says. A sound like air coming out of a sack. "That was too arcane of me, and I should have corrected when I realized we were at odds."

Oh. No argument? Well, that's... really nice, actually.

As Eros walks past the plants, Psyche finds herself following her. Eros is tall enough that Psyche has to strain to keep up. "There are going to be times I don't want to talk to you."

"Is now one of those times?" Eros says. She turns her head, gesturing toward the window. "I'll leave if so."

"No," Psyche admits with a sigh. "I'm actually happy to see you again."

"Good," says Eros. "I'm pleased to see you, too." She stops, studying the yellow-leaved deliciosa.

"I'm underwatering," Psyche says, suddenly self-conscious. Rather than linger on the matter—and sensing she will make no progress on the matter of Eros's appearances—she seizes on a new subject. "How was...work? Is everything all right, back at the Court?"

Eros rights herself. She walks to the window, parting the curtain with one hand. The view isn't anything to write home about. In the movies you always get a clear shot of the city skyline from anywhere in Brooklyn. Psyche has a view of the building's courtyard from one side of the apartment and a view of the street from the other. She likes them both, but compared to the glittering stars Eros has as a canopy, this isn't much.

"My mother called me to settle a matter between two old friends," Eros says.

"Nothing too terrible, I hope?" Psyche says. "Sometimes relationships can make things more complicated. The older the relationship the worse it can be."

"This is new. Very new. Well, one of them is, at any rate," Eros says. "Technically, all of this rightly belongs in the Court of the Wild, but as my Domain overlaps the rest of them, I was asked to adjudicate."

Psyche picks up a notepad and pen and sits on the couch. No morsel of information is going to escape her unrecorded. "Is the Court of the Wild new, or are the people?"

"One of the people," Eros answers. She remains at the window. "The other is the Queen of the Wild. A woman I've known for quite some time."

"Are the two of you friends?" Psyche asks. "Or coworkers?"

"The opposite," Eros says. "Of all the Courts and all the Domains, I see hers the least. She goes out of her way to avoid me."

Psyche hums. "Is it because she hates your sense of humor?" she jokes.

But that's lost on Eros. "No. It's because she's afraid of my influence."

Afraid of Eros's influence? Psyche writes it down, underlines it. *Influence.*

"I'm curious as to what makes you say that. It's a strong assertion, but you seem very confident in it," says Psyche.

Eros turns and takes a seat on the other end of the couch. There's a touch of absurdity to it—this masked, armored woman sitting on Psyche's old Ikea couch.

"I can't lie," Eros says. "None of us can. She admitted this to me herself, that she wanted nothing to do with my Domain. But it's too late—she's already entangled."

Psyche sets the pen down. How to phrase this next question? Though Eros seems a woman who prefers things honest and straightforward. Perhaps that's the best approach. "Are you a soldier?"

This time there's a touch of bitterness to Eros's scoff. "You could say that, though not of the kind you're used to seeing," she says. A pause—one Psyche allows to grow as it likes, to fill the space between them. Prodding will only make things worse. Sure enough Eros elaborates. "I told you the last time we spoke."

"When you told me how you felt about war...?"

"I will answer that, in time. However, I did not come here to talk of such weighty matters—I came to visit you," Eros says. She turns her head, surveying the rest of the room. "If it's permitted for me to explore?"

"Of course," says Psyche. "I mean, there's not much to explore. You're probably used to mansions, but there's no space in New York—"

"I didn't expect a mansion. I expected to learn about you," Eros says. Once more she stands. This time she walks to the kitchen. The family photos on the fridge seem to catch her attention. "These are your relatives?"

Psyche follows her. "Yeah."

The photos staring back aren't anything fancy: two of her sisters at camp as children; one of Psyche with her mother at high school graduation; one photo each with Cid and Laura. Smiling faces abound—though Laura's never been one to smile with her teeth.

Eros hums. "Your sisters..."

Psyche braces herself for Eros to talk about how pretty Laura is, or how athletic Cid used to be. She knows the thought is irrational. Dumb. But it's there, and she wishes more than anything she could shut it up.

"They resemble you, don't they? But there's a softness to you. Like the clouds at dawn."

Psyche's chest flutters. "You really think so?"

"I do," says Eros. "Will you tell me about your life with them? It's such a novel thing to me—to have siblings you enjoy."

"*Enjoy* is..." she begins. *Complicated* is the word she reaches for first. But is it the right one? Laura might not be the sensitive type, but she did come to check on Psyche when she went missing. And Cid didn't hesitate to help her out, either. Is it really complicated—or does Psyche just have a complex of her own?

It's a question to which she's long known the answer.

"Sure, yeah. I can tell you whatever you like," she says.

Eros wraps an arm around her shoulder. It is the easiest thing in the world, and yet the comfort it brings Psyche is...

"What is the difference in years between you? Do you all have the same parents? Have any of you waged war against the others? What was it like, watching them age alongside you, watching them change? Forgive me if there are too many questions, or if I'm overstepping. It's only that I know so little about you other than how you make me feel, and I want to know more. I need to. As a fire needs air."

By the time she finishes speaking, Psyche is looking straight up into the mask's eyes.

As a fire needs air.

She feels so happy that she has to stifle a laugh. How ridiculous, to think of Psyche that way! And yet, what a joy.

Yes, it would be better if they got to know each other, wouldn't it?

"Answer for answer?" Psyche offers.

Another laugh, soft as the dawn.

"Yes. That will do."

Psyche smiles. "Then that means I've got a four-question head start!"

When Psyche was in Eros's Domain, the time passed at odds with her sense of it. She opened her eyes and three days had passed.

When she's *with* Eros, time passes quickly and slowly all at once. It's as if every moment, every happy little discovery, is its own eternity. Psyche has to take care not to fall in.

Eros's odd, straightforward questions—and her even more straightforward answers.

The smell of her, like a campfire.

Her steady gait, and in its wake the dulled footfalls of Latte following.

The comfort with which they can sit on Psyche's bed together, talking, and the questions Eros asks her. How a woman who only yesterday wielded such world-shattering power strokes Latte's fur with all the delicacy of lace.

"Do you have a favorite color?" Eros asks her, as if they are fifteen, and for some reason it delights Psyche just as much as it would have back then.

"Blue," Psyche says, "but blue like the sky in the morning, when everyone else is asleep, and it's almost violet."

All of this is so cozy, so impossible. And yet.

Is this what her bravery has won her? Perhaps she can be a little braver.

She sits in Eros's lap. "Do *you* have a favorite color?"

"Before I answer that, I'd like to ask you something," Eros says. Her hand drops to the small of Psyche's back. "What are you most curious about—what's beneath the mask, my daily life, or what I could do to you on this bed of yours?"

Psyche's cheeks go hot. "Our agreement is to answer honestly," she says. "So..."

She takes a steadying breath.

"If I had to rank them, it'd be more about your daily life and who you are as a person first. Zephyr *did* ask me to look after you, and I intend to do that as best I can. But..."

"But...?" says Eros. "Psyche. Are you *teasing* me?"

In *that* tone of voice?

Oh, it's difficult to say it out loud now.

"But it's hard to focus on that when I keep wondering about...the last one you mentioned. I don't even know what you look like, and I keep thinking about how your skin feels against mine," she says. "And if never looking under that mask is the price of being around you, then it's a price I'm happy to pay."

A soft sound of consideration from Eros. Her hand slides higher, beneath Psyche's sweater and against her skin—an advancing heat that sends ripples through Psyche's whole body. She bites her lip to keep from making any sound.

"You didn't answer my question—" Psyche starts.

She doesn't finish. How can she, when Eros changes their positions so quickly? One moment Psyche is on her lap, the next Eros has set her down and is kneeling before her. Two strong hands on her thighs part them, making space for that mysterious face. Eros rests her head right on Psyche's mound—her chin just below Psyche's navel. Meanwhile she reaches up for Psyche's full ass.

"If I told you that I wanted to do this instead of answering any more of your questions, what would you say?"

Oh, oh, this is just cruel. To be held like this, to be *squeezed* like this...She feels so small in Eros's grip. Blood goes everywhere but her brain. Eros's breath is hot against the fabric of her sweatpants. All it would take is a slight lift of that mask, and Psyche's sense will leave her, she's sure of it. It's already taking everything in her not to roll her hips along with Eros's groping.

But one thing occurs to her above all.

"I—I would say," she stammers, "that as... much as I like this... I don't think we should right now. I think... it's a little too fast."

Eros tugs at Psyche's pants. She pulls them down just enough to reveal the strawberry-print panties beneath. The cool night air and Eros's heat mingle on Psyche's skin. "And if I did this? Would you feel the same way?"

Psyche takes a breath; it comes out more ragged than she'd like.

Great heroes travel far in search of something to lend them strength. Some find it in fountains that lend them eternal youth. Others study ancient tomes to learn secret spells. Still others pay any price they can, betraying friend and family alike in search of the next ancient relic.

They all pale in comparison to Psyche. For there is no potion coursing through her, no divine blood in her veins, and no sword in her hand—yet she summons the will of a warrior all the same and pulls away.

To her credit, at the slightest indication of discomfort, Eros lets go. Eros stands once more and walks a few paces away—the yard between them as good as a mile given the circumstances.

"My apologies," Eros says. "I should have stayed my hand. That was unbecoming of me. Your safety should come before my curiosity."

Psyche strains to try to catch her breath amidst the blood rushing through her ears. "It's—it isn't... If it happens for us, then I want it to happen naturally."

Silence from the other woman—a deafening silence this time, one that cuts at Psyche's tongue. Part of her wants to cross the room and kiss her again—to press herself against Eros and show her how badly she'd wanted to continue.

"I'm sorry," Eros says at length. "It was thoughtless of me."

"My turn to ask a question," Psyche says. Eros looks up from the floor, a certain stiffness coming into her posture, like she's found herself in the headlights. "Were you testing me?"

Few can brag of making a god flinch. "Yes," Eros responds.

"Why would you do something like that?" Psyche asks, wounded.

Eros turns away again. Her shoulders tremble, her hands flex open and closed. Soon, she begins to pace. "I don't have much experience with other people wanting to speak with me. To really speak with me. And I wanted to be sure that you did."

"You'd already asked me," Psyche points out. "And you said you know when I lie."

"My Domains are Love and Passion," Eros says. The words come out of her like a murder confession. "Everyone who meets me loves me. They can't help it. Do you know what it's like having to keep yourself at arm's length from two worlds at once? I can detect *lies*, Psyche, but I can't detect *earnestness*.

I've had people promise to sell out everything they've ever known for a chance to be with me, and I've had to stand there knowing they meant every word. That all I had to do was agree, and they'd shatter their life into millions of pieces. Not because of who I am, but because of *what* I am."

Her voice is cracking. Psyche stands.

"I needed to know," Eros continues. "I needed to know that if I tried, that even if I pressed the issue, you meant what you'd said. Before I told you what I am, I needed to know that it didn't matter to you."

A lump forms in Psyche's throat. She knows what it's like, holding yourself apart. No one wants to talk to the girl whose mother is sick, whose father hasn't kept a steady job in twenty years. Misfortune brings with it miasma; people are always happy to help, but only ever from a distance. There comes a time when they realize there's too much going on, a point where they leave.

"I understand," Psyche says.

"How can you?" Eros says. It comes out of her mouth quick as an arrow and, when Eros sees that it has landed, her whole body seems to shrink. "Sorry, that was—"

"I think you should go," Psyche says.

Eros touches her hand. She, too, squeezes. But then extricates herself, turning too fast for Psyche to get a look at her. Eros stops only when she's reached the door.

"When..." she starts, then shakes her head. "If you want to see me again, burn a piece of honeycomb over open flame. I'll come."

Chapter Thirteen

Psyche thinks of Eros in the mornings when the sky is campfire orange; when she feels the heat of a coffee mug against her skin; when she goes for a walk and sees the flowers blooming; when she surveys like a queen the stacks of books she's ordered to learn more about the Courts.

All of these things remind her of her Oathsworn. And she craves summoning Eros to her.

But then she remembers the awkwardness. The testing. The sharpened teeth, the unnatural strength, the descriptions in all those books of what a god can do to a human.

She remembers, and she thinks, *Maybe it's better to wait?*

Maybe I need to catch my breath. Maybe all of this is happening too fast.

Bacon sizzles on a pan. The sound of rice being tossed in a wok. Bright licks of flame lending her and Laura alike their nourishment.

She eats her fill. Mike stops by to say hello for once in their lives.

"Is it true?" Psyche asks him. "That you got an invitation to the Courts. Is it true?"

He glances up at Laura. She's taking a business call. Maybe that's what lends him the courage to answer honestly. "It is. Our company works with one of theirs."

"They have companies?" Psyche asks. She shouldn't be surprised, but given what Zephyr said about how old-fashioned they can be, it is a bit of a shock.

"Humans run them. Or, at least, I think they're human. I can't be sure. Tantalus International has been run by only two generations in the past couple hundred years, so maybe they're only part human. Still. They like to maintain their influence on us. On this world."

"But why?" Psyche asks.

"It's all some kind of game to them. They can't wage open war against one another without one of them breaking a rule first—so they use us instead."

Psyche frowns. Would Eros be involved with something like that? She doesn't care about most things in the human world at all. But just how deep does all of this go?

Laura starts to double back from her phone call. Mike spots her and waves.

"If you want my advice, though," he whispers to Psyche, "always remember they're not like us."

As Laura arrives, he stands up to give her a kiss on the

cheek. They exchange some whispered pleasantries before he takes off—but not without a last look at Psyche.

But she doesn't have any time to process his warning, because Laura's got questions of her own.

"How has it been with you? Are you recovering well?"

Simple enough questions. Ones that Psyche has asked plenty of people herself. On the other side of her desk or looking after her mother—she's asked these same questions.

But now she doesn't like being on the other end of them.

"I think so," she says. "I started streaming the other day. Like Cid does?"

"That's a good distraction," Laura says. As the dishes are set before them, Laura drapes the napkin over her lap and slices into her eggs. Yolk runs over the rest—rice, bacon, charred garlic.

"I was thinking it could be more than that," Psyche ventures. "Cid does it . . . well, not full-time, but sort of. Doing this gets her the attention to get her the sponsorships she needs to enter tournaments—"

"That doesn't make it a job. You need stability, Psy," Laura says. She dips a bit of bacon into the yolk. "A routine. When your routines slip—"

Psyche knows exactly the report Laura is going to quote, and never wants to hear a line from it again. "I can make it a routine. If I set my alarms to the same times I'd usually go to work, and if I do it regularly, then that's routine, right? That's structure?"

Overhead a plane sails west across the face of god. The people aboard have no idea what's going on beneath them. Is it like that for Eros, too? Waging those wars she spoke of, does she have any idea what's going on in the real world?

Or maybe this isn't the real world at all. Maybe it's all a matter of point of view. Eros must have spent much longer in her world than Psyche has here.

She perches her head on her hand and looks at the red morning sky.

"Streaming could be good for me. Having control of my own schedule, talking to people. That was always my favorite part of my therapy jobs—getting to know my clients and helping them out. I can do that this way, too. It doesn't just have to be video games. I was thinking I could host question time, or maybe I could bring on couples I know and we could talk about their different relationship styles."

Laura hums. "She's a bad influence on you."

Psyche sighs. "Cid's not as lazy as you think she is. She works really hard at this gaming stuff. It's not just hanging out with people. You have to promote yourself, make merch, figure out scheduling. And she's doing all of that on her own. It's kind of incredible she manages—"

"I wasn't talking about Cidippe," Laura says. She takes a sip of her mimosa and crooks a brow. No one—not even their dear departed grandparents—ever called Cid by her full name. Except Laura, who seemed to delight in doing it. "It's the woman you're seeing. The predator."

"Predator?!" Psyche shoots back. "How can you say something like that? Eros would never hurt me—"

"That's only the impression she's given you. You haven't seen her face yet, have you?"

"No, but—"

The sharpness of Laura's gaze could split timber. "Whatever oaths she has sworn to you, Psyche, if you have not seen her face, then she does not think of you as an equal. And neither should you. You have nothing in common with her and *can* have nothing in common with her."

Psyche grits her teeth. She wants to argue the point, but she thinks back to Eros's hold on her, to the test she'd never agreed to take.

"I think that deep down, you know that I'm right," says Laura. "One of Michael's friends was asking about you the other day—someone in the legal department. Antigone's got a stellar reputation, the pay to match it, and she's fond of those games you seem to like so much, too. I took the liberty of making the two of you a dinner reservation in a week—"

"You what?" Psyche snaps. "You didn't even ask me?"

"All I'm asking," Laura says, "is that you give her fair consideration. At worst you'll meet someone new and have a free meal together. Is that really so bad, Psyche?"

Psyche grits her teeth. Of course it's that simple to Laura—she hasn't seen the things Psyche's seen. Going on a normal date feels like going into a kiddie pool when she's used to diving into the ocean.

But a free meal...Psyche still has a fair bit in her savings account, but knowing Laura, this might be at a place she'd never be able to afford on her own. Would it be so bad to enjoy the food? And with the stunt Eros pulled, maybe it'd be nice to just...try something else.

See how it felt.

"Where's the reservation?"

Thanks to subway troubles, Psyche blusters into her date (should she think of it as a date?) fifteen minutes late. Antigone is already seated with a glass of wine. Everything about her screams that she's one of Laura's friends. In the same way a stone in winter and the snow have much in common, so do Antigone and Laura.

"I'm so sorry," Psyche says. "Someone let out a ton of crickets on the Q over the bridge, and they had to evacuate, it was a whole thing."

Antigone studies her from head to toe. How strange it is to feel someone appraising her. Eros hadn't, not even at the start. Psyche can't shake the feeling that Antigone is mousing over her character to check her stats.

"Crickets, hmm?" says Antigone. "What on earth could have brought that on?"

"She said it was performance art or something," Psyche answers. She drapes her jacket across the back of her seat. "Have you looked at the menu already?"

The menus lay face down on the table. Antigone doesn't

glance at them, looking out at the bar instead. "Oh, there's no need. We come here often and I get the same thing every time."

"Ah, you're one of those types?" says Psyche. She picks up the menu, glances at the prices, then sets it right back down. Too rich for her to make any decisions. "Laura said you like *Crystal Dragon Knight XIV*?"

Antigone lets out a low laugh, one that suits her gloomy features. "Did she? I play it on the weekends. I'm not in a guild or anything—to tell you the truth, most of the time I stay in the character creator. Sometimes I'll go out to take screenshots, though."

Oh. That sounded... quiet. Psyche has to hide her surprise. Who played a game with such intricate combat only to run around taking photos instead?

"I love the quests," Psyche says, feeling a little shy. "I mean, it's so exciting, isn't it? I've never played a game that really made me feel like I was saving the world before."

"I get enough of that at my job," says Antigone. "I don't need any extra stress. Better to take in what's already there."

A pause. Psyche drinks a little of her water. "What kind of work do you do?"

"I work with the legal department of Kaminsky Corp to establish relationships with underserved communities throughout the world." She says it the way someone might say they're left-handed. "It's good work. But it is draining."

Psyche nods. It really was good work. She can see now why Laura set them up, but something feels... off. And from the way Antigone is studying her, maybe she feels it, too.

"Laura said you were vivacious," Antigone continues. "That you were always finding your way into trouble."

Psyche tucks a strand of hair behind her ear. "I guess she would say that about me."

"The strangest thing is that you don't look like a trouble-maker at all. You look like you speak in lowercase and spend most of your time in stationery stores." Antigone sips from her wine, drumming her fingertips on the table. "I'm babysitting you for the night, aren't I? That's what this is?"

Now it's Psyche's turn to laugh, and to sigh, and to wish that she had her own glass of wine. "That's…exactly what this is. No offense or anything! It's just, I hadn't really…I'm sort of…"

"You're already seeing someone," Antigone supplies. She rests her head on her hand.

Psyche feels a pang of regret. "Yeah. Laura doesn't like her."

"Laura doesn't like a lot of people," Antigone says. "What's wrong with this one? I'm guessing she stays out after eight on Friday nights or something?"

"God, Laura's the same with everyone, isn't she?" Psyche says. "Something like that. This person…I guess she's a little dangerous. Her family is, I mean. She's…"

Can Psyche really say Eros has been nothing but kind after last night? Perhaps not.

"Trying to be better than the way she grew up. And I don't think Laura gets that part. To her it's all the same—she's super deterministic. Sometimes I think she decided on what sort of people me and Cid would be when we were born."

"This person you're seeing," says Antigone. "Are you happy with her?"

"When we're together, yeah. Work keeps her busy a lot of the time. It's a little long-distance that way. But when she can make time, she does, and it feels like . . . like she's holding me up. Making me better just by being there."

The server comes by and asks what they'll have. Antigone confidently orders the chicken marsala. Psyche opts for one of the specials instead—she'd rather try something the place is known for. Soon there's a round of wine for them both.

"That's strong stuff," Antigone says. "That feeling. Have the two of you been together very long?"

"Hard to say. It feels like a long time, even if we only met a little over a month ago," Psyche answers. The wine is rich on her tongue. "To be honest, we kind of had a fight when I saw her last."

"Which is why you're here," Antigone says. "Trying something else out."

"It's that obvious, isn't it? I'm so sorry. I really didn't mean any harm, and Laura was so insistent I try."

Antigone waves a hand. "It's all right. I knew it from the second you walked into this place that you had someone else on your mind."

"What gave me away?"

Antigone hums. Once more she studies Psyche. Her dark brows narrow over her darker eyes. Then, with a sort of tired levity: "I couldn't tell you if I tried. Just the way you hold yourself. No one who's been dating around in the city stands that way; we're all too crushed by the monotony of it. But you seem like someone's given you hope. Was the fight bad?"

Psyche considers. Was it?

"I don't think it was bad on its own, but it leaves space for worry. It's an opportunity, I guess, to talk about something we haven't. Part of me worries about what it might mean for us, though—what if she can't shake those old habits? What if she does end up being like the rest of her family?"

"If Laura can have a sibling like you, then I think your person there can break free, too," Antigone says. "You just have to be sure that she wants to. Are you?"

Psyche answers without a moment's thought. The day she shot the bow left no doubt in her mind. "I think the parts of her that are like her family are the parts she hates the most."

"Then talk it out. Spend the time getting there," says Antigone. She gestures with the glass. "Give her the chance to prove that she can be different, and if she does—there you go. It might be hard, but you'll get there."

Psyche lets the moment stand. Something compels her to touch the candle on their table. Instead she floats her hand above it. As the heat washes over her palm, she wonders if Eros can see her here.

Warmth in her chest. A shift across her skin, like the caress of a lover.

Maybe she can.

"Thank you, Antigone," Psyche says. "And I really am sorry to waste your time."

"Don't be sorry. Helping people is what I do," Antigone says.

The next morning, Psyche goes out to buy some honeycomb.

When she emerges from the store, she spots the brown dove perched prettily on the lowest branch of a dogwood tree. It cocks its head, watching her.

Enough is enough.

Thus, Psyche—human, mortal Psyche—approaches the bird she suspects is a god. She plants her hands on her hips to make herself feel powerful enough to do what she's decided to do.

Which is to call the bird out.

"Why do you keep following me?" she asks.

There are people watching her—but this is not the Psyche of a few weeks ago. Awakened to the happenings of the courts, she's willing to look a little silly if it means getting answers. Besides, no one is going to stop her.

The bird, too, stares down at her—yet it says nothing, only preens.

"I know it's you," says Psyche. "The Queen of Flame, right?"

The preening stops.

Psyche smirks. "Aah, I wasn't supposed to know yet, was I?" she says. "Well, I do. And I'd really like to know what I've done to earn your attention. Is this about Eros?"

For a moment she worries the bird really is a mundane creature and that she's misread this whole thing. It stands still and bobs its head in a very ungodly fashion. But then it flaps down to land on her shoulder.

Now people are really staring—and Psyche herself feels a little odd. Smoke rises from Psyche's hoodie where the dove grips tight.

A voice whispers into her ear—one so lovely, so bewitching that the world loses its color and meaning all at once. As Psyche stands on the uneven sidewalk, there is nothing but the bird on her shoulder and the endless, eternal sky. The child in her wants to weep; the adult wants to cast aside her life in adulation.

"Your place is not at her side."

And then, the bird is simply gone. A curl of ash, as if someone had burned a stick of incense on her shoulder, is all that remains.

Psyche takes a deep, rattling breath. What was that...? And why...?

There are questions. Dozens of them, perhaps a hundred, rattling around in her brain at once.

But there is only one answer.

The voice had been wrong. No longer is her place among the timid and the afraid. She will live among the brave, among the knowing, or she will not live at all.

It's time to speak with Eros again.

Chapter Fourteen

Psyche takes a breath and surveys her apartment. The plants are in good order. Her PC's cleaned up, the wires hastily managed. Latte has a full plate of food she's chosen to ignore. Psyche's passed the lint roller over every lint-rollable surface. On the kitchen counter are two plates of roast chicken and rice; the smell of spices and rich broth permeates the apartment. The glimpse she catches of herself in the mirror is good, too. She's taken the time to do a full face of makeup and even spent twenty minutes trying to figure out the best perfume for the occasion.

She's about as ready as she's going to get. More ready than she was the last time Eros turned up.

Right. Honeycomb over open flame. Simple and straightforward. The intent had to count for a lot, didn't it? Probably more than the actual flame itself.

But it didn't hurt to do something special. Psyche picks up her mortar and pestle. She fills it with crumples of paper, the dead leaves from her plants she's cleaned up over the past few days. Over this she pours a small amount of olive oil—the real stuff her aunts shipped from Greece twice a year in unlabeled glass bottles. Lastly she opens a bottle of wine and sprinkles a few drops of that on top.

The concoction looks terrible. It smells strange. No one in their right mind would do this on purpose.

It's perfect.

She lights the stove.

As the burner heats, she smooths out a piece of her favorite paper. Intention time, per the rules. But what is her intention?

A breath.

I want to make my peace with passion, she writes.

The paper catches the second she touches it to the flame. When she drops it onto the mortar and pestle, the whole thing goes up in fire—the oil and alcohol first to ignite. Heat flushes her skin and she wonders, idly, if Eros will feel this way, too.

Her heartbeat picks up.

The honeycomb is soft in her hand, her fingers already coated in sticky sweetness.

Last chance to back away. Does she really want to see Eros again? To be part of that strange world, to put herself in danger's path?

Yes. She's never wanted anything more than this—to feel special, to feel alive, to feel loved.

Psyche throws the honeycomb onto the leaping red flame.

Her doorbell rings immediately. Is that…? Eros didn't use the door before. She doesn't seem the type to be fond of them.

Yet the timing is hard to deny. Psyche keeps one eye on the fire as she heads to the peephole.

"Who is it?" she calls.

But she knows the second she looks—it's Eros. There she is, wearing her armor, standing in the apartment hallway. Is it Psyche's imagination, or are her shoulders trembling? And she's got a box of something in her hands...

"I'm the one you summoned," Eros says. Yes, that is her voice—as warm and rich as the honey on Psyche's fingers.

Psyche smiles and unlocks the door. "You could have just come in, you know."

Eros stands at the threshold. Now that they're face-to-face, Psyche can see the box better: gold, about the size of her forearm in length and width, but thin. "I don't know that. You might have called on me to tell me you never want to see me again."

How is it that someone as large as Eros can sound so small? A crack opens in Psyche's heart. People need comfort, and who is she to deny it? She hugs Eros tight, swaying from side to side, as if she's greeting an old friend. Eros stiffens—then relaxes, letting out a sigh of relief.

"Psyche, you don't have to..." she starts.

"I want to," Psyche says, stepping away. "Like I wanted to see you again. Now quit standing out there and come in, I made us dinner."

Eros's footsteps are quiet and measured. Eros catches sight of the shoe rack near the door and looks down at her own booted feet. A moment's consideration, a snap of the fingers—in a flash of light she's wearing far more appropriate socks. Only then does she walk farther in.

Psyche watches her with a smile. Is this the woman Laura was so worried about? The world's most sheepish god of love? She picks up the plates of food and lays them on the coffee-slash-dinner table, along with a cup of wine each.

"This is a traditional family dish," Psyche says. "If anything's good enough for gods, it's got to be this." She winks at Eros. "Though don't ask me for the recipe. I won't give it to you, not even for all the love in the world!"

A slow, considered nod. Eros sits on the opposite couch from Psyche full of virility. She keeps her hands on her own knees and doesn't so much as reach out for fork, knife, or cup. She's left the box to the side of the food. On the counter, the fire is burning out, the flickering making Eros's mask look nervous.

"Thank you for your efforts," she says. "It does smell delicious."

"Tastes even better," Psyche says. "Please, help yourself."

Eros hums. She picks up the plate alone—no utensils—and lifts it under her chin. "I don't eat the way you do," she says. "Will that trouble you?"

"As long as you aren't going to turn it back into a chicken and eat it in front of me, I don't mind," Psyche says. "I have kind of a weak stomach when it comes to blood. But wait. What about that fruit we ate in your Domain?"

"That's different. You see that as food, but it isn't, really.

It's something else," Eros answers. "But you may ask me not to eat this way again if it disturbs you."

Eros pinches the tip of one of her arrows. A trapped worm of flame wriggles between her fingers. No mercy from love—she drops it onto the plate. In an instant it spreads and consumes. As Psyche watches, Eros takes a breath of the smoky tendrils that follow. Then Eros taps the plate with her other hand and the fires die away.

The plate she lays back on the table is empty and clean, as if no food had ever touched it.

Psyche blinks. "You can really eat that way? Tasting the food and everything?"

"Yes," Eros says. "And you were right—it was delicious. You made judicious use of fennel. Most people overdo it with that or with the dill, but you've got a steady hand. Excellent char on the chicken, as well. It doesn't trouble you?"

Psyche beams, sitting a little straighter. "Are you kidding?" she says. She takes a sip of her wine, then gestures with her fork. "Meeting you, shooting that bow with you, the way you eat. Everything about you is incredible."

Eros sits still on the other side. The plate reflects her mask back at Psyche as she eats, bite by bite. What an inefficient process! If only she could consume everything in a rush of fire, cooking would be a lot easier.

"You meant that," Eros says. Psyche is so used to her sounding loud. This quiet—it pains her a little. "You think of me that way?"

"I wouldn't have invited you back if I didn't," Psyche says.

She sets the fork and knife down. "I think you and I share something in common. Something that makes me want to help you."

"What's that?" Eros asks.

"We don't get much chance to be our own people," Psyche says. "Growing up, there was always someone arguing in my house. My sisters have always been like oil and water, so I had to keep the peace between them. Then my mother got sick, and things got hard between her and our father."

Psyche drinks a little more wine to drown the lump in her throat. *Be brave, Psy.*

"We never really stayed in one place even before that. My father worked for the military, so there was always a new assignment somewhere or another. I went to thirteen different schools. Not exactly the best way to make friends, you know? Even if I did, I wouldn't have had the time for them. I had to be there for everyone else. My sisters got to have friends, both of them, but me..."

"There was always something to be done," Eros fills in.

Psyche nods. "Sounding a little familiar, huh?" she says with a sodden smile. "I thought it might."

In life there are as many silences as there are sounds. This one is comfortable, a companion to their thoughts.

Psyche isn't used to silence. Growing up there was never any room for it. Thus she is the one who banishes it. "You said that love was a terrible thing. A weapon. Now that I know how close you are to it—how much you have to think about it and interact with it every day—my heart aches for you. I can't imagine what that's like. The fact that you're still standing when something so comforting has been taken from you is..."

"Troubling?" Eros fills in.

Psyche shakes her head. "No, not at all."

She's on her feet before she quite knows why. The distance between them—the table, the plates, the dinner—now seems too great. In a moment she's crossed it to sit at Eros's side. Even from a respectable arm's length away, the god's radiant heat is enough to warm Psyche's cheek and light her courage anew.

She takes Eros's hand. That simple touch is a spark spreading through her. Eros turns toward her, her body turning, too. The mask's solid eyes take on the cast of one who has long since lived in the dark.

"Eros," Psyche says. As the drumming on a great oarship that has just sighted the shore, so is the beating of her heart. "When Zephyr asked me to help you, I didn't know what the trouble was—and when I saw the Court, I didn't know what kind of person you'd be. The last time we met, you showed me the kind of person you didn't want to be—aggressive, manipulative, selfish. If you'll let me, I want to help you find the person you *do* want to be. I want to help you bring her home."

There is a storm of emotion behind Eros's mask, one apparent in the gentle tremble of Eros's hand, in the sound of her lips parting, the rise and fall of her throat as she swallows away her doubts. Eros can have whatever time she needs to navigate these things—Psyche will wait right here for her.

"I'm not sure who that person is," Eros says.

"That's all right," Psyche says. "We can figure it out together. Sometimes it's easier to start from the kind of person you don't want to be, or the things you want to change about yourself."

Eros squeezes Psyche's hand in return. "That's a long list," she says. "Are you certain you have time for all of that?"

"I might be able to fit you into my schedule," Psyche says. She flashes a smile, then strokes the mask's cheek. The warmth of it surprises her. What would it be like to press her lips against these, she wonders—would they kiss her back? A question for another time.

"And if the things I say frighten you?"

"Then I'll tell you so," Psyche answers.

"We don't live lives like yours," Eros says. She leans forward. "What you think of as a great crime is to us a passing amusement. My father's arena is the most popular place in the whole Court, the pleasure dome aside, and the things you'd see there would haunt you. Murder is a trifle to him."

"But you aren't him," Psyche says. She strokes the mask's cheek—Eros's cheek—again. "You don't want to be, either. I'm certain of it."

"How is it that you aren't afraid of me?" Eros asks. She covers Psyche's hand with her own, turns it over in the warm light of the apartment. "Your flesh is so pliable, Psyche. I could tear this arm out of its socket in an instant. Do you understand that? Do you understand what I am?"

Psyche can't quite answer that she's always been the sort

of girl who spent more time watching the lions and tigers at the zoo than the penguins or the sheep. When Eros holds her like this, Psyche is more aware than ever of how small she is. How vulnerable. And yet how she delights in this—in giving someone so powerful her trust.

Psyche sidles closer. "I'd like to," she says. "Though I can say for certain you aren't the type to tear my arm off. I think you'd rather do other things with it."

A small laugh from the god. She presses the palm of Psyche's hand to the mask's marble lips. "You would allow me?"

Kisses trail up Psyche's wrist, smooth and warm. Her skin tingles all the way up to the shoulder—then down, down, down. How heady it is to have love itself attending to her like this...!

"I might," Psyche says. She takes a breath, then cups Eros's face. Her fingers land half on the edge of the mask and half beyond it—the ear between her fingers is sharply pointed. To touch Eros's skin sends another wave of heat coursing through her. "Eros."

Eros stops in place, turning her mask toward Psyche's face. "Yes?"

"I'd like you to swear an oath to me," she says. Her cheeks warm, her throat loosens. The tongue in her mouth is a heavy thing—unwieldy for talking, but for other things...

With the very tips of her fingers, Eros traces arcane designs on Psyche's forearm. Is it some kind of spell—or is it something far more natural that prickles Psyche's skin? "Hmm. What is it you'd ask of me, oh fearless one?"

Psyche reaches for Eros's collar—the burgundy arming coat peeking out above the rim of her armor.

"Swear to me," she says, "that no matter how much either of us may want to, neither of us will fuck the other for another two months."

Eros's deep, rumbly laugh echoes all along Psyche's stomach. Has she ever been so close to anyone before? Not like this. Eros's presence asserts itself every passing second; she will not let herself be ignored. Everything about her demands worship and adoration.

And somehow *Psyche* is the one making demands. Is this how witches felt in centuries past? Swathed in power from beyond the veil, surveying the world from atop their broomsticks? She sees now why so many of them would have rather died than give this up.

"Now that's bold," says Eros. "Very bold."

Psyche pinches the pointed tip of Eros's ear, earning a pleased purr. "Too bold? I thought it'd be best for both of us. We can get to know each other without any added pressure or complication."

"Oh, I think it's a good idea," Eros says. "But you've phrased it so vaguely that, well, a malicious actor could slither right through that boundary."

Psyche raises a brow. Without realizing it, she's spread her legs further. "And how might they do that?"

Eros hikes up Psyche's shirt with her long-fingered hands. Between the cool night air and the blazing contrast of Eros's touch, Psyche's skin turns to gooseflesh. Higher and higher

Eros raises the shirt, until she uncovers Psyche's nicest bra—a lacy blue number she bought as "self-care" last year.

"Are you certain you wish to know?" Eros asks her. She slides one hand beneath her mask, lifting it ever so slightly—not enough for Psyche to see beneath it, but enough for her lips to be freed from their confines. "I could tell you, of course. Or I could demonstrate."

Anticipation is an army at the gates of Psyche's heart. Drunk on adoration, she looks down from her rampart toward the god and knows there can be no other answer. "You can demonstrate," she says. "A little."

"Very well. As my lady commands, I shall enlighten," Eros says. "Should you wish me to stop, you need only tap my shoulder twice. Is that understood?"

Psyche nods. She's biting her lip so hard she worries it might bleed, but it is a distant worry, one that she has no particular care to indulge. All she wants is to see what will happen next.

But she feels it before she sees it—Eros adjusting Psyche's posture as easily as Psyche fluffs her pillows every night. Eros unclasps her bra with such quickness that Psyche doesn't register it until Eros is pulling it gently, gently away.

"The trouble is," Eros says, "that you said 'fucking' without specifying. As a bit of an expert in the matter, I can point out that there are many ways to fuck. Most agree that kissing would be permitted, but what about..."

When Eros's full lips close around Psyche's nipple, warmth doubles, triples, and turns toward wicked ends. Just when she thinks she's gotten used to the heat, Eros's tongue flicks over her nipple.

Psyche's not fast enough to catch the moan that leaves her lips.

Eros first smirks, then laughs—lifting her mouth only as much as she needs to in order to speak. "You sound even better than I thought you would, like that," she says.

Eros's mouth is on her again, her efforts redoubled—teasing, sucking, licking. Meanwhile her free hand is tweaking Psyche's other nipple in turn. Before she knows what she's doing, Psyche is starting to writhe. Has the world always seemed so cold? For now she wants nothing more than to feel more of Eros's incredible warmth.

The break earns another moan from Psyche—and another smug chuckle from Eros. She sits up, pulling the corner of her mask back down.

"That's enough of a demonstration. Tell me, Psyche," she says. "Did you think of that as fucking? Should we avoid it for the next two months?"

Psyche's still trying to catch her breath. Her cheeks are hot and her pussy is hotter. Yet Eros doesn't press the issue—she sits there, head perched on her hand, and awaits Psyche's answer.

"A little overheated? Need a drink?" Eros says, offering Psyche her own wineglass.

"P-proud of yourself, aren't you?" Psyche says. But the waver in her voice undercuts the joke. She takes a long sip of the wine. Rich bitterness coats her tongue and roots her to the present. A deep breath and she can think. "No. I don't think we should avoid that."

"Oh?" Eros says. "Your boundary's a little further south, then?"

"You might say that," Psyche says. Another sip, another breath. No matter what her body wants, she has to think clearly. "I think I understand the point now. How about…" Difficult to think of this without letting her mind wander. Psyche bites her lip. "Neither of us will touch the other's genitals," Psyche blurts out. "For two months."

Eros hums. "You may want to clarify that," she says. "Without a mask I can see exactly where you're looking. Specificity is key with beings like myself."

Psyche takes a third sip of her wine. She keeps her eyes pointedly on Eros's, or at least on her marble substitutes. "That includes groping over clothing," she says. "A-and the use of toys. N-no penetrations, of any kind. Only kissing and groping above the belt."

"That's better," Eros says. A beat of consideration, a beat that leaves Psyche longing for a cold shower. "I find that agreeable. There are only two parts left—the reward for keeping to it, and the punishment for wandering."

Psyche drains the rest of the cup. She sets it down on the table, closes her eyes, and tries not to think about the way Eros is sitting with her legs spread wide.

"If either of us breaks the oath, then they may never see the other again, unless the other allows it," says Psyche. That part is easy enough to say. That part doesn't require her to run lust's sharp blade across her skin. "And if we keep to the agreement, then two months from now—"

"Two of your months, or mine?"

"How long are your months?" Psyche asks, tilting her head.

"About a decade, in your time," Eros answers. "That's the impression I've gotten, at any rate. We aren't to keep humans in our Domain any longer than that without letting them return."

A decade? Psyche swallows. Twenty years? No, it's out of the question; there's no way she could make it that long. She glances at the date on her phone. "Our months, then. Let's say . . . September fifteenth."

Eros nods. "And on that day . . . ?"

"On that day, we drop those restrictions, and I'll do—"

Eros holds up a warning finger. "Don't you dare say 'whatever you like,' that might as well be a death sentence."

How'd she know? Psyche takes a second to consider. "We . . . can touch each other all we like, so long as we don't cause any harm."

A chuckle, then: "All right. Do you remember how we seal our oaths, Psyche?"

She does. Oh, she does. Her enthusiastic nod says it all.

Eros plucks an arrow from her quiver. With her other hand she reaches for the box she'd brought along and sets it in Psyche's lap. "Open it," she says. "It's turned out to be very convenient for us."

Inside is a collection of chocolates. Even love herself can default to something so reliable sometimes, hmm? But Psyche has to admit she's never gotten one this nice before. Each chocolate is decorated with gold foil or intricately shaped. One of them is a slumbering dragon, another is a golden bow and arrow. Chocolate-dipped fruits, fudge—there's a wide array before her. The included card is handwritten and illustrated in brown ink. The handwriting is neat, but very formal, something like a teacher's.

"Did you make these for me?" Psyche asks.

"I asked Hestia," Eros says. "In all our lands, she's the second best when it comes to parties, and the first when it comes to cooking. No one's more in demand than she is. Hmm. Except perhaps me."

"There's that narcissism again," Psyche says. She picks up the bow and arrow. The note says it's meant to "evoke the heart-piercing sensation of realizing you've fallen in love." Hestia has also noted: "Vegan and cruelty-free," which feels a little strange. Hadn't they wanted to eat her...?

"I'm simply stating a fact," Eros says. "Everyone wants love and passion at their parties, just like everyone wants good food. I suppose there are some that would take Hestia over me, though. Like the Queen of the Wild."

Psyche bites into the bow and arrow. She isn't sure what she was expecting, but it wasn't *this*. Rich, deep chocolate combines with a complex citrus. The roof of her mouth tingles. Creamy nougat—notes of vanilla and honey—then coats her tongue. She finds herself moaning and smiling, having to force herself to return to the subject at hand.

"You mentioned the Queen of the Wild before," Psyche says. "That she was having some trouble with a human?"

"She still is," Eros says. "But she's declared it none of my business, so unless she makes amends for calling me an 'addle-brained hardener of pricks,' I won't be helping her."

Eros picks up one of the chocolate-covered fruit slices and pierces it with the arrow.

"You might be the least addle-brained person I know," Psyche says.

"I see you agree that I'm a hardener of pricks," Eros says. The arrow roars to life as she holds it between them. "I'll get you for that later."

"No you won't. I've specifically forbidden it," Psyche says. She watches the flame consume the chocolate with a smirk. "I like this part."

"I thought you might," says Eros. She lifts her mask just slightly, then clears her throat. "I, Eros, the Loosener of Limbs, swear an oath by sacred flame: for the next two months the only adoration I shall pay to Psyche shall be above the belt, and the same shall be said of her toward me. If I err, I shall cast myself forever from her sight; if she errs, then never again shall I allow her my grace. But if we are loyal and faithful to this oath, then on the fifteenth of September, we may partake in love's festivities at last."

"It...sounds a lot better when you say it that way," Psyche admits.

"I've had several thousand years to practice," says Eros. "Do you swear this oath, Psyche?"

She pulls closer to the burning fruit. "Yes," she says. "I swear this oath."

Eros is the first to consume the fruit—but in an instant their lips are together again. Fire flows between them, setting Psyche alight, transforming her from an ordinary woman into something more. Something beloved.

Yes, that's the truth of it. No matter how in demand Hestia is as a cook, she's already made one mistake—that chocolate isn't at all like falling in love.

This is.

Melting into Eros's arms, their lips joined, their breath one—the utter safety and the dizzying power of this embrace. Knowing that there is no one else on earth to whom love has given their attention so fully, knowing that she alone has compelled these oaths—and knowing that there will be months more of this. Kisses just like this.

Yes, she's sure of it. *This* is falling in love.

Chapter Fifteen

Tides rise and fall. The sun rises and sets.

Psyche sees Eros.

Eros waits on the fire escape for Psyche to discover she is there. Psyche mistakes her for the sun well into the afternoon.

"You like staring at me, don't you?"

Psyche rolls her eyes. She crawls out of the window to sit next to Eros. Before them, the city is already awake, already bustling, though not entirely of its own free will. Below them one of her neighbors is shouting at her boyfriend over the phone. A woman walks a Great Dane. Two men dap each other up and exchange bags of what are definitely, absolutely, one hundred percent normal gummy worms.

Psyche tips her morning tea to her lips. She hands Eros her cup, too. "You know I do."

There's something of a cat's preen in the way Eros rests her head on her hand. "I wanted to hear you say it." She holds the cup below her chin and waves it. Psyche tries to see the vapor, but she knows it's a lost cause. "My Domain is one that thrives on adoration."

Eros leans back. Latte leaps into her lap, content to bask in the warmth of Eros's presence. Those two have been getting along almost too well for Psyche's liking.

"I've got a question of my own," Psyche says. A moment's hesitation. *Are you worried I'll change my mind?* That had been what she wanted to ask. But that might put too much tension in this red-fruit moment, this peace. There's still so much she wants to know about this woman. "If you could have picked any Domain, what would it have been?"

The neighbor downstairs is truly screaming, her voice harsh. The dogs have stopped to stare at her.

Eros reaches for Latte's stomach. *Her* scritches never seem to get her maimed. "I think," she says, "that I'd like to have Zephyr's. He can have mine if he likes. He's always been too charming for what he is."

Psyche raises a brow. "And that is?"

Latte begins to purr. "Zephyr belongs to the Winds. All the Courts are open to him so long as he doesn't offend. And, as the West Wind, he's the nicest of all his siblings, so people like to keep him entertained."

"Except for Glaucus," Psyche says.

"Glaucus has it out for everyone," says Eros. "But yes, especially Zephyr."

Psyche draws her knees up to her chest. "What'd Zephyr do?" she asks. She can't imagine a man that nice doing something that upsetting.

Eros hums. "The short version? Glaucus thought Zephyr had been a little too friendly with a woman he saw as his own."

Psyche leans on her shoulder. "I don't have to stream until later, so I'm all ears. Will you tell me why you want to be the Wind so badly? Seems like he's gotten into his own share of troubles."

Eros wraps an arm around her waist. Latte lies between them, now, sprawled from one lap to the other. "The Winds," Eros says, "go where they like and heed no one. This is a story about the warmest of these Winds, the bringer of spring..."

"Why do you talk so much about streaming when I've never seen you swim?"

Psyche can't suppress the laugh. "Oh god, where do I start?" she says. She can't tell if Eros is pouting, but she likes to imagine that she is. "It's...it's an internet thing."

Eros crosses her arms. Oh, she is pouting, there's no doubt about it. "Show me," she says.

Psyche calls her over. Eros, much larger than her, sits on her lap in front of the computer. That this is a preposterous arrangement does not seem to occur to her. Much like Latte—if she fits, she sits. "This is your electronic tablet device."

"Right," Psyche says. "My PC. So do you know what cameras are?"

"A little," says Eros.

Psyche points to the webcam. "That's one right there. When I turn it on and go to the right page on the internet, everyone can see me, and what I'm doing. It's like we're all in a room together."

Eros leans toward the camera. She picks it up and brings it close, staring directly into the lens. "I can understand why you have so many followers. Zephyr told me you've a small cult to yourself."

Psyche flushes. "I—I wouldn't call them a cult," she says, waving a hand. "We're more like a community. We play games together, they ask me for advice."

"They seek your counsel?" Eros says. She sets the camera back down, caring not that it tumbles off its perch. "Do you grant them favors? Espouse a common philosophy? Do they pay you tribute, Psyche?"

Psyche clears her throat. Is it getting hotter in here? "It's not a cult," she says. "We're all friends."

Eros hums. "I see. Will you let me attend one of your not-a-cult meetings?"

"Sure," Psyche says. "Everyone's been asking about you, anyway, so I'm sure they'll be excited to meet you. Maybe in September?"

Eros stands—only to wrap her arms around Psyche from behind. "On that day, they will love you as they've never loved you before," she coos. The heat is back again, and making itself very known. "When they gaze upon your face, my Psyche, they will see what I see. And they will love you from the depths of their hearts, a love that fills them near to bursting. You will collect such tributes from them that you need worry for nothing, for the rest of your life."

What a dizzying prospect, to rule over them like that. And what powerful wine it is to have a god whisper such things to her...

But ultimately, she reaches up for Eros's cheek. "I don't want you to use your powers on my followers."

A quiet that, at first, could be mistaken for displeasure. But then Eros leans into Psyche's touch. "You," she says, "are unique among humans."

"Promise not to use your powers?" Psyche says.

Eros squeezes her. "For you? Anything."

Rhythms emerge.

In the morning they have breakfast. Since it turns out Eros has no idea what she's doing in the kitchen, Psyche cooks for them. She does make a habit of standing around and asking Psyche all manner of questions as she works, though. Psyche thinks Eros will be attempting it before long. Maybe they'll start with something nice and easy. Scrambled eggs, or toast.

The conversation is easy, too. They're at their most teasing in the mornings. Eros asks Psyche about her dreams and promises to fulfill them; Psyche laughs and says she will do just fine without. Psyche asks Eros about the other gods, and sometimes she gets funny stories. Sometimes, they're tragedies. But Eros starts avoiding those after Psyche goes pale the first time.

Their afternoon meeting is always a surprise. Eros appears in all manner of places—supermarket aisles, the bed, once in the mirror without appearing in person. She never announces herself. Instead Psyche will hear a familiar voice asking a question about whatever it is she's up to. Why that brand of cereal? What is this playing over the speakers? What is she running from? Eros seems to take interest in all of it. For an unknowable god, she's fascinated by even the most mundane details.

But it is the evenings that are the most difficult. Eros only ever appears on the couch then, her shoulders sagging and her voice heavy. Psyche shares what food she can, what comfort she can—a hand on her shoulder, cuddling, whatever comes to mind for her. Only when some of the tension has gone from her does she ask what it is that has caused Eros's troubles.

There are only ever three answers—work, her mother, or her father.

"Are you trying to scare me?" Psyche asks, throwing two packs of salmon into her cart.

Eros's mask is turned away from the meat and fish, toward an endcap stacked with toilet paper. She appeared only moments ago, materializing from the door to an employees-only area. "If the Court doesn't frighten you, then nothing can. But I like to try. You make such cute faces when you spot me."

"The Court did scare me," Psyche admits. "If it wasn't for you, I would've died there. But…"

"But…?"

"I'm a braver Psyche now," Psyche proclaims. "Everything

out here seems so boring in comparison. I don't know how you can stand shopping with me when you've got all those delights back home."

Eros picks up a pack of Angel Soft and places it gently into the cart. Psyche raises a brow.

"I'm fond of winged figures," Eros says in explanation. Then: "Would you like to visit again?"

"Eros..."

"Is something the matter?" Eros asks.

Psyche frowns. She considers how best to phrase her thoughts—and which brands of cereal she'd like to have on hand this week. "You never have anything kind to say about your Domain. You spend so much time with me that it feels like you're trying to get away from it. Your comfort's important to me, and I don't want to impose. I'll always have my memories. So if it's safer for you to visit me here, and I can provide that rest for you, then we should keep doing that."

The deception, such as it is, does not last long. "Spoken like one of us. That isn't a direct answer."

A Kacey Musgraves song comes on over the tinny store radio. Psyche thinks that she could get used to this sight—standing in a grocery store with her strange masked woman, the two of them picking out whatever pleases them. Neither of them have stopped over the course of this conversation.

"If we can do it safely, yes, I'd like to go back. I want to see your favorite places, hear all that new music, see things other people only dream about. I want..."

To understand you better, to shoot your bow again, to see a sunset in a sunless place. I want to be the Psyche who finishes her bravery list.

Eros places a box of spicy hot chocolate in the cart. Is it the flames on the box that did it this time?

"Then we will go again."

On the night of September 1, Psyche returns home from a walk around the block to find herself elsewhere. She turns the key in the lock, pushes in the door, steps over the threshold and—

On the other side she finds not the carefully manicured coziness of her studio apartment but an endless beach. Beneath her feet the sand is soft and dazzling white. Salt air clings to her skin and prickles at her tongue with every breath. There are sand dollars and starfish and streaks of jagged seaweed.

Overhead the sky is forest green, fading to grass, and where it meets the sea it has taken on the color of a lime's rind. The sea itself is not the blue she knew when they lived in California, nor the murky green of Florida, nor even the imposing gray of Massachusetts's shores—it is a deep, churning red. Looking at the horizon, she can't escape the feeling that she's found herself inside someone's bottle of wine.

A certain lightness fills her chest. She smiles wide as her heartbeat picks up. As she steps out of her sneakers and pulls off her socks, she surveys the shore around her.

"What is this one, Eros?" she calls. "The Court of Romantic Views?"

"The Court of Waves," comes the answer.

Eros is at her side. She wasn't a moment ago, of that much Psyche is certain, even though there are no footsteps near her on the sand. In place of her armor or even her relaxed modern clothes, Eros wears a loose crimson tunic trimmed with intricate gold. The colors bring out the warm tones of her brown skin—and there is plenty of skin to be seen. Her sculpted arms and strong collarbone are bare, as is a tantalizing amount of leg. Blood rushes to Psyche's cheeks when she catches sight of Eros's strong, thick thighs.

"O-oh," Psyche says. "You're…"

"I thought it best to dress for the occasion," Eros explains. Is she smirking behind that mask? What a shame that she's still wearing it, even now, but it can't be helped—Eros draws her own boundaries.

"I-if I'd known, I would have put on something fancier," Psyche says. In her sweatpants and tour T-shirt she feels woefully underdressed. But at least the sand is comfortably warm between her toes.

Eros reaches into her tunic. In so doing she jostles the fabric. Is the teasing glimpse beneath it something she's offering on purpose? Either way, Psyche is too distracted to notice what Eros pulls from beneath until it is being held out to her.

"I thought you might say as much, so I took the liberty of having one made for you, too."

A matching tunic—gold with red instead of the other way around. The fabric is soft and supple, like jersey, but as richly beautiful as velvet.

"Do you like it?" Eros asks.

Psyche nods. "Could you... I'm not sure how to put it on?"

Eros is only too happy to help. Not that she's inappropriate about it—far from it. As Psyche sheds her clothes down to her underwear, Eros keeps a respectable distance. When draping the fabric, she touches only where she needs to—wrapping a braided red cord around Psyche's waist, pinning the fabric in place, tucking and adjusting. She makes short work of it.

When she's done, she looks Psyche from her toes to the tip of her head.

"Do *you*... like it?" Psyche asks. It's been a long time since she wore anything this nice—or this short. She isn't sure of how to stand.

Eros doesn't say anything. For an awful moment, Psyche wonders if Eros is having second thoughts about all this somehow, if the sight of so much of Psyche has made her realize she's the same as so many other girls.

But then Eros scoops her up off her feet, and that doubt dies with an arrow in its throat. "You're the most beautiful thing in this place."

"Eros, the sea is right there."

"I meant what I said. I'd rather look on your smile than on all the seas of the world. This world, or any other," Eros says.

Psyche barely has any time to recover before Eros steps into a small wooden ship. Still cradling Psyche, she sits down on a bench. Before them is a table and upon it, a cloche.

"What if I told you I don't know how to swim?" Psyche says with a giggle.

"Then I would call you a liar," says Eros. "And I would be right."

Eros snaps her fingers. At first Psyche thinks nothing has happened—but soon she hears the chirping and the clicking of dolphins. A pod of six emerges from the red sea, their hides almost silver, their teeth needle sharp. If Psyche weren't in Eros's strong arms, she might have been frightened by their flat black eyes.

But she knows there's nothing to fear, even as three of the dolphins approach from each side. Like horses before a carriage, they pull the ship out onto the reddening waves.

Psyche's mind is swimming with questions. She blurts out the easiest one she can think of. "Is it allowed to travel between Courts like this?"

"The King of the Waves owes me a favor," Eros says. "Otherwise, no. Not without the permission of that Court's ruler."

"You used a favor from a king just to impress me?" Psyche says. "Eros, there must have been something else you would have liked to do out here. It's beautiful, isn't it?"

Eros looks out onto the sea around them. "I never had cause to redeem any favors before this. Court politics have never interested me, despite my mother's best efforts. And as for beauty—as I said, I'd rather stare at you."

"I bet you say that to all the human girls. Maybe even some of your own kind, too?"

The silence that follows is not pleasant. Its sharp edges threaten to cut the delicate peace they've found together.

"S-sorry," Psyche says. "I just—"

"I understand. Mortals spend so much of their short lifetimes worrying about what they already know. You need your reassurances," Eros says.

"Huh. You sounded almost like a therapist there," Psyche says. She's joking, but only to hide her own embarrassment. "You don't usually let people get this close, do you?"

"For a single night? Perhaps. You'd be surprised how many leave afterward," Eros says. "Unlike you, most can't bear my company outside of my Domain. The fantasy they have of me shatters quickly. They expect... a certain joy from me. And they're disappointed when I don't conform to that."

She gives Psyche a squeeze. Around them the dolphins continue their work; the sailless ship skates smoothly over the surface of the sea.

She squeezes Eros back. "I can't imagine why. I mean, you've got such a sparkling sense of humor."

"So I'm told," says Eros dryly. She lays her hand between Psyche's shoulder blades. Her warm skin sends a shock through Psyche, one she has to swallow. "Now, you should eat your meal before it gets cold."

Beneath the cloche are two sumptuous salmon fillets, drizzled with a lemon-honey glaze; a crab served whole; shrimp in a spicy sauce; half a dozen oysters; a vibrant salad. Two bowls of fruit flank the plate. The plate itself is solid silver, as are the fork and knife. Despite the ship's movements, the tableware doesn't rattle—not even as Eros pours them each a glass of wine.

"I wasn't sure which you liked best," says Eros. "But Zephyr mentioned these are all choices worthy of you."

Psyche's stomach rumbles. "God, I don't know if I've ever been this hungry," she says. "Though we have to work on your human skills. This is enough for, like, five people. Maybe more if they're light eaters."

"Eat what you like," Eros says. "The rest will find use elsewhere."

Psyche scoffs—but she picks up her fork all the same. " 'Find use elsewhere.' What's that even mean? You're going to recycle it?"

The first bite of crab melts in her mouth. She's so overwhelmed by the sheer unctuous joy of it that she almost misses Eros's response.

"The King of Waves will take whatever's left into himself," she says. "And make from it something new."

As the meal continues—as she gorges herself on the delicious food Eros has prepared—a question swims below the waves. And it isn't long before she has to give it voice.

"Is this his whole Domain?" Psyche asks. "Or is there more under the water?"

Eros makes a pleased sound. "The majority of it—his palace and the Court itself—lies beneath the surface. Clever of you to have noticed."

Psyche smirks and tosses her hair. "Oh, you know, I didn't get a master's for nothing."

"A master? You already belong to someone?" Eros says. There's a strange urgency in her voice.

Psyche waves her hands, her ears flushing. "No, no, no, not like that! A master's degree; it means I'm a master of what I studied."

Eros settles, then nods. "Ah…I see. Forgive me."

"Never ever," teases Psyche. Then, to keep the sarcasm from lingering too long, she loops her arm through Eros's and continues. "But I know how you can make it up to me. Bargain?"

"You're learning this entirely too fast, do you know that?" Eros says. She picks up a slice of fruit and feeds it to Psyche, who is only too happy to take a bite. Juice dribbles down her chin. "Let's hear it."

Psyche wipes some of the juice away with her thumb. "If you take me to see the Court itself, then I'll forgive you."

In this world there are certain people who have always gotten their way. The minds of these lucky few cannot fathom that anyone might deny them, as no one has, and so their convictions, once voiced, are always decisive.

Eros is one such woman. She picks up Psyche's thumb and slips it between her lips with the absolute confidence of someone who knows how much she's wanted.

Thoughts dissipate like so much foam. Eros's mouth is hot and her tongue is hotter, swirling over the smooth skin as if savoring the remnants of the juice. Blood shoots straight to Psyche's aching core. She can't keep her breath from catching or her cheeks from flushing.

"Y-you're…making a good argument…"

Eros hums around Psyche's finger. Then, smiling, she begins to suck.

It's no use trying to fight it—not that Psyche wants to. She starts to grind in Eros's lap, and Eros holds her tighter. For what feels an eternity, Psyche gives herself over to this lick of flame—until, at last, Eros withdraws.

In that instant Psyche notices two things.

First, the world is so, so much colder when she isn't consumed by the fires Eros provides her.

Second, just before Eros withdraws, Psyche feels the pressure of teeth. *Sharp* teeth. Not enough to cut, no, but enough to make their presence known.

Her mind races along with her heart. Psyche swallows, trying to catch her breath. "D-does that mean…?"

"A question for you before I answer yours," Eros says. She rights her mask, but for a moment there Psyche thinks she sees her tongue. "Do my teeth frighten you?"

She doesn't have to think to answer. "No," she says. "I want…I want to feel more. B-but not now!"

Eros nods. She sits up, allowing a little space to come between them, then looks out onto the shore. "Beneath the waves, everyone's teeth are even sharper than mine," she says. "And while no harm will come to you while you're with me, they will press their luck so far as the Law allows. Are you certain you wish to see?"

Psyche's blood does not yet cool. That pinpoint feeling… what would those teeth be like on the other parts of her? No, no, she has to focus.

"As long as I'm with you, there's nothing to fear," Psyche says.

"Then I will gladly show you. But," says Eros. She holds aloft a finger. Psyche considers turning the tables on her.

Wouldn't it be fun to get *Eros* to moan, for once? "We will need permission from the King of Waves himself. He granted me only the use of the surface; anything more will need negotiations."

Eros moves Psyche off her lap to stand—but Psyche stops her with a hand on the chest. Straddling her, Psyche waves a finger. "I want to try talking to him."

"The King of the Waves?" Eros says.

"If I'm the one asking the favor, then I should be the one to speak to him. I did a bunch of reading! You know, they have all sorts of manuals on how to talk to you guys these days. Most of them are kinda…weird. But it's how I summoned you the first time."

She leaves out her little discussion with the Queen of Flame—best, she thinks, if Eros doesn't have to worry about that.

A moment's silence. The giddy impossibility of what she's requested brings her joy; she looks out onto the waves expecting any moment to see a sea monster cresting them.

But there is only Eros staring up at her with unblinking eyes, Eros drawing long, considering breaths, and the churn of the red sea.

"I know it's probably impossible," Psyche says. She cups Eros's face. "But I really want to try. Will you let me try?"

The sun paints Eros's mask with its unnatural colors. Its expression does not—cannot—change. But she does touch Psyche's cheek.

"Psyche," she says. "Never look to me for permission. I

would have you doing what you like, being who you like—or I won't have you at all."

How can she say such things without a hint of irony? For her voice is warm and confident and full, and hearing it makes Psyche feel like she's the god in this relationship. Her mouth opens, but she can think of nothing to say. Eros has struck her between the ribs with tenderness.

Eros's thumb traces Psyche's cheekbone. "I would love to see what you do with it. And should anything go amiss, rest assured you'll be in no danger. I'll save you."

Warmth blossoms in Psyche's chest. She nods. "All right, then," she says. "I won't let you down. What's this guy's name?"

"Poseidon," Eros answers. "Though we don't usually address the Court Sovereigns by name. My mother being an exception."

Psyche clambers off Eros. The boat shifts beneath her feet as she walks to the bow, but she takes it slowly. Part of her wonders if the oldest parts of her blood are happy with the situation. Somewhere in her lineage there is a sailor beside themselves with joy at the sight of her. What would her followers think? Maybe she should take a photo or two...?

No, it can wait until after she's settled matters with Poseidon.

She takes a breath. "Oh Lord of the Waves, Watcher of the Seas! To test my own bravery, I want to visit your court, and I'm willing to offer you a deal!"

For long moments, nothing: only the gentle breath of the sea, the chirping of the dolphins, and her own breathing. Had she erred? Perhaps she wasn't formal enough? Doubt creeps in.

And then the roiling of the sea shakes it loose.

Gone, the calm—the waves are rippling now, beating against the little boat's hull. The red beneath pulses with unnatural light. Yet when she gazes down upon the light, she sees that it is banded, not solid, as if she is between the ribs of a massive body.

She does not hear the voice so much as feel it: her bones rattle within her flesh, her lungs spasm. When she was a teenager, she'd always stand as close to concert speakers as she could get. This being's voice is louder, heavier than any of the stacks she'd stood near before. It is less a voice and more a force.

"Who calls upon the King of Waves, and what does she offer in exchange for safe passage?"

Psyche staggers backward. Her hands rise to her ears, though it's no use—the voice echoes throughout her body. Yes, she is afraid, but there is a giddiness in her heart, too. She is at the top of a roller coaster staring down at the drop.

So it is that with her hands covering her ears, she nevertheless shouts back at the god, "My name is Psyche. I swore an oath with Eros of the Court of Flame and am under her protection. She tells me the two of you go way back!"

The sea rumbles once more; the dolphins can no longer pull the boat along against the current. "Ah, her Oathsworn. I have heard tell of you, Psyche of the mortals. Eros has been kind to me where others have not, and at great peril to herself. That is why you have such bounty before you. You would ask more of me?"

If she squeezes her thumb, it's a little easier to bear the onslaught of Poseidon's voice. "The food was delicious, thank you so much! Definitely five stars!" she shouts back. "But that was a favor you granted Eros on my behalf. I'm humbly requesting a favor from you on Eros's behalf. Completely different."

The sea underfoot rises and falls like the laugh of a sleeping giant.

"So it is," comes Poseidon's voice. "What is it you would offer me, Oathsworn?"

Psyche takes a moment to think, standing at the bow of the ship, rubbing her chin. What would a god want? What would *this* god want? She casts a glance at Eros. Her masked companion stands within arm's reach, looming, saying nothing.

Sometimes when you start a sentence, you know what you mean to say by the end of it. Maybe she'll find her way to something proper.

"In exchange for a single mortal's day within your Court and safe harbor there, I offer you..." Psyche begins. And just as she expected, she realizes there's only one thing she *can* offer. "Pleasant conversation and company for that span!"

A diplomat's upbringing is not an easy one. As a hilt is shaped on a lathe, so are they shaped for their duty—using people as a means of getting what they want. A diplomat of ten years would have extracted from Poseidon a deal that brought bounty to her home; a diplomat of twenty would have used this opportunity to seize untold power with a carefully worded request.

Psyche has been shaped. She has had the disagreeable parts of herself trimmed away, the rough parts smoothed, and what is left is a polished carving that the world cannot help but enjoy. She knows this. And she knows that, with enough time, she could have found a way to strike a better deal.

But more than that—she knows she doesn't want to.

Eros has taught her how tiring a god's dealings can be. If Poseidon is anything like Eros at all, he must want something simple. Something he doesn't have to worry about.

Someone else—someone more prone to worrying, more calculating—may have trembled in anticipation of the answer. Psyche does not. She merely takes Eros's hand, smiles at her, and waits.

The sea rises and falls. She hears the raucous bray of laughter.

"Eros, you've chosen an interesting one, haven't you?" he says. "It has been centuries since someone spoke to me in such a way."

"The most interesting of all," Eros answers. "Utterly without fear. Do you accept her terms, within the confines of her oath?"

"I do," he says.

A great pit opens in the sea beneath them—and at its base, the Court.

Chapter Sixteen

On wings of flame, Eros carries them down to the Court of Waves. Psyche holds her as if she were the mast of a great ship, and Psyche trying to weather a storm. Even surrounded by the sea, Eros smells of a campfire, of burning, of temptation. The farther in they float, the less Psyche can believe that any of this is really happening—yet she clings all the same, unwilling to wake up from what might be a dream.

Walls of water churn around them. Strips of seaweed flow like banners in the wind. Fish swim as if nothing in the world has changed for them—as if there is not a sheer cliff face of water only inches away. Yet these are not the fish Psyche has seen on the other side of the divide. There are no swordfish here, no marlins; instead, there are twisting, glittering things. Some are fish-shaped, but with dazzling ruby scales, or a head on either end of their bodies. Some are more fantastical. As Psyche holds tight to Eros, she spots something like a long, undulating dragon gently traversing the wine-red sea.

"Impressed by the view?" Eros asks.

She's not sure if *impressed* is the word. She rolls it around in her head. *Impressed.* Does the sight of the uncanny sea creatures impress her, or merely frighten her? What about the creatures with women's faces where their stomachs should be, the ones that swim at the very forefront of the water. Do those impress her? These things that no one else has seen, the rapid beating of her heart, the tingle at the back of her head... Eros seems to think she's fearless, but is that really the case?

Psyche, the therapist, stares her own emotions in the face. *What are you?* she asks them.

The answer comes to her when she feels Eros tracing a circle around her back, when her eyes fall on the glittering abalone city beneath them.

Fear, yes—but excitement and wonder, a sense of the sublime.

"Yes," she says.

The Court of Waves lies beneath a gleaming, iridescent dome. Its surface reminds Psyche of a soap bubble. As they approach, she wonders if there will be a gate or something similar for them to pass through—but there isn't one in sight. Curiosity prickles her senses and she laughs amid the eye of the wine-red sea.

Eros shifts Psyche's weight to one arm. With the other, she fetches a slice of fruit she'd tucked away in her tunic. This she holds before the wide-eyed Psyche.

"Be a good girl and open your mouth for me," she says.

Oh. Is *that* how she wants to play it? The flush comes back to Psyche's cheeks. She doesn't need any introspection to know what *that* voice, *that* phrase, does to her. Nor can she fight it—she opens her mouth. Eros lays the cut fruit on Psyche's tongue with all the reverence of a priest. She clears a shock of hair from Psyche's face and caresses her cheek.

"Now, don't swallow it until we're through the barrier."

And before Psyche has time to ask what that means, Eros sends them plummeting toward the Court. Faster and faster the wind whips against Psyche's face until, finally, she's only a hairsbreadth away from the iridescent surface of the barrier.

Eros takes them through feetfirst. A good thing, too; Psyche's not sure how she would have liked being thrust face-first into a layer of ice-cold seawater. She holds her breath reflexively. Her traitorous mouth nearly swallows the precious slice of fruit she's been given—but she holds on, and when they break through, Eros rewards her by planting a kiss on her forehead.

"We're here," she says. "You can swallow now."

And so they are.

Before Psyche's eyes is a place unlike any she's seen before—even the debauchery of the Court of Flame has little in the way of comparison. Where Eros's home is a circus of passion, this is more like some sort of strange family reunion. The space in front of them resembles a campsite near a river, with kelp and seaweed in place of grass. Groups of masked gods cluster around tables throughout—some playing games, some stirring iron pots over green-hued flames.

Around the perimeter are lanes not unlike those Psyche used to see in some carnival games. Ornate white fences separate them from one another, the lanes themselves composed of smooth pebbles. As Psyche watches, an ichthyic humanoid figure shoots by on one of the lanes, astride a seahorse taller than Eros. At the edge of the lanes, there is seating for those watching the races—mostly feminine shapes to Psyche's eyes. And most of them are cheering at the sight of the racer.

Rivers and streams cut through the field in places—some white water rapids, some placid streams. Boats and swimmers alike course through them. It occurs to her that there are far more people here than there were in the Court of Flame, but that they're all less human in appearance. Gills, fins, and fangs that protrude from mouths all are just as common as the impossible beauty Psyche's come to expect from gods. What's more, most of these people are clothed in tunics like she and Eros are wearing. Not all—some cavort in the rivers naked as the day they were made—but most. The masks here conceal less, too; those in the Court of Flame wore mostly full-face masks, but here the dominoes are far more common. One of the women swimming along the rivers wears only a thin strip of cloth. Even from a distance, Psyche's teeth hurt when looking upon her.

Smaller figures—children?—tumble and play in the center of the field, at the foot of a great throne. Atop the throne sits a man—and an impressive man, at that. The throne's got to be the size of a small house, but the man who sits on it with his legs spread wide and his head balanced on his fist is even larger than that. His skin is a pale green; gills along his neck accentuate the strong lines of his muscles. Scales fleck his forearms and barrel chest. A billowing beard of kelp seems to float in the air before him. Psyche can't see much of his face—only the beard and his likewise flowing hair—given his domino. Shaped from coral, it protrudes from his forehead, giving the impression of two great horns on his brow. Resting across his thick thighs is a golden trident, the length of which would rival any skyscraper, encrusted in pearls.

As they land near the center of the field, the man on the throne laughs. All around the world trembles, but the other revelers don't miss any steps. Does this happen often?

"Eros," he says, "you did not tell me she was so small!"

"Lord Poseidon, with all due respect, you say that to all the mortal women. And some of the men," Eros says. She rests a hand at the small of Psyche's back. "In any case, I present my Oathsworn: Psyche."

Eros doesn't need to tell Psyche that there's a protocol for this sort of thing. She bobs a curtsy. Or tries to. It's a lot harder than it looks, and her cheeks burn when she considers what she must look like to him, but it's the thought that counts, isn't it?

"A pleasure to meet you, my lord, King, sir!" Psyche says. Despite Eros speaking normally, she finds herself shouting. Surely he can't hear her from all the way up there?

"All the pleasures in the world stand at your side, little Psyche," booms Poseidon. When he smirks, she catches sight of his teeth. Needles. Do all gods have mouths like that, or only those of this Court? "I commend you for withstanding them. There aren't many who can be so composed around our Eros."

"Psyche is an uncommon mortal," Eros responds. "Are you hosting a gathering, Earthshaker?"

"Indeed. A man likes to look on his family, from time to time. And so many of them are unmarried, I might as well spear two fish at once. Or forty! Ha!"

Psyche tries hard not to raise a brow. There have to be at least a hundred people gathered on this field. Are they all Poseidon's relatives? That'd be nearly impossible. And what did he mean by talking about whether or not they're married? While it's a relief that even divine families face that kind of nagging, Psyche can't help but feel something's amiss. Yet she stands and smiles, all the same. Wouldn't want to offend a god.

"I'm shocked not to have received an invitation," Eros says—cold and flat, but in the way Psyche has come to know means she's joking. "I'm something of an expert in the subject of marriages."

"What you're an expert in isn't marriage, dear girl, it's making children. And I have plenty of those already!" he says. He laughs, the ground shaking again. "Speaking of, your sister's around here somewhere, Eros."

Sister? Psyche looks toward Eros. She'd never mentioned a sister. Her mother and stepfather, yes, but never siblings. A dozen questions manifest at once. Psyche bites the inside of her cheek to keep from voicing them. Maybe it just never came up?

Eros's posture stiffens. "Is that so."

"It is," says Poseidon. He cups a hand to his mouth. "Herophile! Speak up, will you? Your sister's here, with her Oathsworn!"

Only now do the assembled turn toward Poseidon. All share a similar look of annoyance at the distraction. Psyche scans the crowd, wondering which could be Eros's sister. It isn't as if she has much to work with when it comes to determining a resemblance. Dark skin and red hair are all she knows—and no one here has red hair.

Yet there is a figure coming toward them from the rivers, one whose skin is only a shade lighter than Eros's. She wears long, flowing robes, embellished with small shells at the lapels. In her hands, four scrolls; her fingertips are stained black with ink. And there is another important commonality: she, too, has concealed her face entirely beneath an ornate mask. This one is as placid as Eros's, but decorated with abalone in place of gold.

"There we are," says Poseidon. "Herophile, have you any portents about this meeting? Anything we should know?"

Herophile's head dips in consideration. Then she turns her face up toward her... father? Psyche's not certain of their relationship. Is Poseidon Eros's father, or do the two women share a mother instead? Yet the thought does not last long in Psyche's mind—there's something more distracting to consider.

Light shines from within Herophile's mask, pure white and bright as the sun itself. Arcane symbols glow—eyes, all of them, blinking even as Psyche watches. The light flows out from Herophile and curls around her, like ink in a glass, hovering there.

"The night," says Herophile, "will end in a victory for you, Father."

Again that bellowing laugh. It does little to muffle the strange, ringing quality of Herophile's voice, which reverberates in Psyche's ears for long moments after.

"Then move forward with my blessing. Herophile, keep your sister company. The Oathsworn has promised to be mine," says Poseidon.

"But can't we all stay together?" asks Psyche. Worry compels her to speak; bravery means she does not think through what it means to argue with a god. "It'd be lovely to meet more of Eros's family. I don't know very much about any of you."

Poseidon rests his head on his hand again. The smile he shows her makes Psyche's blood go oil thick in her veins. "You offered company, did you not? You did not specify that I needed to entertain the two of you as a pair. And I have my own questions for you, besides. Eros is not the sort of woman to make an oath."

Psyche looks to Eros.

"Uncle," she says, "Psyche is not yet fully accustomed to our ways. Her intent was that we should be together the whole while."

"Then that is what she should have said," says Poseidon. "Here—as a gesture of my goodwill to you, Eros, I will promise that no harm shall come to her. Besides, my oath promised safe harbor. I shall do nothing that encroaches on the boundaries of your protection."

"A moment, if you would, Uncle?" Eros says. The giant man grants it with a dismissive nod and wave. Eros throws an arm around Psyche and pulls her close. "You have my apologies. I should have realized you weren't specific enough. I should have amended it there and then—"

"It's all right," Psyche says. She cannot bring herself to make an argument of this, and besides, she's well aware that her own hubris has led them here. If she had stopped to ask Eros for assistance, they might have avoided this fate. She caresses Eros's mask, her fingers tracing the warm porcelain brow. "I'm sure it won't be so bad. I wanted to learn things, and I already have, right?"

"Psyche..." Eros says. Like wax she melts at Psyche's touch.

"He's already given his word he won't cause any harm," says Psyche. "I can handle myself, at least for a little while. Besides, you get to spend some time with your sister this way."

Eros hums, deep and low from the bottom of her throat. "If you have need of me, call, and I will answer you. No matter where you are. Even if you're in the depths of Tartarus itself, Psyche, do you understand? I'll not miss a breath before finding you."

Such intensity would have forced even the fiercest soldier to drop their shield and spear. Psyche is no different. Her defenses and worries fall to the ground with the clatter of bronze; she embraces Eros long and tight. Tartarus holds no meaning for her. No, that's not quite right. Tartarus, she thinks, must be the place where she can no longer see Eros.

"I will," Psyche says. "I will."

The soft creak of shifting leather—Eros's mask rising high enough to let her kiss Psyche's forehead. There, where lips meet naked skin, all of love's fire seems to blaze.

"Then I will see you before long," Eros says. "Go with this warning: my uncle is not so gracious as he appears. There are few who have caused more terror than he. He cannot break his promise—but mind that you give him no reason to look for a loophole."

Nothing in this place is ever as it appears, is it? The warning settles in Psyche's stomach like a too-heavy meal. She nods. Then, she stands on the tips of her toes and presses a kiss to the underside of Eros's jaw.

"I'll stay aware," she says, "so long as you try and enjoy your time with your sister."

"Herophile is a terrible conversationalist," Eros whispers.

"So it runs in the family?" Psyche teases. She pinches the pointed tip of Eros's ear, then pulls away with reluctance.

Only then does she present herself to the Earthshaker.

"Have you resigned yourself to the woeful fate of being my companion for a day, Psyche?" he asks.

"I have, Your Grace," she says. "You only have to tell me how we begin. We can't exactly share a seat at the table, can we?"

There—that laughter again. He takes his trident. When he lays its tip at an angle to the ground, it and his arm form a bridge.

"Come right along, little Psyche," he says. "Your table shall be the foundation which has borne cities—my very shoulders."

It is an absurd thing, one that should not make sense. Part of her wonders if she is dreaming. Yet it'd be a strange thing to wake up now when there's so much more she's looking forward to. However the company proves to be, it will only last the span of a human day—this she specified.

Psyche takes one step forward. She casts a glance behind her at Eros. Herophile stands at her side, her head hanging down, her fingers hooked around the edge of her mask. She must mean to take it off once Psyche's gone.

Will Eros? she wonders.

She steps onto the tip of the trident. The King of Waves lifts her several yards in an instant. A chill of disgust runs through Psyche. If she wanted to run away—if she'd had any doubts about this man's intentions—she'd be out of luck now. Only a painful fall could free her.

He has sworn his oath, hasn't he?

She swallows. Another step, another.

Before long she's there on the god's shoulder, sitting near the yawning canal that is his ear. Beneath her feet his muscles give the impression of springy earth. If she were to close her eyes, there'd be no differentiating them.

"You can swim, can't you?" he says.

He does not wait for an answer from her before catapulting them both into the water.

Here is what happens when one holds one's breath: The first ten seconds pass without a care in the world. One hardly has to think on them. The bet that compelled this behavior, or the dare, is a trifle.

The next ten seconds require a little attention. The nose wants to breathe where the mouth cannot. One must stifle this by force of will.

By thirty seconds, one's lungs begin to burn. Where this fire came from is beyond mortal ken, but its presence is undeniable.

Forty seconds—the lungs are screaming, the eyes beginning to spasm, sense beginning to flee. All but the most determined will cease their challenge here.

Psyche must do this with water flooding into her nose. Torrents of it rushing all at once—the great red sea staking its claim on whatever parts of her it can reach. Like cloth to wet skin, she clings to the King of the Waves; through the twists and rolls. Where Eros sank slowly to keep a better eye on her, Poseidon has no care at all. The great god has made a torpedo of them.

And all the while he laughs, and laughs, and laughs.

"You must understand my confusion, Psyche," he says. "It's rare that my niece should have dalliances at all. To hear that she'd sworn an oath was quite the shock."

They hurtle past a building-size squid, its unblinking eye like the pit of an uncovered manhole.

"When I saw you, I understood a little of the matter. Among mortals you are fetching, aren't you? Were I a younger man, I'd try to seduce you away from her."

Revulsion wriggles up Psyche's throat. She tugs, sharply, on the strand of kelp to which she's holding.

"Oh, don't be that way. I have my charms. Do you think I have all those children because I don't know my way around women? Bahaha!"

Her lungs burn. Water rushing against her threatens to pull her away from him, but she knows what's at stake if she lets go. Poseidon only said he would *cause* her no harm—letting her drift away into the ocean is a different matter. He could not be said to have caused that, exactly, only permitted it. Safe harbor meant only that he would catch her at the end of such wanderings.

"At any rate, I told myself—well, there must be more to her than her good looks. Eros has had her choice of the beauties for centuries now, and while she hasn't always taken that opportunity, she has on occasion. But never for long. What, then, makes you different...?"

A fish slaps against Psyche's face. Her concentration flickers, her fingers loosen, and her mouth opens. In rushes the water—filling her nose, her lungs, pulling her away from the kelp that's secured her. No, no, no—this can't happen. It won't! Coughing and sputtering, she pulls herself closer once more. What a groan of effort it takes for her to do this! Now it is not simply her lungs that burn, but her whole body.

"Imagine my surprise when I saw the two of you arrive, and she was still wearing her mask! Ha!"

Salt water fills her throat. Parts of her body are no longer her own—she coughs and finds herself breathing in even as everything within her screams that this is the wrong thing to do.

Yet an eerie feeling comes over her. A heat. Against the ice-cold waters, it is shocking. Her brows raise; her stomach spasms. Yet the heat flares hotter and hotter, making steam of the water she's swallowed.

"Now I understand. Better than you do, at that—I'll take that wager any day. That is why I wanted this chance to speak with you, Psyche. Because I understand the position she's put you in. I can't imagine she's told you everything about herself if she's done this to you."

A moment's peace within the maelstrom is not enough to process what Poseidon is telling her. Not that she cares to. The whole thing sounds too much like an abusive boyfriend for her taste—looking to isolate and to sow doubt. No wonder Eros warned her about him.

No—Psyche's only concern is getting through this.

Eros wouldn't lie to her.

"She's given you powerful enemies—more powerful than you can imagine. There will come a time when you need to confront them. She won't be able to help you, not in the way she wants. When that time comes, I hope that you remember the Earthshaker. Only one other stands above me—and even he would tremble if I turned my trident against him. When she cannot lift a finger to help you, I will shatter your chains. And I will do it gladly."

More of this nonsense. He can't be serious with this peacocking, can he? Psyche's stomach twists again. With a relief born of the gods themselves, she spots the Court of Waves coming up ahead of them. She just has to hold on a little longer…

"The only thing I ask of you—the one thing I want in return—is to see my sister's face when I do. Now brace yourself, girl. I've never been known for gentleness."

A crash, the world around her shaking.

A flash of light.

Black.

The first thing she sees when she wakes up is a sunflower. The largest of their kind she's ever seen, with the petals that might arouse jealousy in the sun itself, stares down at her.

The first thing she hears when she wakes is a heaving sigh—the sort that belongs to a Victorian woman lamenting her husband's drowning.

The first thing she feels when she wakes up is a pair of cold, clammy hands on either side of her head.

It is not until the sunflower turns, and she spots a pale blue neck where its stem should be, that she realizes all three of these things are connected.

"Cousin's awful, isn't he? How I despise him…oh. Why are you screaming?"

Psyche only stops when the sunflower-woman points it out. Breath comes raggedly; she is covered in sweat. She pushes herself upright and finds she's in a medical tent. Or something of the sort, at any rate—she's on a bed much like one in a hospital, but where she expects medical instruments, she finds only bowls of fruit.

"What…what's going on? Where am I?" she stammers.

The sunflower-woman, wearing a robe of deep blue, turns and sighs toward the flap. "You are being kept somewhere safe for mortals. Cousin's return to the Court…" A strange choking sound, her voice now strained as she continues. "Proved too much for you to bear. You tumbled away."

Psyche's hand flies to her temple, to her legs, to check for any signs of harm. She'd fallen? But from such a height and so fast, she should have been dashed against the ground.

"Your Oathsworn caught you," the woman continues. "It was *terribly* romantic, at least until you cracked your head on her forearm. All that blood rather ruined the image."

Again Psyche touches her head. She knows what harm a head injury can do—but there's no tenderness anywhere, no sign of any damage at all. She stares at her clean fingertips.

"Oh, you should have seen her demanding we look after you. What a fury! Why, you could see Ares's fire in her right alongside her mother's. And while Cousin argued—soundly in the eyes of the Court, might I add—that you had caused that trouble yourself by letting go, your Oathsworn would not hear it. It nearly came to blows! What a fight that would have been, swift Passion against the Tides themselves! All for the sake of romance…"

Another forlorn sigh.

Psyche takes a breath. "Where's Eros now?" she asks.

The sunflower-woman wrings her hands. "Well…"

Psyche tries to hop off the raised bed, but she can't catch her balance and falls back immediately. "What do you mean," she rasps, " 'well'?"

"When there's blood in the water, the sharks are sure to find it," the sunflower-woman says. "And this little argument, it's blood. So much blood, which has gotten on so very many hands..."

Just what is this woman saying, and why does she talk like this? She sounds as if she's always on the verge of crying. And what a strange mask! A sunflower is so plain for one of these creatures.

But those are small worries compared to what might have happened to Eros. If she calls out now, will Eros answer...?

And what will Psyche do if she does not?

"You're very rude, you know."

Psyche frowns. "How so?"

"You haven't even asked my name. I know you don't know it. I'm telling you all these things about your Oathsworn, and you haven't even asked."

Well, that much is true, though the woman's name seemed a secondary concern. Psyche puts on her best client-soothing voice. "You're right, that is rude of me. My name is Psyche. What's yours?"

A pause, then the smell of fruit. A moment later a slice of it is against Psyche's lips.

"Clytie of the Court of the Deep. Or, I guess, the Court of Waves. Cousin is insistent we call it that now. Won't you eat more? I wasn't sure how your Oathsworn prepared it for you, so I thought raw was the safest bet, even though the strands always end up in your teeth, and it's such a bother..."

Psyche takes a bite of the fruit. Clytie's right—it does end up stuck between her teeth. And the flavor isn't quite like the ones Eros always feeds her, either. This one tastes almost like salted caramel.

"While Cousin and your Oathsworn were arguing, certain people decided to bring up their grievances so that they might be heard. Not me, of course. My grievances have already been 'addressed,' according to Cousin, so there's no need to talk about them anymore. But other people, they brought things up."

"What were your grievances, Clytie?" Psyche asks. She can't stop herself—she speaks with her mouth still half-full.

"That the Light's Sovereign has turned from me, despite all I've done to earn their affection. That *your Oathsworn* was the one who bespelled them to do so. But it's all right. You see, the Court of Wisdom ruled that I've gotten my comeuppance, and that all parties in the matter of Love and War have received their justice. So no one cares."

She frowns. "Clytie, I'm sorry. It's awful when people sweep away your concerns like that. Especially when it sounds like you caught the short end of things. I'd be happy to listen if you want to talk about what happened, but I do have a question for you first, if that's okay?"

Clytie hums. "Hmm. All right. Since you're being so nice about it."

Psyche makes herself open her eyes. Now that she's sat

down for a little while, her head isn't swimming so much. "Thank you, I appreciate it. Could you tell me what happened with Eros? Was there some kind of fight?"

"*Is* there," Clytie corrects. After consideration, she continues: "Your Oathsworn has gotten into her share of trouble, but this latest thing is new. Seems she went and killed one of our compatriots. A fellow by the name of Glaucus. Used to be human, like you, which is almost as unbelievable as her—"

Once more Psyche sits up, once more a little too fast—but she must, all the same, for what she is being told is dire indeed. She fixes Clytie's sunflower mask with curiosity's burning look.

"She killed Glaucus?" Psyche says. Her voice has shot up half an octave. "Eros said that you... that your kind can't die. That you couldn't even be hurt. She cut herself to show me, there wasn't any blood—"

"Oh, we can still be hurt," says Clytie. Such venom in her voice—yet such resignation. "Some of us more than others. Hurting Cousin would take some doing, and so would hurting your Oathsworn, radiant solar that she is. But for the younger, smaller Domains, it is a simple enough thing. Like... Glaucus.

"The easiest way is for an older Courtier to kill a younger. That's nearly always how it happens. Convincing a Beast of Legacy to do it also works, but then if they catch the poor thing, they tend to put it down, and give its hide to some hero who doesn't deserve it. A terrible fate, isn't it? To be cast aside like that."

A part of Psyche—the part of her concealed behind the castle walls—wants to ask what Clytie means by that, why she would phrase things in that particular way, but she can't. Not when there's a siege afoot.

"What happened with Glaucus? How did she...?"

The sunflower's petals take on a reddish hue. Clytie sits atop a fanciful coral chair, crossing her legs as she does. "You'd think it'd be the first, wouldn't you?" She toys with her fingers, twists them, wrings. "But it wasn't. It never is with her. Passion can't moderate itself. You understand that, don't you?"

"Clytie," Psyche whimpers. "Please. Please tell me."

"Glaucus had many lovers, and only one woman who ever cast him aside. One of my sisters from the old Court. To be honest she and I never got along—she has terrible taste in men, really, some of the most awful taste you've ever seen. But that's beside the point. It's just easier to talk about if I take little tangents." Clytie wrings her hands again. "Glaucus wanted Scylla more than anything in the world, but she wouldn't hear of it. You probably never saw beneath his mask, but it wasn't a pretty sight. Scylla humiliated him, and he went to another of the Courts for help. The Court of Enchantments."

Psyche can't help but wonder how many Courts there are. And, as Clytie pointed out, such diversions make it easier to deal with the mounting dread in her stomach.

"There he met another of the old ones, who made for him a potion that he could use to change Scylla's heart. But this wasn't the Queen of Enchantment, mind, it was her gangly idiot daughter, and she spilled a few drops of the potion onto her own skin. *That* ensnared her to Glaucus, ardently so. Why, you never saw a plainer girl more possessed by the fires of love. It made her almost beautiful."

Psyche has trained herself to be patient whenever a client's going on about a story. She's made herself a good listener. But it is hard to summon those skills now, with the battering ram echoing through the halls of her heart.

Still—if she does not try, she will lose something of herself. "What happened with the two of them? Did you dislike that girl, for some reason?"

Clytie laughs. The petals of her mask sway. "Oh, everyone hates the Court of Enchantments. Slipperier than eels they are, with all the haughtiness of the Court of Wisdom. You never know what they're up to. This daughter, though, she was younger than the rest of them, and that made her pathetic. A small thing in the company of giants always seems pathetic, don't you think?"

"I'm not sure I'd call anything pathetic." Psyche pinches the bridge of her nose.

"Then you're far more kindhearted than I'd expect from Passion's Oathsworn." Clytie hums. "The girl told Glaucus how she felt. You'd think he'd know what humiliation felt like, but he didn't have a bit of sympathy in that body of his. Not a bit. He told her trees would sooner grow in our Court than he would consider being with her, and she, well..."

"She didn't take it well."

Such pain enters Clytie's voice, such wavers, that it is a wonder she continues speaking at all. The most coldhearted could not have heard her without setting their eyes aglimmer, their lips aquiver.

"Not in the slightest. Men have no idea what they're doing when it comes to love. They consider themselves pursuers in a hunt. Never mind that love isn't a hunt at all; if they think they're being pursued for even a second, they'll turn on you. Mark that, Psyche. Mark it well. There is no fate more terrible than striving for a man's regard. Even among the gods."

Psyche reaches out for the sunflower-woman. "Clytie, I'm so sorry for whatever happened to you. A broken heart is a terrible thing, and it takes so much time to work through. You don't deserve to be treated like that."

Yet she receives a scoff in answer. "You only say that because you don't know who I am."

"I don't, but—"

"You wanted to hear the rest of the story, didn't you?" Clytie says. "Love is the most beautiful thing in this world and the most terrible, too. And when this girl from the Court of Enchantments realized that Glaucus would never look on her as she looked on him, she found herself crushed by it. Do you see all the water above our heads? Imagine that every drop of it is a love as ardent as you've ever felt. Imagine all of that pressing down upon you at once. The sheer weight of it. That is the love that this girl felt, the love that beguiled her. And if anyone should condemn what she did, then I challenge them to live under that pressure themselves.

"This potion, this kindness, that she had once thought to grant Glaucus—she twisted it just as he'd twisted her kind affection. The potion within became as poisoned as her heart. When this girl fed it to Scylla—who never met a drink she did not want to try—it was not cruel love that filled Scylla's heart.

"We all saw what happened. Scylla exploded upward in a great cloud of flesh. It was as if a giant squid had let out all its ink at once, except the ink was Scylla. She howled, and howled, and howled, and there was nothing anyone could do to save her. Not even Cousin could keep her from changing. When it was all said and done, there was no question what was before us: a monster."

Silence in the hut. Splinters of a broken gate in Psyche's throat.

"What...what happened to her?"

Clytie turns toward the door. "Cousin placed her at the border of his Court, where intrepid mortals sometimes make their way in. Scylla eats them now. I think she's happy, though, since it means she doesn't have to see Glaucus. Or didn't, until very recently."

Psyche does not want Clytie to continue. She wants to run. She wants to leave this place. She wants to be anywhere but here, anywhere but among these people. She wants to open her eyes and find herself beneath the blankets with Eros, watching a shitty sitcom and having to explain all the jokes.

Even before Clytie says it, part of Psyche knows what's coming.

"Do you remember what I told you about the wars between us—older Courtiers and younger ones? It's the same with love, you know. And with seeing each other's faces. Older Courtiers learn to conceal their power somewhat to the point that we can all get along, but it doesn't always work. Scylla was *much* older than Glaucus. She needed to downplay herself for the two of them to speak. Now, with what she is, she can't do it anymore.

"If someone were to leave Glaucus before Scylla, he could no more resist flying toward her and embracing her than a moth can resist a flame. And she would consume him as readily as the fire does the moth. All at once, just like that, for her hatred of him has had thousands of years to grow.

"No one knows about love the way your Oathsworn does. When, during their fight, he drew blood and swore he would tear the heart from her body, she answered him that she would return his heart to him, and drove an arrow into his neck. An arrow that compelled him to walk to the border of the Court of Waves and embrace his old love."

Clytie crosses her arms. "Scylla ate him. One of the Rivers saw it happen with her own two eyes, and brought word to the Court today."

The battering ram breaks through the gates. All of malaise's soldiers spill forth into Psyche's heart: doubt and fear, guilt and disgust, a shame unlike any other. Had Eros really…?

Before Psyche can even begin to formulate a thought—let alone an answer—a muted horn rings through the air.

"Hmm. They've reached a conclusion. Your Oathsworn should be returning shortly, if she's to return," says Clytie. "I see I've frightened you. It can't be helped. So near to the flame you're certain to get burned. But it is lovely to burn, isn't it?

To be consumed in that way, to give yourself over to a thing that is greater than you could ever imagine? I'll be cheering for the two of you. I always cheer for love."

"Clytie..."

"There's one last thing I want you to know, Psyche. One very important thing." She closes the distance between them in only two steps, a fingertip beneath Psyche's chin. "Love and Passion can never unmask before mortals. It would drive them as mad as it did Glaucus. As mad as it drove me."

It is only then, with so little distance between them, that Psyche realizes something important.

Clytie isn't wearing a mask.

That sunflower...really is her face now. It's been grafted onto whatever face she might have had before, judging from the jagged scars at Clytie's neck. And that sunflower is smiling at her.

A scream dies in her throat as the door opens. Eros bursts through like a bull breaching a fence. "Psyche? Psyche, are you all right?"

Clytie drops her all at once and draws back, as if she'd never said anything at all. Psyche can no longer bear to look at her—but she finds she can no longer bear to look at Eros, either. Her eyes land on an intricate carpet and do not leave it, not even as Eros's arms wrap around her.

"Clytie, what did you say to her?" Eros booms. "Look at her. Look at what you've done. Poseidon tasked you with healing her and no more!"

"Is she not healed?" Clytie answers. "He did not forbid me

from speaking with her, and she seemed *so eager* to talk. What a kind soul she is. How could I resist?"

It is like a conversation she is hearing from a different room. Distantly she knows what's happening. Dissociation. A shock response. How pitiful, she thinks. Most people react that way only to trauma, and this isn't trauma, is it? To be beneath the waves like this, to be held in the arms of a god? To be loved by Passion herself—that is no trauma.

Is it?

"We're leaving," Eros says. "Just hold on to me a bit longer, Psyche, and I'll get you home. You're going to be all right."

The world around her begins to shift.

"Ehehehe. Goodbye, Psyche. I'll look forward to talking with you again."

Chapter Seventeen

"Are you certain?"

They stand not on the Court's impossible shores but on the rusted wrought iron of Psyche's fire escape. Eros crouches birdlike on the rail. Her fingertips caress Psyche's cheek.

Psyche doesn't have the will to move them away. She's not certain if she wants to, anyway. What is she certain of, right now? The question repeats. *What are you certain of, Psyche, what do you know for sure?*

"I think it's for the best," she says. She does not look up at Eros. "Maybe. I don't know."

"Whatever Clytie told you..."

"I need time to think about it," Psyche says. Her voice rises. Like a too-sharp blade wielded by a novice, it cuts her as much as it cuts Eros.

Both of them flinch.

"Psyche."

Psyche stares not at her face, not her false face. Anywhere

but there. Instead she fixes her gaze at the oyster-shell clasp of Eros's ornate robe. So like the one they'd shot at together. Had that been Poseidon's symbol they lit aflame? Was that why he'd treated Psyche in such a way?

"Psyche, you know I would never hurt you. My heart would stay my hand, even if my Oath failed."

"Do you have a heart?" Psyche asks. Knowing she is treading on dangerous ground, she tries to mitigate the blow she's struck. "Your kind, I mean. Gods. Do gods have hearts?"

A silence. Eros's head tilting downward. Her hands drawing back from Psyche's face. Yes, the wound has struck true.

"If we can be said to have them, then mine beats within your breast."

The blade passes once more between them; now Psyche is the one bleeding.

A touch from Eros now would tip the balance—a physical truth to reinforce the spoken one. Refutation of the things Clytie had told her, of the things she'd seen; warm refuge in the cold bitterness of these new doubts.

But doubts are the bright colors on an adder's scales; they are there for a reason. And until Psyche's had time to sort through what hers might be, she can't allow the serpent to coil around her throat.

No matter how much she may want it to.

"Eros, thank you. It means... it means a lot to hear that, but..."

"You still need time."

That Eros's warmth is there even now only makes Psyche

feel worse. How can Eros speak so tenderly in these circumstances? Isn't she upset? She should be upset, she should be angry, she must hate Psyche for doing this so close to the day they'd chosen together. Isn't she angry?

A hand on Psyche's shoulder, a squeeze so gentle it might be a dream.

"Then whenever you are ready to call on me, I shall be ready to answer."

With the rush of fire, she is gone, and Psyche is alone.

It is early September—and this is already the coldest night of the year.

Eros killed someone.

The woman who held Psyche as gently as a bird in hand had sent a man to be devoured by a woman he once loved. *Would it bother you to know that I've gotten my hands dirty?*

A question once asked in jest. Psyche repeats it to her water-stained ceiling, holding her own hand above her face. Her olive skin matches the stains, in places, and she tries to connect one to the next as best she can.

It is better than imagining herself coated in blood.

Tonight she has done all of her favorite things. After throwing the duvet in the drier downstairs for five minutes, she fluffed herself up inside of it and watched a bunch of meaningless sitcoms with Latte in her lap. Latte's kind enough, or perhaps wise enough, to behave. She listens to *Golden Hour* on repeat.

She wanted to take a long luxurious shower, too, but after her little outing to the Court of Waves, the feeling of water against her face makes her scream, and so she returns to the duvet. Heated it up again, too. Good as new.

Wouldn't it be nice if she could be the same? A tumble in the dryer and set to rights just like that. Everything in its place. All her tension gone, all her questions answered.

Life is not so simple. She has always known this, and always despised it, and she cannot sit and break down what is going on in her mind. So she stares at the ceiling, at the stains, and she asks:

"Did I get someone killed?"

But the air has no answers.

She doesn't get out of bed the next day. Internet distance makes it easy to pretend to her closest companions that she is fine, that nothing has happened, that she has no questions about reality or righteousness or justice. She sends pictures of Latte; everything must be fine.

When she posts that she's not going to stream because she isn't feeling well, she receives two messages.

The first is from her sister Cid. Lol is your stomach doing flips because you decided you could totally handle eating an entire pint of ice cream in one go again?

This one merits no reply except a lazy lmao sent without so much as an emoji. Psyche would rather the duvet swallow her whole than try to explain this to either of her sisters.

The second is from Bondi. They only invite you once, but they know how to stick around, don't they?

Cold shock against the back of her neck. I don't know how to go back to being normal again.

Psyche waits for an answer—but it doesn't come until long after she's fallen asleep. By the time she sees it, Bondi's offline again.

> It took my friend a long time to forget. Trashy slasher movies might make it easier. Movie date tomorrow night? Or tomorrow morning, for me.

In tiny, gray text next to it: Edited 4:33 am.

She wakes up after noon, crawls out from under her sheets, and microwaves herself something a factory spat out. She tends to her plants, and they don't die, but they don't thrive. She tends to Latte, who spends half the time on her shoulders and the other time mewling for her attention. In the evenings, she holds her own makeshift Court. Her viewers come to see her and ask her, Psyche, can I fix this?

"You can fix almost anything, Tief," Psyche says. She's playing a different game today, *Chronicle of the Sky Knight*. The player character is preset. "The question you need to be asking yourself is whether it's worth it."

Smiling for her followers is exhausting. It's as if she's found a mask of her own to wear—one of iron and lead and finely carved marble—and must bear its weight. Her head throbs at the temples; the ring lights ahead of her are spears leveled at her pupils.

Yet she smiles. They need her to.

"The first and most important thing is to figure out what you're looking for in a situation like this. Your partner forgot your birthday. Are you looking for reassurance from them that you're important? Do you want them to make amends? What would make you feel like you're being seen and heard; what would help you move forward?"

The main character of *Sky Knight* picks up a bow and nocks an arrow. Psyche's palms itch. It's a plain bow this time, carved from a yew tree in the family's backyard. Nothing transcendent. So why does it feel…?

"Then ask yourself what's practical. Let's say the two of you agree to pick out a new gift together—do you think you'll be able to forgive them for forgetting in the first place? If there's a pattern of things, you might want a bigger gesture, but that can only go so far before it's unreasonable. You have to ask yourself if what would make things better for you is practical, and if it's healthy for your partner to try and do, too."

The village's best hunter, the main character's dashing older brother, comes up behind him. He has a few tips about good shooting form. Buttons pop up on-screen to press in time with his suggestions.

"Sometimes the amount of effort it would take to make things right is unhealthy for both of you. In that case, it's healthier to try and part ways as painlessly as you can.

Breaking up doesn't always have to be painful if you both go in with open eyes."

Psyche misses a press. The main character's shot goes awry, and the hunter laughs softly at his earnest efforts.

"But sometimes it's worth trying again."

If they had met in the game's village, what would Psyche have thought of Eros? A hunter's hands are stained from the start. Eros told her outright that they were. She hadn't tried to hide it.

But could Psyche have gone hunting with her? Could she, when Eros returned with a carcass slung over her shoulder, have helped her clean it?

She imagines herself doing it. At first she can't fight her disgust at the animal laid out before her, but Eros is as patient as she's always been. Her cuts are swift and certain. Her broad shoulders hide part of the carcass from view.

"It's all right," she says. "Tell me what's for dinner tonight, and I'll put all the best pieces aside for you."

The exercise has its limitations. It isn't really Eros standing next to her, only Psyche's concept of her; she isn't confronted with the smells or the sounds or any of the viscera. It's only an exercise.

But the strangest thing about it—aside from the calm that it brings her—is that this false Eros is still wearing her mask.

Bondi doesn't want to talk about what she meant by that middle-of-the-night text, so Psyche doesn't pry. They watch that terrible movie together. From opposite sides of the earth, they share a couch, all thanks to the power of the internet. Since Bondi doesn't mute her mic when she eats, Psyche can even hear her chomping away on popcorn the whole time. Latte bounds out of her cat tower right at the climax; Psyche scrambles to catch her own bowl of snacks before it clatters to the ground.

She isn't successful. Kernels scatter across the hardwood. She lets out a sigh.

"Bon, could you pause it a sec while I clean up?"

"Sure. You're definitely not checking under the sofa because you're scared right?"

"Fuck off," Psyche says with a laugh. Teens running around a summer camp fearing for their lives are quaint in comparison to feuds among the gods.

So is picking up popcorn. Too lazy to get the broom she squats down to shovel it all onto a sheet of paper.

As she reaches, she spots the dove on the fire escape. Not unusual in and of itself. Why is it, then, that her heart skips a beat at the sight of it? Shadows are shifting as it paces the railing. Impossible to make out the colors of it for sure, but...

Psyche stands. In two steps she's made it to the window, cleared away the curtain, and gotten close enough to get a good look.

Pale, pastel brown.

It chirps and flies away, and Psyche realizes—she can still be spooked.

Her next stream goes long. Searching the fridge confirms the deepest and most worrisome of her fears: there is nothing she can heat up in the microwave. Maybe tonight's a night she can cook?

Psyche looks to Latte and shakes her head. "That isn't happening, is it?"

Her sleeping cat rolls over. She paws at the air. Dreaming of a cat toy, perhaps? Either way, it's an agreement. That much is certain. Cooking *won't* be happening tonight.

But there is a late-night Greek diner she could hit up for a little taste of home. Doesn't she deserve that after all this? Of course she could order, but it's only a couple of blocks away, and she always feels bad about other companies getting a cut of the profit. Plus, she likes the old cooks and servers who run the place. It might be nice to see familiar faces.

Summer nights in the city are nearly as humid as the Court of Waves—but only nearly. The breeze saves this one from such an ignoble fate. As she passes men playing dominoes and women talking on stoops, she allows herself to float among the sounds of the city. Clattering tiles and distant, tinny music; cars honking in rounds; gossip in half a dozen different languages. Fireflies flit above sewer grates, and children play at skelly boards.

It is September 14, and it is a good night.

She's sure of it.

Psyche turns a corner. Here the lights give way to shade: a row of sprawling oak trees obscure the streetlamps. The lack of shops means there isn't much in the way of ambient lighting, either. It's all dimly lit brownstones for the next two blocks, then another turn to the diner.

A couple of years ago it might have frightened her. When she first moved here, everything about the city was so overwhelming; it was hard to tell good busy from shady busy, or peaceful quiet for the sort that meant you should never wander there after dark.

Well, no matter. She's got other things to worry about. The date is a firebrand in her mind. Tomorrow she swore to see Eros again. Oaths are sacred; she can hardly break hers. But when Psyche does summon her, what will they say?

What does Psyche need to make this work?

As she walks, she tries to sort through her thoughts. She wants answers from Eros. How often does she have to do things like what she did to Glaucus? What makes such acts necessary? Does she regret having done them?

But what if Psyche doesn't like the answers she receives? Easy enough, the therapist part of her says. If she doesn't like them, she should call off whatever this is and go about her life. The city will be here for her; her followers will be here for her. She could leave, if she wanted.

But could she really?

That warmth around her, that steady, reassuring presence.

The pure adoration of Eros's glance and the gentle possessiveness of her grip. Her world is so much more beautiful and so much more dangerous than Psyche's own.

Can Psyche forsake all that? Does she want to go back to the way things were before?

She crosses the street. Overhead she hears birds flapping their wings, building nests.

She thinks she *can* forsake it. Oh, it might take time to get used to things again, but she could. A childhood spent moving around the world has taught her plenty about starting over.

But does she want to…?

Or does she want to learn more about Eros's favorite things—what kind of music she likes, which places in the world are her favorites, the movies that can hold her attention?

She imagines this world, too, and something in her heart aches for it.

"Are you the one?"

The voice stirs her from her thoughts—a rich timbre that sets her spine tingling. Psyche can't help but turn back to see who's speaking. She spots three tall figures behind her, all wearing matching leather biker jackets. One has golden flat studs, one has silver spikes, and one has no adornments at all. The dark makes it hard to see their faces. Maybe they're big fans of *The Warriors*?

Psyche keeps her head down. If they're trouble, it's best not to give them a reason to talk to her. She hurries along her route—but when she hears their footsteps, she knows she hasn't lost them.

"Are you the one they call Psyche?"

She stops midstride. Are they some of her followers? Alarm bells are ringing in her head, but maybe if she's kind enough and asks them nicely, they'll leave?

"If you guys want a selfie together, sure, but after that I really need to be going. Will that be okay?" She talks as she turns—and finds them standing shoulder to shoulder, strangely still.

"You are Psyche," Gold Studs says.

"We have found you, then?" says Spikes.

"The tempter," finishes Plain.

Fear's cold fingers wrap around her heart. Shit. Why didn't she bring her pepper spray? Shit, shit, shit. Okay—think it through. Panicking will only make matters worse. First things first, she can call for help or record whatever's about to happen with her phone. She reaches for it within her jacket pocket.

Her hand finds only worn cloth. Fuck. She must have left it back at the apartment!

Psyche swallows. Might as well make it clear she doesn't mean them any harm, right? She holds up her empty hands, palms out.

"I don't know what you're talking about," she says. Slow, firm, but not aggressive.

"You know what it's about," answers Gold Studs. They take a step forward, passing between the gaps of the branches. Moonlight illuminates a simple leather domino mask, a sharp jawline, and sharp teeth. Despite the danger, Psyche can't deny their beauty—how painful it is to behold them!

And painful, too, to realize what is going on.

The Courts are here.

"Who do you serve?" Psyche asks. She takes a step back, her hands still in the air. "I—I haven't visited in days, and I've caused no offense. You don't have... This isn't your Domain!"

Spikes steps forward, feathers clasped between his fingers. His skin is the color of rich clay, his muscles only barely contained by the leather. "So great is our Queen's power that it extends here. Her feathers guide us."

Plain is the next to step forward. The most horrible of the three, she pulls a lighter from her jacket. A flick of her thumb, and the flame is lit.

Another step back. When Plain pinches the flame and conjures from it a sword, Psyche knows in her heart what this is. The Court of Flame, the revelers who carried her to disaster.

"What do you want?" Psyche asks.

Gold doesn't have an answer for her. Instead, they lower their head and grunt. It's all the warning Psyche gets before they lunge in her direction. Psyche screams and leaps backward, but Plain closes the distance with a reckless slash of the flaming sword.

Shit, shit, shit. She has to get out of the way!

Another hurried step back, a scramble, only to stop when she walks straight into what feels like a brick wall. Spikes hooks his arms beneath her shoulders and pulls upward. Psyche's feet leave the ground. She kicks at Plain, but Gold Studs grabs her leg.

Once more Plain raises the flaming sword. "Breaker of compacts, temptress, here ends your—"

"Unhand my Oathsworn!"

A familiar flash of gold, the whistle of an arrow! An arrow of light pierces Plain through the chest. She staggers. Her jaw hangs open, her hand rises to what should be a wound—only there's no flesh torn. The light might as well be projected onto her skin. And then, like a woman gone too long without rest, she collapses to the ground.

Behind her stands Eros with flaming bow and arrow. "I'm sorry about the trouble, Psyche."

"You would raise a hand against us, Sister?" growls Spikes. Everything in Psyche's body wants to bolt when she hears him speak. She tries to stamp on his instep—but though she brings all her weight down upon him, he doesn't flinch. Instead he squeezes her so tight her ribs creak. "For this?"

"I will raise more than a hand if you continue," Eros says. How easily she draws that bow! "Let her go. You have no business terrorizing her."

"Mother says otherwise," Gold Studs giggles. "Mother says you've been naughty, Eri. She said we could torment you as much as we liked."

"You will do only what you dare, and what you dare isn't much," Eros answers. "This is your last warning. Let her go and we may call this matter forgotten."

S-she's raising her bow against her own siblings? Psyche's eyes fall in horror at Plain, still crumpled on the ground. Her heart hangs between beats. Has Eros really killed one of her own siblings so easily? No—Plain's still breathing. And breathing deep, now that Psyche's watching, as if in a deep sleep.

Silver laughs. The deep rumble of it resounds against Psyche's back, like the tremble of a building about to collapse. "And if we kill her instead?"

It's then that she feels it—the prick of something sharp against her throat. Needles? Claws? Psyche can't so much as wriggle without cutting herself. She tries to take a deep breath to soothe herself, to meet Eros's steady glance—but her fear is getting the better of her.

Is this how all of it ends? Killed in a petty squabble between the gods, one that she doesn't even understand? She wants to scream. Oh, she wants to scream, but what good would it do? All she can do is look to Eros and pray they can get out of this together. More than anything she wants the safety and comfort of those arms.

"E-Eros," she calls. "Eros, I don't... I don't want anyone to die."

"No one's dying today. Close your eyes for me, Psyche. You'll be safe when you next open them."

"Ha! Fat chance of—"

Before Spikes can finish his taunt, a burst of light paints Psyche's eyelids red. The whistle of an arrow follows. Spikes's grip goes slack; he, too, tumbles to the ground. Psyche feels a strong, warm arm take hold of her. "Tell me where to take you."

Could she go back home knowing these three had found

her? No, no—she'd spend the night watching the windows and living in fear of the door.

"To your place," Psyche says.

A small sound before the whistling of another arrow. At first, she thought it amusement—but when Psyche feels wetness against her arm she realizes the truth. It's pain.

And Eros is bleeding.

"As you wish."

Chapter Eighteen

When Psyche next opens her eyes she sees not the brownstones and oaks to which she's accustomed, but the statues and tapestries that adorn Eros's Domain. A curious silence replaces the bustle of the city. Disturbing it: Psyche's still-pounding heart, and Eros's pained breathing.

Eros sets Psyche down on a divan. Despite her injuries, she does this with gingerly care. The only sign she's hurt at all is the way she's breathing—and the way she clutches her fingers to her rib cage. Perhaps, too, in that she does not linger to stare at Psyche. Instead she scoops a fruit from the bowl on the table and holds it out as an offering.

"Here," she says. "It'll calm your nerves."

Psyche looks from the fruit to its laboring owner. "Eros..."

"I'm sorry I failed you," she says. "I should have intervened sooner. You must be shaken, dealing with those three. The second I felt them leave, I should have known..."

Psyche takes Eros's wrist and tugs her closer. The god of passion kneels. Were it not for the mask, their eyes would meet. What would Psyche see within them? And what would she think of it? Questions for another day. Psyche, still shaking, holds the fruit out to Eros. "I think you need this more than I do. It heals you, right? I thought I saw you bleeding."

A wince. Eros bows her head. "You...are very sweet to think of me at a time like this."

"Eros, don't be hardheaded," Psyche says. "It's okay to accept help if you need it. You think this is your fault, but I can't see how. You can't control what other people do. We made it out okay, right?"

Eros grunts. From between her grasping fingers, golden blood drips like sealing wax onto the floor. Psyche's heart aches. She holds out the fruit again. "Please. It hurts me to see you in pain."

The weight of Eros's hand on the fruit makes Psyche's dip. Yet Eros does not yet claim this for herself—she only holds it. "The fruit...won't help with something like this."

Now it is Psyche who kneels next to Eros. The fruit won't help? But it's meant to keep the gods immortal, isn't it? She scrambles to try to think of a solution; all she comes up with are the memories of her mandatory first aid classes. But do those work on gods?

Better to try than to abide the pain. Psyche tries to move Eros's hand to get a better look at the wound. By now, most of Eros's arming coat is soaked with the thick gold of her blood.

"Psyche..."

"Was it the sword?" she asks. "Fire's supposed to cauterize, but maybe it doesn't hurt you, since you're from the Court...? Oh."

Beneath Eros's hand is not a wound in the traditional sense—the flesh there is not ragged, nor torn. Instead it is simply missing. A chunk of her flesh is just...gone. Worse, it may not have been flesh to start with. There's no sign of bone or any other organs—only molten gold beneath her skin. Gold that now oozes from her more and more by the second.

Well, fuck.

"I...Eros, what...what happened?"

Eros clutches the wound again. Sweat drips from the chin of her mask, the first time Psyche has ever seen such exertion from her. Is this how a god dies?

"I would do it again. No matter what happened to me, I would do it again. I couldn't just leave you to them."

Psyche presses her hand over Eros's. The blood pours over her, too. "Talk to me. Let's try and figure it out together, okay? We just need to stay calm, and we can find some way to fix it. It's going to be okay."

"Are you talking to me, or yourself?" Eros says. Between the pants, she lets out a tired laugh. "Because I know how this ends."

"No, you don't," says Psyche. A firm certainty comes over her; her clay has been fired and set. "Because you seem to think this is going to end with you dying, and that isn't going to happen."

"Going to argue with old Thanatos himself are you?" Eros says. "Ah... Psyche. Never change."

"I'll argue with whoever it takes, so stop it with the fatalism!" Psyche says. She presses as hard as she can. "Tell me what I can do to help, and I'll do it. You aren't going to die!"

Eros lifts a hand to Psyche's face. To her horror, Eros's fingertips are ice-cold.

"I can't," she says. "It's against... against the Law."

"Fuck the Law!" Psyche says. She earns another sputtering laugh from Eros.

"Psyche," she says. "I really can't tell you. I can't. You have to... you have to figure it out yourself, or else it doesn't count."

"You're bleeding to death and—" Psyche starts, but she grinds herself to a halt. Shouting and arguing aren't going to fix anything. Shit, she always thought she'd be calmer in a situation like this, but here she goes losing it. Okay, circular breathing—think, think, think...

"It's the way we are. I can't tell you any more than a fish can breathe air. It'd kill me. Or do the rest of the job, anyway."

"All right," Psyche says. "Please, just hold on, let me think."

"I've got no complaints about holding on."

Psyche wants to whack her for making a joke at a time like this, but she worries it would hurt Eros further. She didn't see Eros get hurt—so maybe the injury wasn't caused by a weapon? Clytie and Eros both said gods couldn't kill each other that way. Beasts of Legend had to be involved, whatever those are.

"Did you fight a beast?" Psyche asks.

"Only if you count my siblings as beasts. And most people don't."

It was worth a try. "No one wounded you?"

"You might call it self-inflicted," Eros says. Then she winces again. A fresh spurt of blood wells over Psyche's fingers. "The Law doesn't like me giving you hints."

"Well, then it can find me and file a complaint in person," says Psyche. What else does she know about the gods? Courts and Domains, masks, powers, and…

Oaths.

The piece falls into place. Eros blaming herself, swearing she'd do it again if needed.

"You came to me before I called for you," Psyche says. "You broke the promise we made to each other about space."

This laugh sounds weaker than the others—but prouder, too. "Fuck the Law, indeed. Got there on your own."

Psyche has about a thousand questions. Given the bleeding, she's going to need to figure out the right one to ask, and fast. If the Law forbade Eros from telling her what the problem was in the first place, it likely also forbids her from talking about the solution. Glaucus and Zephyr's fight had been about a broken oath, too, hadn't it? Eros herself had put a stop to it, and she'd done it by killing Glaucus. Maybe removing the offended party is key?

"If I leave, does it help?" she asks.

Eros shakes her head. Though weak, she clutches Psyche closer. "Please don't."

A twinge in Psyche's heart. She kisses the mask, wishing

more than anything that she could kiss the skin beneath it. Marble makes for cold comfort now.

"Don't worry, I'm not going anywhere. You're stuck with me for a while yet. I can't have you dying before you tell me more about this world," she says. "Or before our date."

"Almost made it, didn't we?"

"And we still will," says Psyche. She's sure of that now—whatever happens here.

"You've always been so confident, ever since I first met you. But not just…confident. Optimistic. I think the world is better for that," says Eros. "For having someone who always sees the best in it. And the best in everyone she meets. I wanted… I wanted so badly to be worthy of that. No one ever looked at me the way you did. Not as a tool or as a weapon but as a person with her own wants and needs. No one ever…"

"Zephyr did, or he wouldn't have invited me," Psyche counters. But she hates the distant tone Eros is taking, the way her voice is starting to waver. Once before she heard a voice just like this. A hospital bed, rain on the windows, her sisters waiting outside because they couldn't bear the weight. Only she could. "You're going to make it out of this."

"Do you know the strangest thing?" Eros says. She nuzzles against Psyche. "I'm not afraid. I always thought that if I died it'd be in battle, or espionage. Something insipid. But to die like this, with you…I can be happy with this."

It's like swallowing glass, listening to her. How many years had Psyche spent mending other people's ills, smoothing over the rough, only to be powerless when it mattered? No amount of talking could save her mother. No amount of trying saved her first career.

When she lost everything—when her mother died, her father grew distant, and her sisters started to stray—Psyche had no one but herself. Laura found solace in the arms of her adoring suitors; Cid retreated into her own world; Psyche had no other long-term friends because she moved so much and spent so much time taking care of everyone else.

It was just her. For years, it was just her. Through college and grad school both, through the burnout, through everything…it was just her, desperately trying to keep other people's lives together to make up for her own.

All she had for company were the games she played when she got home, the ridiculous RPGs where the main character got swept up in a larger-than-life narrative, where the world was awful but in a way they could change, where no one had to die of cancer and her father kept them together instead of getting a separate place for himself because they were "old enough," and…

Hasn't she lost enough already? Hasn't she rebuilt enough already?

Can't she be selfish, just this once?

"Eros," she says. Tears fall on Eros's shoulders. To Psyche's cold horror, there is less of her with every second that passes. The clay she'd so eagerly fired is now starting to crack within her arms. Pouring out into a pool from Eros's shattered skin is pure, molten gold. "Please don't die. Please, I won't be able to forgive you if you do."

Eros reaches for Psyche's face again. Her hand shakes, circling, touching nothing. "What would you…forgive me for…?"

Another spasm of pain takes her; another spurt of gold. Eros, god that she is, groans in agony.

Another hint? What could she forgive her…oh!

Psyche clasps Eros's shaking hand tight. With the other, she cradles the masked face that she's come to know and—yes—come to love.

"I forgive you for breaking your promise to me," she says.

Light fills the room again. Eros gasps and groans. Missing flesh stitches back together—and while her blood does not flow back within her, it does stop flowing out. Eros arches as her body comes back together; she holds tight to Psyche.

"Thank you," she whispers—the woman with bloodied hands speaking in gentle tones of reverence. "You saved me."

Psyche sniffs. The tears that fall from her now are grateful, joyous ones; the fear has gone away. She buries her face in the crook of Eros's strong shoulder. "You saved me first."

"No, it was you—the first time you spoke with me, you gave me someone to be," Eros says. She tangles her fingers in Psyche's hair. The mask presses against Psyche's ear, once more warmed by divine skin. "You saw something in me I thought long dead."

"That's a romantic way to say I nagged you into committing murder," Psyche says. She can't keep back the sob. So much has happened—how are they to sort through it all? Yet as adrift as she feels, she knows she has Eros alongside her.

And there is the reassurance she needed—Eros's mask shifting, a kiss on the tip of Psyche's ear. "Glaucus tried to poison Zephyr. If I had left him to his own devices, as I planned, I would have lost my only friend within the Courts. You saved him when you saved me."

"Poison . . . ?"

Another kiss, this one softer than the last. "There is a creature that dwells within the depths of the Court of Waves, one of Poseidon's forgotten children—a beast. His poison leaves us in such irreparable pain that we will do anything to stop it. That includes making an oath just to break it and die."

"Clytie told me you killed him," Psyche says. The rush of emotion has left her in a daze—but when Eros picks her up, she does not protest. "I thought . . . I felt so awful about it. It didn't sound like you to do something like that. I know that you told me what life was like for you before, but I hadn't . . ."

A rumble deep in Eros's chest as she hums, considers. Can a woman without organs breathe? Psyche tries not to let her mind wander too much. All that matters is that the two of them are here, together, and safe.

"Are you still comfortable with me?" Eros asks.

A good question, a fair one. But after all this time to think, Psyche's certain she knows the answer.

"Yes," she says. "I don't know if I'm comfortable with the Courts, or the politics, or any of that. Not when it involves killing. But when I'm with you, I feel like we can do anything. Like we could fly to the stars. Even with the others, they're not all bad. Don't get me wrong, you've all lived so long and under such intense pressure that you really need therapists, all of you do, but I think beneath all the trauma you've inflicted on one another, there are good people."

Eros strokes Psyche's cheek. Sitting like this—in Eros's lap, straddling her—Psyche's all too aware of the warmth that's flooding back into her divine guardian. And of the slightest movements.

"You believe that after my siblings tried to kill you?" Eros says. "You are that certain in your belief?"

"Well, I mean, I wasn't happy about it. Pretty terrified, honestly. I don't know what I would have done without you. Die, probably," Psyche says with a nervous laugh. She'd rather not think about that possibility all that much. "But...your mother put them up to it, didn't she? It sounds like she doesn't leave any of you with a choice in the matter when it comes to dirty work. When an abused dog bites someone, you don't blame the dog."

Quiet—a thoughtful one. Eros lifts Psyche up and carries her to the divan. There she sits the two of them down once more, Psyche on her lap. For a little while the two of them bask in the comfort of one another's presence—Psyche's hands wandering the firm course of Eros's renewed body, Eros holding her tight. There's no need to talk about it; both know how badly they need this shred of peace, of reassurance, of love.

Now, having seen Eros on the verge of death, Psyche finds herself eager to touch her all the more. Who is to say how long it will be before someone tries to kill her again? Though that does beg the question...

"Eros?"

"Yes?" she answers, slipping a hand beneath the hem of Psyche's tunic. "Would you like me to stop?"

Should they? It is after midnight—officially the fifteenth. Maybe they should talk about all this, maybe they should slow down, but...it doesn't feel right to after what they've been through tonight. "No. But...why would your mother try to hurt me? I've never met her."

Eros hooks a finger beneath Psyche's chin. "You'd like to hear about that now? I'll tell you, if you like. But it may cool your blood."

At least she's being honest about it. "Maybe you can tell me after," Psyche says. "There's other things I want to focus on right now."

Eros hikes her hand up to the small of Psyche's back. The caress of her skin, her warmth, the possessive pull of her hand... Oh, there's no doubt they'll be working through things.

"I am at your command," says Eros. She presses a kiss to Psyche's temple, to her ear. "Distraction is one of my many, many talents."

Is it the brush with death that's sending shivers through her? "Is that so?"

Eros tilts Psyche's chin up and plants a kiss on her throat. "Oh, yes. By the time I'm done with you, death will be the farthest thing from your mind. You'll be too busy begging me to finally let you come."

She draws a sharp breath. "I never knew you were such a tease."

"It isn't a tease, Psyche, it's a promise," says Eros, gripping her thigh. "I've waited long enough to hear your moans—I'm going to take my time enjoying them."

It's enough to hitch Psyche's breath in anticipation. "A-are you sure?"

"I've never been more sure. Let me show you what pleasure can be like," says Eros. Her hands travel higher; she hooks Psyche's panties onto her thumb. "You want it so badly already, don't you? I can smell you from here. Tell me, Psyche. Tell me that you want me to fuck you."

Every one of Psyche's senses is alight. Blood rushes through her ears and down, down, warming her, readying her for what is to come.

"I... I need it. God, there hasn't been a single day I haven't thought of fucking you."

Eros tugs at Psyche's underwear. "Every day, hmm? And every time I touched you, you thought of it. My fingers inside you, and my tongue..."

Those things and more. So many more. "K-keep going, big talker. It's going to take more than that to make me break."

"Is that a challenge?" Eros asks.

"It might be."

Something hot and insistent at Psyche's ear—Eros's tongue flicking at her earlobe, the pressure of a sharp-toothed bite. "Close your eyes for me."

Oh, she doesn't want to. But when a woman tells you to do something in a voice like *that*, you do it.

"Good girl," purrs Eros. "Don't open them until I tell you it's safe, all right?"

"But I want to see," Psyche whines. "You must be beautiful. I want to see your face when you're fucking me."

A rich laugh that only stirs her further, only makes her more eager to see. What does she look like when she laughs? What a smug look she must be wearing.

"Bold and bolder. I'd like for you to see, too, Psyche, but it isn't safe. Not tonight. Tonight, when it comes to my face, all you need to worry about is soaking it."

Oh god. Psyche's breath catches. Before she can think of anything to say, Eros is picking her up again.

"We're going to the bed. I want to have space to spread you out beneath me."

"You're the one who's getting bold," Psyche says. She's pressed up against Eros's front, supported by one of the god's forearms. So graceful is Eros's gait that Psyche doesn't feel the swing of it at all. Of course, the kiss distracts her, too. Full lips and a rich, sweet heat filling her mouth—that tongue, the dangerous promise of those teeth. A hunter's mouth.

And Psyche longs to be her prey.

"Now, now, you've seen what happens when I break my word. I promise you that no one ever has or ever will leave you quivering like I do," Eros says. A heavy thud—the mask, torn off and flung aside.

A firm tug at Psyche's belt, her tunic undone. The air is cool against her readied skin but soon warmed by Eros's own body pressing against her. That hot mouth trails kisses down from her neck to her collarbone.

"You're as perfect as I imagined," whispers the god. "Every bit of you."

"I don't know about every bit—"

Teeth drag gently, but insistently, over Psyche's nipple. "Will you argue with me in matters of passion, too? You'll find I'm the authority on the subject. Every bit of you, Psyche."

She grinds her knee against Psyche's crotch, eliciting a moan and a tremble. God—shouldn't this be the other way around? Shouldn't Psyche be the one adoring Eros? There's something so terribly lewd about the inversion, about knowing it is the god who is servicing her.

"You want to learn a little of what I know, don't you, Psyche? A lesson in pleasure, and fire, and sweet release."

Psyche grunts and nods, wrapping her arms around Eros. "P-please."

Eros starts grinding in earnest—long, slow strokes that leave Psyche panting. She plants one hand on the bed, and the other she wraps around Psyche's waist. Soon the two of them are moving in perfect, languid time.

"I want you good and ready for me," Eros whispers into Psyche's ear. "You're already trembling, but I want you begging."

"T-take more than . . . more than this . . ." Psyche manages.

She hears Eros's cocky laugh and wishes she could smack her on the shoulder for it. No—it's all she can do to focus on her breathing, to cling tight, to feel the roll of Eros's muscled body against her.

"Not much more," Eros teases. "Look at you. You're so *wet*. My brave Psyche, how much more of this can you stand?"

Pleasure rolls through Psyche's body with each thrust. She tilts her head back, the moans coming steady, growing louder. Being against her like this is…

"You sound incredible. Such sweet little moans," Eros says.

"F-fuck you," Psyche says, laughing. Eros laughs, too—and then kisses her again.

For a while they stay like this, the steady pressure building and building, their mouths joined together. Psyche offers herself for consumption and Eros takes—her tongue slides into Psyche's mouth, hot and hungry.

But soon, Psyche's breath begins to catch, and Eros starts to slow. She breaks off their kiss only to slide her tongue farther down Psyche's eager body.

"I can taste how much you want me," Eros says.

Eros's mouth closes around Psyche's nipple. Her tongue flicks over it as she sucks, and sucks, her free hand toying with the other. Psyche has to bite on her knuckle to keep from moaning like a virgin. What's gotten into her? All this teasing and she's about to come already. This impossible heat…

"Mm, there's my good girl. So eager. I knew it the second I saw you—that I had to have you just like this."

"But I'm just—"

The teeth again, the bite only sharp enough to throw the pleasure into relief. Psyche writhes beneath Eros's body.

"You are everything to me," Eros says. "Never forget that."

"Eros…" Psyche moans.

Eros trails her fingers lower, lower, to the thatch of hair hiding Psyche's needy pussy.

There she stops, spreading Psyche's legs apart, planting kisses on her inner thighs. "I've risked everything I've ever known to look at you like this. To taste you. You've taught me that love isn't always something to fear, and that is why I love you. Why I'm going to fuck you right into the ground."

Before Psyche has time to fit the proper words together in response, Eros is already on the attack. That same eager tongue now finds its home between Psyche's legs.

Oh god, it's all too much to bear. With her eyes closed, every sensation is so much stronger—and that's before she factors in the ecstasy of those three words. Psyche's spent so long on the precipice; how is she meant to muster her willpower now? The first lick is enough to send her crashing over the edge of pleasure—Psyche's thighs quiver and spasm around Eros's head. The stars that Eros promised her dance behind her eyes as she falls, falls, falls.

And Eros is there to catch her. Strong and steady, she weathers the vise grip of Psyche's closed legs with a pleased moan of her own.

"I've never seen a woman look so enthralling when she comes," Eros says. "What a good girl you are. My Oathsworn..."

"Eros!" Psyche pants—breath only now returning to her. She reaches in the dark for Eros's braids. Instead, her fingers graze something yet more tantalizing: the bare skin of Eros's face. A fresh wave of lust runs through her when she realizes she's touching a cheekbone. "Eros, oh god. I... I love you, too. Please, let me see you. I want... I want to see your face..."

Eros tenderly squeezes her hand. She presses a kiss into Psyche's palm, then rests it against her cheek once more.

"Another night, my love, another night. We need to make sure you're ready for it. I promise you, one night, I will show you. But it can't be tonight," she says.

Sweat plasters Psyche's hair to her face. She tries to sit up but it's no use—she's far too out of it to manage. She plops back onto the bed. "But if you're my Oathsworn, isn't that like being married?"

Eros kisses Psyche's still-shaking inner thigh. Psyche feels the curve of her smiling lips. "Hmm, I suppose we are, aren't we? Marriage is what mortals would call it."

The thrill that runs through her is only partly because she can feel Eros's tongue licking at her skin again.

"If we're... fuck, Eros... why can't I...?"

"It would drive you mad, and I will have no part of it," Eros says. Once more the press of her teeth against delicate skin. "That will be the last I hear of this tonight."

Damn, there's no arguing that, and why would she, anyway? Eros is certainly making up for the mystery. As Psyche writhes on the bed, Eros trails her way closer and closer, her hot breath on Psyche's pussy almost enough to send her over again.

"You're ready for me now, aren't you?" Eros says. "Tell me how you'd like me. What shape shall I wear for you—my bride?"

All the blood in Psyche's brain has gone decidedly far from the places that make decisions.

"W-what do you mean?"

"Gender is no limit," Eros says. "Pleasure is my Domain, and pleasure I will grant you, in whatever shape you choose."

O-oh. Oh god. Psyche hadn't even considered—how is she supposed to make a decision like that at a time like this? She can hardly think! All she wants is more, more, more. She has to force herself to breathe just to summon an ounce of critical thinking. But when she does, she's glad she did.

"Whatever... whatever makes you comfortable," Psyche says. "This is about the two of us, isn't it? I'll never... make you become anything you don't want to. As long as you're the one fucking me it doesn't matter the shape. J-just please, please fuck me, I don't know how long I can—"

She doesn't have time to finish the thought.

Or much time to think, after the fact, at all.

Eros pushes into her with heady eagerness, her free arm once more around Psyche's waist.

"I love you," Eros whispers. "I love everything about you."

Thrusting, fucking, being filled—Psyche's head lolls back. Her hips rock against Eros, against that flame that so longs to consume her.

"The faces you make, your moans, your mouth, your pussy..."

Harder, harder, the pace rising, Eros groans, too; sweat drips onto Psyche's forehead.

"Your heart, your soul. My Oathsworn, my bride."

Building, building, a roaring inferno around her; flames along her arms and her legs and so many right at the core of her, so much—

"Come for me, Psyche."

Eros promised her it'd be the hardest she ever came.

And—true to her word—it is.

How long do they spend consumed in such a way? Psyche has no way of knowing. It might have been a day, it might have been a year. All she truly knows is by the time they collapse in a mess against one another, she is not entirely certain she's alive. How could she be? The living have never known such bliss as this.

In the dark lands of pleasure and contentment, Eros wraps an arm around her and pulls her close. They lie on the great bed, curled against one another, a perfect set, the stains below them a distant concern. Just how did gods get come out of sheets? Well, tomorrow she'll have to find out, but for tonight, she's happy for all the evidence she can get that this really happened.

She could lie like this forever—but there is something that has crept back into her mind.

"Did you mean what you said?"

Eros laughs. "And here I thought I'd left no room for doubt about my feelings."

Psyche smiles to herself. "It's like you said—humans need reassurances. Even me."

A kiss on the crown of her head. Her hair's a mess, but she can't bring herself to care.

"I am your humble servant," says Eros. "Tell me what you'd like to know."

The questions cycle through Psyche's head. She doesn't bother to sort them out. "Did you really know the first time you saw me? And what are you risking being with me like this? Why does your mother hate me? There's just so much I want to ask..."

Eros hums. She smooths Psyche's hair, perhaps out of guilt for having left it in such a state. "Never fear asking me things, Psyche. As for your questions, it's all part of the same story, if you'd like to hear it."

"Our story?"

"Our story," Eros says with a nod. "Though from my side of things."

Psyche cuddles up tighter against her, and Eros gives her another squeeze. "Tell me," she says. "It'll be my bedtime story."

Eros kisses her again. "Here is the truth: when we first met, my mother wanted me to execute you."

A pause to let her words sink in. It wasn't quite a surprise to hear, but... there's still something of a shock. Eros traces circles on Psyche's skin with a fingertip.

"Would you like me to continue?"

"Y-yeah, I think so," Psyche says. "I mean, I know it ends happily."

"So it does," says Eros. "You were her sacrifice for the night.

The second Glaucus ruled his compact with Zephyr broken, you were unprotected, and she claimed you. That's why they were carrying you to her. She wanted me to calm you down beforehand. I've always hated jobs like that, and when I saw you..."

"When I was arguing with you?"

"Yes, even then. I knew that for the first time in my life, I was going to break an oath. I couldn't do it. Not with the way you looked at me, the way you spoke to me. All these years I've been piercing others with passion's arrows, I never knew what it felt like to feel it in the pure way. Not until you stared down a god and made her do your bidding."

It seemed such a small thing at the time. No, more than that—it had been the *right* thing. Yet in retrospect it had been bold, hadn't it? If she knew then what she does now, would she still have spoken to Eros in such a way?

Yes. If it meant saving a life, always yes.

"But if you break an oath..."

"I was willing. Meeting you felt like coming to the end of a journey. But as I spoke with you, I wanted to know what the rest of it would be like, so...I needed to do a little scheming. For which I hope you'll forgive me. Shall I continue?"

No one had ever thought to check in on her like this. All her other partners were happy to take and take without giving in return. But Eros? Eros always stops to make sure she's okay.

Psyche curls her fingers around Eros's. "Yeah. I want to know the rest."

"So, I'd decided I needed to scheme. I am not naturally

given to scheming, as you might have already realized, but there was nothing for it. You were already designated a sacrifice. To save both of us, I needed to do something my mother would never expect."

"Is that why you had me swear the oath?" Psyche says. "You said it was just so that we could see each other again, you liar."

Eros laughs. Beneath, the bed thrums with the sound. "And it was. Oathsworn share a unique bond. Other mortals are granted only a single journey to our courts; any more will overwhelm them. With the oath in place, I could bring you back, but more importantly, the others couldn't touch you. And since I couldn't possibly kill my own Oathsworn, my mother's orders would not end me. It was a perfect solution to the problem. The only trouble was getting you to agree."

"So you turned on the charm and fed me those tasty fruits," Psyche fills in. She playfully bats Eros's shin with her foot. "Seducer!"

"You say that like it's meant to be an insult," Eros teases. She kisses Psyche's head again. "Yes, I turned on the charm."

"But I don't understand," Psyche says. "My mother would have been so happy to know I was getting married. That I'd found someone. No matter how upset she was with me. Why was your mother...?"

A squeeze. "Your mother loved you. My mother *is* love. But that does not mean she has to care about me," Eros says. "No one has ever sworn an Oath like this without consulting their Domain's ruler before. And my mother's Domain is not just flame, but Love itself. By offering it to you, I was contradicting her about as strongly as I could. That mattered more to her than my being her daughter."

"Eros... I'm so sorry. No one should have to deal with something like that," Psyche says. Her voice goes soft. "I wish my mother were around. I think she would have liked you."

"Everyone likes me," Eros says, with a squeeze. "But it does honor me to hear you say that."

"Are things going to be okay with your mother now? I can try to help when it comes to smoothing things over, but if she already hates me..."

"Please don't trouble yourself worrying over that. I knew what I was doing when I swore my oath to you," Eros says. "I don't care, though. I'd swear it a thousand times. Even if there was never a world where you came to care for me the way I cared for you, I would swear it happily time and again. Just to preserve you for the rest of the world and watch over you."

Eros turns Psyche around in her grip. This time, she kisses her properly—a promise of eternity without words. With her eyes shut, Psyche is all too aware of how warm she feels, how safe.

"So, in the end, it's very simple," Eros says. "She hates you because I've been with you instead of carrying out her cruel work, because I've sworn myself to you until the stars fall from the skies. You were right—I would catch them all for you. She hates you, Psyche, because I love you enough to forsake the Courts."

Though she lies in the safest arms she can find, away from all harm, sleep still finds her. Surrounded by such warmth and tenderness, she does not notice its grip around her neck until it is too late. The unseen assailant wins. She falls, gently, into a blissful slumber.

Where sleep goes, dreams are sure to follow. The curtain falls, the stage is set, and—of all things—Psyche finds herself at dinner. Sitting across from her at the far end of the table is her father. Laura and Mike take up the right side, Eros and Cid take up the left. The wood siding and shag carpet tell her that this must be the house in Austin, the house she always liked best. Before them is a Thanksgiving feast—her father carving up the turkey, Cid heaping potatoes onto her plate, Laura opting for cranberry sauce and pie. Mike exchanges turkey carving tips with her father, who hears them with a curt grunt and not much feedback. Holiday music plays from the other room.

She blinks. Without thinking, she blurts out a painful question: "When's Mom coming downstairs?"

Laura scoffs. "Psyche, please. First you bring that weirdo home, and now you're asking about that?"

"It's been years, Sis," says Cid. "C'mon, not at Thanksgiving."

What else had she been expecting? Even in dreams she cannot be granted another visit. A hope she hadn't known was there dies. Pushing her food around her plate, she heaves a sigh. No matter how many people they invite to holiday parties, Psyche has always felt lonely.

A heavy hand on her lap. The soft lights of this old home

lend Eros's mask a warmth it does not always have. She leans in, smooths a lock of hair away. "Keeping hope alive is a beautiful thing."

Yet short-lived is this tender moment. Laura, as always, cannot keep her thoughts to herself. "God, couldn't you at least get a nicer mask?"

Psyche flinches. It does not take a seer to know what's coming next—the fight that will soon follow. She waves a hand to try to head it off. "Laura, please. I told you it's part of her culture."

"Culture or not, I can't believe you married her like that. She has no sense for appearances. Didn't I tell you she was a predator?"

"She's not," Psyche says. She squeezes Eros's hand—partially to comfort her, and partially to keep herself from adding what she really wants to say.

"She seems nice enough, and I think the mask thing is pretty cool," says Cid, mouth full of potatoes. "And I think Laura's being a ripe old bitch like always, but I gotta wonder. Why not show Psyche your face, huh? Do you not trust her, is that it?"

"I trust her with my life," Eros answers. That she keeps a level tone in spite of all this is astonishing. "And that is why she will never see my face. It would only hurt her."

"I dunno," says Cid. "Sounds like an excuse to me. If you're willing to marry someone, that's all about openness and honesty, isn't it? Ain't very honest to cover your face..."

"If the two of you were really equals, she'd show you," says

Laura. "But I guess you must just be one of her playthings. Poseidon said she had so many before you."

Doubt, like ink, darkens the edges of this picture-postcard world. Her father keeps cutting away at the meat. Not once does he look up at them. Neither does Mike, smiling his roguish smile, his empty smile.

"She's the god of passion, Psy," says Cid. "I mean, she must be fucking with you, right?"

Psyche's throat goes tight. "She swore an oath to me."

"sHe SwOrE aN oAtH tO mE," Cid repeats. "You're so lame. No wonder she's toying with you like this."

No, no, no—this is all wrong. Why are they both staring at her like this? Shadows distort their faces into horrific visions; the world begins to spin. Psyche reaches for Eros's hand.

She finds only empty air.

Eros is gone. There is no sign of her at the table, no sign of her anywhere—there is only Psyche and her sisters and the table. Father and Mike have now been consumed by the encroaching shadows. Like birds her sisters hop onto the table and crawl toward her.

"Plaything!"

"Leftover!"

"Idiot!"

"Loser!"

Psyche squeezes her eyes shut and screams.

In the waking world—yet not in the human one—she bolts upright. A thin sheen of sweat coats her naked body. The cold night air raises hackles on her skin. Just a dream, she tells herself—no more than that. Eros would never abandon her like that, never manipulate her like that. The proof is in the light bruises that now dot Psyche's neck and collarbone. They are together now in all the ways that matter. The oath they'd sworn bound them surer than any ring of gold.

Psyche takes a breath.

A dream. No more than that.

Yet…

The analytical part of her is already chugging away. Often dreams are manifestations of stress, the mind's way of confronting an enemy indirectly. So, while it was just a dream, it's also her body trying to tell her something.

"Eros," she whispers, for she can feel the anxiety at her heels, feel it building and getting worse. "Eros?"

The weight at Psyche's side does not shift. For the first time since Psyche has known her, Eros has fallen asleep. Beneath the silken sheets, her great body is nearly motionless. Only the slow rise and fall of her chest gives her away.

Psyche swallows. She needs to wake her. They should talk about this, that's the only way to deal with anxieties like these—

As she reaches out, her eyes adjust to the dark.

She realizes something important. Though Eros is turned away from her, the strap that holds her mask in place is nowhere to be seen. Nor is the edge of it. Had she never put it back on? Come to think of it, they had just held one another for a while, and Eros had never told her to open her eyes… Maybe she'd felt so comfortable that she, like Psyche, had not noticed sleep's stalking hands?

Oh, it'd be so simple now to get a look at her, wouldn't it? Eros keeps plenty of lanterns around. All Psyche has to do is creep out of bed to reach for one. She can even see one from here—a candle burning on her nightstand, its light so dim that Eros would surely never notice it. A simple peek, that's all—enough to assuage her worries. Enough to prove that the two of them really are equals.

Or—and she stops herself to consider this with one foot already on the floor—she could wait. Didn't she promise she'd never peek beneath Eros's mask? Both Eros and Clytie had been clear about the consequences. What if they're right, and the sight does drive her mad? What if she must wander for all eternity with a sunflower's face stitched over her own? The sight of Clytie's jagged flesh comes to her again, and her stomach twists.

No. No, Eros would never hurt her like that. Can't ever hurt her like that. The oath is clear about it, isn't it? And she already saw what happens when Eros breaks one. It's impossible. The oath will protect her.

Both feet on the ground, she reaches for the candle. The flame flickers in her hand, but does not go out.

One step around the bed, another. She keeps her footsteps quiet.

Eros does not stir.

The third step, the fourth.

A clatter.

Shit! She's knocked into a piece of Eros's armor and kicked it beneath the bed. Her foot aches—but worse than that is the knife-edge of knowing what will happen if she's caught. Lying won't work. What is she going to say?

A moment suspended between heartbeats, staring at the sleeping god.

Eros does not stir.

Here she could cut her losses. Here, she could put the candle atop Eros's nightstand and forget she ever felt this urge. There's still time. And yet—if she does, she will never know the truth. She will never know if she really is worthy. She will live out the rest of her life, wondering, wondering...

An unbearable thought.

The fifth step brings her to Eros's side. All she must do now is lean over, and the dark will be banished. Eros—her somewhat wife—is curled toward her like a child, her face half buried.

Psyche takes a breath. She leans over.

And the candle does its work.

Much has been written of beauty. It and love beguile the imagination across cultures. Though few agree on precisely what is beautiful, all agree that beauty is desirable. Humans reach for beauty as much as they reach for the stars.

But just as to hold a star in your hand is to welcome complete and total incineration, to behold true beauty is to welcome complete and total transcendence.

Before her—a sight not meant for human eyes to understand. A beauty so all-encompassing that it forces her to confront every face she has ever seen, all at once. Such is its divinity! For no matter where her eye lands, the flesh there seems to shift, the features blurring from one to another. A noble set of brows become those of a gentle maiden, only to grow into the pleasantly unkempt pair that might adorn a young warrior. Her lips, so full when they pressed against Psyche's, change from pillowy to narrow. All of it is shifting, and all of it—every single combination—is as beautiful as the cosmos itself.

Sweat sticks to her brow, her blood goes cold, her hands tremble. Within her breast, her heart surrenders to the horrible sublimity it has beheld and falls silent. Her knees knock together and a terrible, choked cry falls from her lips.

As does the candle.

Hot wax spills on Eros's shoulder. The god, roused, thrashes and reaches for her mask.

It is then that Psyche beholds her eyes.

No flesh lies within those sockets—only an eternal, burning flame.

Psyche screams, and all goes black.

Chapter Nineteen

"There's no time for you to keep slumbering, little mortal. You've got too much to answer for."

Once, when she was a child, she needed to have her tonsils removed. Too many throat infections too often, and with how often they moved, her parents tired of having to deal with them. Off to the surgeon with her. When Psyche was strapped to the operating table, the doctors clasped a mask onto her face and told her to take a deep breath.

Oblivion followed.

And then she awoke in the recovery room with its vestiges clinging to her like spiderwebs. No waiting, no sleeping, no dreams—only nothingness and then the rush of awareness.

So it is now. The voice is a rainbow burst across the darkness of Psyche's mind. It is the first thing she remembers thinking or feeling in...she's not sure how long.

Her head pounds, her throat aches, and breathing fills her with a strange burning pain. But for better or worse, her senses are returning to her.

First there is the woman's voice. As the wind through a rose garden, as the ardent melodies of an enamored musician, as the whisper of a secret lover—so is this woman's voice. Every syllable seems to hang in the air around her and sparkle before fading into the ether. Yet as lovely as it is, there is an awful pain that follows in its wake, a throbbing of the head. Too much more of that voice and she's going to burst, she's sure of it.

Touch comes next when she reaches up to rub at her temples. Her skin is cold and bizarrely rough—but that is the least of her troubles when she's in such pain. She paws at the ground only for her hand to meet cold, moist air.

A cloud?

No, it can't be. It's supporting her weight. Maybe she's dreaming?

She whimpers, still in agony. The taste of honey and roses and salt coats her tongue. Soon, the scent fills her nostrils, too. All the tension in her body melts away, and only the questions remain—what is this place, and how did she get here?

"What an ambitious gnat you are. You can hardly stand to be in my presence, can you? And yet you dared your seductions. Dearly shall you pay for them." It's a voice she doesn't recognize, a terrible one.

Psyche covers her eyes. A pathetic moan leaves her, and she finds herself curling up, turning away, anything to get rid of the sound of that voice. Like drowning in a vat of honey, like flowers growing in her throat, like the strangling hands of…

"Psyche? Psyche, please wake up—" Her eyes go wide, her tongue sticks to the roof of her mouth. Cold memory dulls immediate pain in favor of letting shame flourish. That voice. Eros.

Oh god, she... Psyche had *seen*...

"Er-Eros," Psyche whines. Too frightened to open her eyes again she reaches out into the void. "Eros... I'm so sorry..."

But it is not Eros who answers. "Sorry? That's all you have to say for yourself? The blessings of beauty clearly haven't seeped into you yet. Sorry! Ha. Oh, you're far beyond that. You should be begging."

Psyche's mind is like an oxcart struggling uphill in a hailstorm. Nevertheless she bites her lip.

She wants to say something wise. She wants to make her understand how sorry she feels about all this. But she can't.

"Eros... it hurts..."

"I know, I know, Psyche." A crack in Eros's voice, a pain no less deep than Psyche's own. "Keep your eyes closed for now, all right? My mother's here. She can't hurt you, but—"

"Eros, darling, please don't speak."

Red floods the corners of Psyche's vision. Without meaning to, she rolls away from the woman's voice and toward Eros's. Something clatters around her—a bowl?

"I will speak as I like. I have a right to address my own Oathsworn, and you can't hold me back like this forever—"

"I can, and I will, if that is what needs to be done. You know well the strength of your stepfather's cages. Really, this doesn't need to be so difficult, Eri," says the woman. Metal rattles in response. The cage she'd mentioned, no doubt; the cage that keeps Psyche and Eros apart.

"Why do you hate me?" Psyche asks.

"Hate is anathema to my Domain," answers the woman. "I can no more hate than you can fly."

"You hate plenty," comes Eros's voice. "You don't call it that, but I know your heart."

"Call it whatever you like, but it isn't hate," says the woman. "To prove it to you, let's make this a proper audience, hmm?"

A snap. The ephemeral ground beneath her goes plush solid, and a sudden warmth comes over her. Against the red of her eyelids, she can see the glow of sunlight.

"Open your eyes, Psyche. And help yourself to one of the fruits you knocked over, won't you? It might make all this easier for you to bear. We need you to understand the mess you've gotten yourself into, don't we?"

The fruit…! Her fingertips graze against one of their waxy rinds. Desperate for relief from the pain, she takes a bite. The rich juice and vibrant flesh threaten to overwhelm her senses. Her breathing slows, her head stops pounding. There is nothing weighing her down anymore save her own guilt.

But what a weight, that guilt! The strongest divers could not surface were it to clasp about their necks, nor could the swiftest raptors take to the sky clutching it in their talons. The floor is the right place for one such as her. How foolish she was!

The woman's command rings in her mind: *Open your eyes,*

open your eyes. Yet knowing that Eros is here, Psyche cannot bear the thought. How could she possibly look at Eros, having done what she did? Fear prevents her, yes, but so too does shame. They could have lived their lives happily together had she not looked under that mask. And at such a vulnerable time…

Maybe she really is as bad as Alex thought.

"I can't," she mumbles. Tears well at the corners of her eyes. "I don't deserve to."

A pleased hum, one that thrums within Psyche's own lungs. Why? Why does it leave her feeling so pleased, and so disgusted?

"Oh, sweet girl, you're finally beginning to understand, aren't you? I knew you had it in you."

Is it the fruit that softens the impact of the woman's voice, or is it Psyche's shame accepting the pain without contest? For she no longer wants to stop up her ears. Still, she flinches; still, she tries to hide herself away.

"Everything in this world has its place—from grains of sand to the highest sovereigns. To stay within your place is a beautiful thing, a lovely thing. My siblings and I have always striven to ensure that the paths laid out for you and your kind are the best you could hope for. They're happy lives. Even yours, short though we planned it to be, was happy. Or would you deny that?"

Even if the woman's voice no longer hurts her—these words do. Psyche's face contorts in self-inflicted agony. Any other day she could brighten the situation, she could lie. But today?

"What do you think was happy about my life before that party?" Psyche says. Her voice rises, cracks. "My sisters never talk to me unless they want something. My friends all live across the world and I never get to see them. My followers thought I was someone I wasn't. I had to watch cancer eat away at my mom, and my father left the second things got bad. I've never held a job for more than a year without something going wrong. What about that is happy?"

In the moments before a lightning strike, the air goes tense. Dogs and cats run to seek shelter; birds take to the earth; a certain burning smell comes to the nose. In this way those sensitive to the wrath of the heavens know when it is coming for them.

Psyche has lived her whole life waiting for lightning to strike. Every argument, every snide comment had before it a moment where her hackles stood on end. *Here it comes*, she would think, and in her mind she would imagine the way it would all go. Knowing that the bolt was coming rarely did anything to change how painful she found it.

It is the same now. In the wake of her honesty, the hairs at the back of her neck stand on end; her flesh goes bumpy; her throat starts to close. She is aware of eyes upon her, of wrath building, of a faint rumble beneath her.

"Your life," says the woman, "was a happy one."

"You might think so, but I felt otherwise," Psyche says. She clutches her hands tighter. If she were to open her eyes now, what would she see? What face would Eros's mother wear?

"This is precisely what I worried about, Eri. A sacrifice with undue ambitions. It only hurts you, little human, to dream in this way. You were meant to die upon the altar. The life you've lived beyond that is a boon my daughter has seen fit to grant you. One given without my knowledge or consent, might I add."

Why does this woman think she has such a right to talk about Psyche's destiny? It's infuriating. No wonder Eros has trouble talking about her feelings or loving freely; her mother doesn't want to so much as consider anything Psyche's saying.

Love inspires projects, but spite finishes them. Psyche presses against the ground. Her weak limbs shudder but hold. She sits, then stands. With her hands on her hips (a power stance, she tells herself), she opens her eyes and beholds the god.

Eros's many-splendored mother sits atop a seashell throne. Iridescent abalone glimmers five colors at once, not one reflecting the fires that surround them. A pearl-encrusted seat sits below the fan of the shell itself, with an attendant on each side holding ornate golden jugs. Were these two attendants the only ones in the room, their beauty would be difficult to bear—one lithe and elfin, the other sumptuous and thick. Both wear masks of interlocking shells; both have lips that beg to be kissed.

But Eros, too, is here—just as Psyche imagined, she is encased in a golden cage to the right of the throne. As beautiful as the metalwork is, Psyche feels nothing but hatred for it, especially when she catches sight of Eros's bloodied knuckles. Her love wears only the casual tunic she slept in, not the arming coat and trousers Psyche had come to know so well. Her hair is in disarray, and her mask is riddled with cracks. Still, to look on her is to love her.

And yet Eros is a candle in comparison to her mother's sun. The Queen of Flame is draped across the seat of her throne, her brown skin incandescent. The finest mahogany could not hope to match her for neither luster nor depth of color. Gossamer flames comprise the gown she wears; interlocked feathers form the mask covering her face. Her hair flits and flickers with the breeze—it reminds Psyche of a bonfire. To behold her threatens to bring Psyche to her knees. It is to behold the depths of the sea, the heart of the sun, the dawn over the cloud-crowned mountains.

Psyche's legs begin to tremble. "Eros and I are both adults. We can make what oaths we like. Your need to control her every move is overbearing at best and toxic at worst."

The woman smiles. Psyche's chest spasms, a paroxysm of pain. "You think so little of me, even after seeing me? My, you are stubborn. It's no wonder the two of you get along so well. I'll grant you my name, since I admire your temerity. Know that you address the Queen of Flame and Love, Aphrodite."

Psyche grits her teeth and digs her nails into the palm of her hand, unwilling to yield.

"You're as awful as all the stories I've read of you," Psyche says. "Don't you have better things to do than stalk mortals, by the way?"

"You've more bravery and will than most mortals, and for that, I commend you. How unfortunate that my daughter saved you from sacrifice—I find mortals of your kind to have the best flavor. Like fat sizzling on a hot stone."

"You aren't going to eat me," Psyche says. Her shaking knees tell a different story, but she tries to downplay this by taking a step forward. Eros said gods aren't used to being challenged, right? "You're going to let Eros and me go."

Aphrodite tilts her head. She holds out a cup in her hand; one of her attendants fills it with liquid fire. When she tips it to her lips, gold spills down her cheek. "I don't see any reason a dead woman should be asking me for favors."

"Mother—" starts Eros, but Aphrodite waves, and flames erupt from the bars. Psyche's heart sinks into her stomach. How could any mother do that to their own child?

"Eros!"

A groan, a shudder—but Eros holds fast. "Don't worry about me. You need... to keep all your strength."

"What did I tell you? Hold your tongue," says Aphrodite, as if she were merely lifting Eros by the scruff and waving a finger at her. "If she's so eager to parlay, she might as well have all the facts."

"You don't have them all, either," Psyche says. "I'm not dead. That says something about me, doesn't it? I heard humans don't usually live after glimpsing your faces. You don't know what to do with me, do you?"

Aphrodite scoffs and picks at her nails. "Oh, I know what I'd like to do with you, but unfortunately I can't. Which does bring me to my next point." She snaps her fingers. The plumper of the two servants sinks to their knees before the throne. Aphrodite lays her feet atop their back as if it were the most natural thing in the world. "While I love your confidence—and truly, I do—you shouldn't get so cocky. Think for a second, will you? Eros must have told you that our kind cannot lie. Didn't I just say you're dead?"

Can she really be dead if her heart is hammering so quickly? If the sweat clings to her brow, if the breath still leaves her? Psyche flexes her hands. It can't be true. There's no way.

So why is it she looks to Eros for reassurance of something that should go without saying?

"You're speaking in metaphor," says Psyche. "You're trying to gaslight us both into doing what you want."

"What I *want*," says Aphrodite, nudging the curvier servant closer to the skinnier one, "is for you to lay yourself upon my altar where you belong. But I can't have you do that now, because you're dead. Very dead. Your physical body? Dead. Your spirit? Mostly dead. About ninety-eight percent dead, if I had to gamble. Is that direct enough for you?"

"No," says Psyche. Her voice cracks again. "That's not—that can't be true. Eros can't hurt me. We were just—"

"Lying together? *Canoodling?* I'm aware. I came upon you right after you died, you know. Eros was *distraught* at what had happened. She was cradling your limp body tight. I've never seen her weep like that! And all over a little sacrifice like you. It just goes to show everyone has their own charm."

She snaps again. The servants start waiting on her feet—both of them now, working in tandem.

"Well, with my oldest in such a state, I had to do something, didn't I? If I ate you, it would have solved the matter then and there—she's got no reason to cry over someone she can never see again—but things weren't quite so simple.

"Imagine my surprise when I tried to devour you and found your oath still held. Imagine!" says Aphrodite. She laughs, one without mirth and yet beguiling. "I couldn't believe my eyes. Half an oath! Whoever heard of such a thing? You're so full of surprises, little morsel."

When Psyche speaks, it's with the voice of a reprimanded child. "What do you mean?"

"Oaths are particular things, Psyche. They have to be entered into with clear knowledge, a fact which my daughter here chose to ignore in service of her scheme. When *she* swore to keep you, to feed you, to love you, those things were already in her heart. But when you swore to accept them, they were not in yours."

"I didn't—how could I have—" Her eyes find Eros. The once-proud warrior clasps the bars of her cage with shoulders slumped. "Eros, I love you. You know I do."

"You might now, but you didn't then, and that makes all the difference. Though isn't it romantic she fell for you so quickly? Foolish, yes, but there is a certain beauty to it. Lying, though... we do hate liars."

"Eros... is that true? You meant everything you said?"

Within the cage, Eros nods. "Since the moment we spoke, I knew. I hoped... that perhaps you felt the same, but..."

Psyche screws her eyes shut. Love at first sight? That had never sounded like her, had never made sense to her. You needed to know a person before you could make a commitment like that! But knowing that Eros had thrown herself in so fully, and they were in this mess because Psyche hadn't reciprocated...

Never mind Aphrodite. Eros is the important one now. Psyche turns aside, walking across the plush carpet to Eros's golden cage. No one stops her. Nothing in the world could. To see Eros so broken like this and to know how much of it is Psyche's own fault—no, nothing could keep her from offering what little comfort she can. Not the flames licking the bars, not the oppressive view of a god who does not understand them.

Psyche braves the flames. What danger do they pose to her if she's already dead? She wraps her arms around Eros's strong frame and pulls her as close as she can.

"I'm sorry I lied to you," Psyche says. "And I'm sorry about...about the mask. I know I shouldn't have looked."

"I should have known defying gods applied to me, too," Eros whispers. She pulls Psyche's head close and presses a kiss on her temple—the only place her lips can reach. "We're going to make it out of this."

It drops from her mouth, the question she's afraid to ask: "Am I really dead?"

Eros squeezes tighter. The cage rattles around her, the gold threatening to bend. "Not...not all the way. You've sustained awful injuries. My half of the oath is the only reason you're alive, and Mother can rescind it if it pleases her."

A memory returns to her. The first time she came to know death.

The steady beep of an EKG machine. The bustle of the nurses and doctors and attendants. Her sisters with their wide eyes and their pale faces, unable to make eye contact as they asked her what all of it meant. The answer, a poison on her tongue.

Everything feels cold.

"Who's...who's going to take care of Latte?" she says. Her body shakes into a sob. "Who's going to...she needs her special food or she gets fussy..."

She says no more—a whip of fire circles her waist and pulls her away. Eros grunts and tries to keep her, and Psyche tries to keep hold, but it's no use. Not with the cage roaring up in flames again. Psyche, teary-eyed, is cast upon the floor of the palace before Aphrodite once more.

"Aww, sweetheart. Are you sad?"

How awful of her to speak to people like this. The fires all around them are nothing compared to the disgust, to the agony in Psyche's heart. What is she going to tell her sisters?

Aphrodite snaps her fingers.

The plump servant sits up and walks to Psyche. With a warm piece of silk, they dab away her tears. The skinny one wraps their arms around her from the side. A cruel pantomime of friendship that does little to improve her mood. Yet she cannot bring herself to push them away, either.

"I hate to see a broken heart. Why don't I offer you a boon, hmm? In my infinite grace and kindness. An opportunity to prove to me that you're worth more than the Fates thought of you."

When a boxer has had their bell rung, they can hardly feel the rest of the incoming blows. It is no different for Psyche.

She hears the words, yes, but their impact means little to her. This might as well be another of Aphrodite's tricks.

But...what if it's not? Could she live with herself if...

She laughs. No. No, she couldn't live with herself at all.

"You can save me?"

"I can do many things," says Aphrodite. "And if you do a favor for me, well, I might consider lending you some assistance."

The plump servant wraps a blanket around her shoulders. Psyche's not sure where it came from, but it is plush and soft, fluffy as a cloud. The skinny one hands her a bowl of fruit and smooths her hair.

Psyche picks up a fruit. "Can't I eat these until my body heals?"

"You could try. My daughter's certainly given you enough of them to lend you a certain hardiness. You'll be pleased to note that your body is in one piece—that isn't the case for most mortals who behold someone of Eros's stature. That's the fruit's doing. But it won't matter, in the end; your body isn't the problem. Your spirit is."

The servants part, taking their spots once more at Aphrodite's side. That they said nary a word to her in their ministrations only makes Psyche feel filthy. Like a toy.

She shuts her eyes. "Tell me what happened, exactly."

"So demanding!" says Aphrodite with a laugh. "It's very simple. Your body couldn't handle the shock and died. Your spirit *mostly* left but, since Eros had proper claim to it, could not leave entirely. A tiny bit of you still clings to life, and that is the bit that's animating you."

She crosses her legs.

"Now, since the oath is what's keeping you together, and mine is the Domain of Love, I *could* allow you another chance to swear it. That would restore you—the parts of your spirit that have gone on to Elysium will return, bound as they are by the Law. But I could decide to annul your oath, as it was sworn without my blessing, and by a terrible little liar."

There's no energy left to argue the point. Psyche really is a terrible little liar. An honest and caring partner would not have looked beneath the mask. A loving woman would have been content with marrying a god.

Maybe her sisters had been right about her in that dream.

But she can't leave Eros alone. Not when she's seen what Aphrodite is like, and not when they have so many firsts yet to share. Psyche hasn't introduced Eros to either of her sisters yet, or her online friends. They haven't traveled the world. And there are still so many movies to watch together, so many things to learn about one another.

It can't end now.

She can't abandon the best thing that's ever happened to her.

"What do I have to do?" she asks.

Another snap. This time, the skinny servant manifests a small, pearl-encrusted box. Laura had plenty like it as a teen. Less opulent, of course, but no worse for holding jewelry. This they place before Psyche.

"The Blooming Maiden owes me a tithe of her beauty. You will go to the Court of Earth and find her. Tell her I sent you, and she will fill it without delay. If you return to me with her tithe in that box within three hours' time, then I will consider letting you renew your oath."

The back of Psyche's head tingles as she studies the box; she tastes seawater and wisdom.

"You have to do more than consider," she says.

Love herself grumbles and sighs. "I am offering you a kindness and grace unheard of—"

"And if you don't agree to do more than just consider it, then I'm not going to entertain the offer," Psyche answers. *Be brave, be brave.* "If you only agree to consider it, you won't honor the deal. Obviously, you must want this tithe, and there has to be a reason you can't go get it yourself. I need to know that if I return with it, you'll honor the deal. You'll give us your blessing."

Silence, save for the roaring flames. When she glances to Eros she sees nothing but adoration on her wife's face, and that lends her strength.

Be. Brave.

"I wish," says Aphrodite, "that I could hate you. But instead, I only feel a terrible admiration for your courage. I suppose that's what drew my spineless daughter to you in the first place. Very well—I agree. If and only if you return the tithe as I have said, I will grant you my blessing."

"Three human hours, by the keeping of my own watch—and starting from the end of this conversation?"

"Clever and pretty. Yes, three human hours. You may start the clock just before you leave, so long as I witness you doing it."

There is an honest glow, a sincere joy to Aphrodite's voice. It hits like a bludgeon of pleasure.

"Where is the Court of Earth?" Psyche asks, picking up the box. "I'd like to know where I'm going."

"Psyche—"

"Hush, hush, she's asking reasonable questions, after her unreasonable demand," says Aphrodite. "The Court of Earth lies four dreams and five desires away from here. Never have I set foot in it by mortal means, so I'm afraid I can't give you any more direction than that."

"When I return to the mortal world, will I be dead or alive?" she asks. "If I step foot outside of here and keel over on the spot, it's hardly a fair chance, wouldn't you say?"

Aphrodite, atop her throne, preens. The look she casts down on Psyche is full of admiration as much as it is contempt. But not hate—never hate. "That would be unfair. Hmm. The Lord of Death is my brother. For the next three hours, I shall tell him he is forbidden from touching you."

Psyche holds the box up to her eyes. It's lighter than she expected—lighter than wood, even. A small latch on the front seems the only sign of security.

"Oh, there is one more clause. A special one, just for you. You must return the box to me *unopened*. Should you peek inside, you will break your compact, and my brother will take you right back to my altar. Do you think you can handle that?"

Mockingly—like a cat.

Does she think Psyche is so predictable? That she won't

learn from the scar shame has rent upon her? Let her, then. Psyche will show her the courage Eros so loves.

"I'll do it."

Two minutes. That is how long she allows herself to say goodbye before returning to the mortal world. Any more than that, and she's sure it'll come back to bite her in the end. With her life and Eros's happiness on the line, there can't be any room for mistakes.

One kiss with Eros, shared between the bars.

"I'll be back before you know it," she says.

"Impossible. Every second without you will be an eternity for me," Eros says. She caresses Psyche's face, her touch tender and soft. "Trust none of our kind any more than you need to, and may the lightning's swiftness return you to me. My Psyche. How brave you are."

"I don't feel very brave," Psyche admits. But she knows they have little time left. One more kiss to seal this promise, a kiss of life and death.

She makes sure it's one to remember.

On the other side of Aphrodite's palace door, Psyche walks into her living room. A glance at her phone tells her that she's been away for only a day. Good news, especially given Latte's empty food bowl. The second Psyche's back, Latte is mewling the mewl of the aggrieved, the dispossessed, the starving. So far as Latte is concerned, *this* is the most pressing issue—never mind Psyche's dying spirit.

Psyche picks the fanciest cat food and pours it out into the bowl, then takes a salmon fillet from the fridge and chops that up, too. The bright orange looks bizarre against the brown-white slurry of the usual—but Latte's overjoyed. She devours it all without waiting for Psyche to draw back her hand.

All right. Two hours and forty-five minutes to find the Court of Earth, retrieve the tithe, and get back to the Court of Flame.

"How hard can it be?" she says out loud. Eros and the gods have their magic, yes, but so does Psyche. You can trick the mind into feeling all sorts of ways if you really try. Saying things out loud is part of it. Magic words and chants have such a place in media for a reason; when you ritualize something, you lend it power.

She picks up her phone and hits record. "I'm going to do this. I can do this. It's within my ability, and once I break it down into pieces, it's going to be easier than I think."

A moment for the words to ring out. She plays them back to herself. The tinny speaker makes her sound like a different person, which only further cements the reassurance.

She can do this. For the first time in months, she breaks out her planner and picks up her favorite pen. Her hand skates over the page.

Step one: Find the Court.
Step two: Get there.

Step three: Talk to the Queen? Ask for the tithe?
Step four: Find a way back to the Court of Flame.
Step five: Marriage!

There. That isn't so frightening, is it? Seeing it all in pale purple on eggshell white, it's less intimidating.

So. Step one. How is she going to find the Court of Earth?

Psyche does what anyone might do in such a position—she googles it. Plenty of video game wikis and fantasy novel references come up. She spends at least five minutes scrolling through them, trying to add different search keys. *Gods* proves too vague, as does *masquerade*. Ugh. Knowing the proper name for them would go a long way here, but...

The Blooming Maiden isn't much better. Psyche gets results for yet more TTRPG supplements and the occasional tavern. And while it occurs to her that she could go to one of these taverns, take something beautiful, put it in the box, and then bring it back, she's conscious of the time, too. The nearest one is up in Ithaca; there's no way she can make it.

What to do? If she had a whole day, she might check a library or spend time on obscure message boards. But with the way things are now, it'll take too long to get responses that way.

Psyche leans back in her seat. If only she could split herself into a dozen tiny Psyches and unleash them upon the internet all at once. Parallel processing, that's what it's called, isn't it? Get all those brains working together on—

Latte meows.

"You're a genius," says Psyche. "I *should* ask my followers."

She flicks on her camera and light. Without bothering to check what's in frame, she starts the stream. Within a minute there are three hundred people there watching her.

Much more than a dozen little Psyches.

"Hi, guys. I'm really sorry, but I don't have time to hang out. I'm here because I need your help. It's going to sound like I'm not well, and I need you to trust me when I say I am, but more than anything I need to know where to find a place called the Court of Earth."

Bells ring as her chat starts swarming. Do they already know what she means? There's over a thousand watching now, surely someone's got to know. Could it be this easy?

But when she opens the chat window, she doesn't see anything about the Court of Earth.

Whoa, you're using effects on your face now? Your eyes look so cool!

Is this an ARG? Why's she look like that?

Anybody else getting a headache from this?

Court of Earth? Psyche if you're promoing a game you can just tell us lol put down the contacts!!

What...do they mean by this?

She takes a breath and glances at her visual feed.

It is only by digging her nails into her wrist that she keeps from screaming.

The face staring back at her has...changed. Where once her eyes were tea-leaf dark, they've now gone solid, blazing gold. It's as if someone filled her skull with molten gold and it's seeping out of her sockets. And in firing this vessel, the potter must have erred, for there are cracks all over her face, each the color of her eyes, each bright and burning.

Oh god. What the *fuck*? Tears well up, but she's not even sure if she can cry anymore, and she certainly can't afford to cry on stream.

Steady breathing, Psyche. Maybe it'll go away when she fixes this. It'll go away and she can look like herself again and everything will be fine.

"Last night's makeup," she says. Self-loathing makes her voice waver. Will she be lying for the rest of her life? Maybe if she lives only another two hours. "P-pretty neat, right? But I really need to know about this Court, guys. I'm serious. It's the most important thing I've ever asked you about."

The ding of a superchat. Tiefling again: If you get here, I can get you in to see her. But you need to get here.

No sooner has she glimpsed it than, all of a sudden, she's forcibly kicked from her own stream. The page refreshes to the log-in screen. A red banner atop the name and email fields reads: You have been signed out by another computer.

"What?" Psyche says. She frantically types in her password. "Come on, come on…"

You have changed your password.

"Fuck!"

She stands. Paces. *Fuck, fuck, fuck.* Does she have any of

Tief's information? No, not without access to the main account. She could check her other accounts and cross-reference her followers, but how long is that going to take? God. Talking to customer care and getting her account restored is right out of the question—

Her phone rings. Bondi? A notification banner accompanies her smiling face: We need to talk.

Psyche nuzzles Latte, then sets her on the couch. She needs to be able to walk all this energy off, and the cat isn't helping.

"Bondi? Listen, please, I know I've been blowing you off lately but I'm really busy—"

"I know how to get you to the Court of Earth."

Psyche stops midstride. "You…what?"

"I can get you there. I don't know about getting you in, or how the fuck you ended up in this much trouble, but let me do this for you. Please."

"How do you know about the Court?" Psyche says. She can't bring herself above a whisper.

"Because I'm the one who got you into this mess. I'm so sorry, Psyche."

Chapter Twenty

Psyche lies on her hardwood floor. Shadows from her houseplants keep the overhead light from stabbing into her eyes. Not that it matters now, with her eyes the way they are, and her mostly dead.

"Bondi," she says. Is she slipping back into Therapist Voice for her benefit, or Bondi's? "I need you to explain what you mean by that. Can you do that for me? I'd like to understand."

On the other end of the line—and several thousand miles away—Bondi sniffs to hold back from crying. "I was the one who told Zephyr about you. You were so down and he needed a friend and I thought maybe the two of you would hit it off."

There are questions Psyche could ask. But here on the floor with the sturdy wood beneath her, it is more comfortable to let Bondi talk. There's more, Psyche's sure.

"I just... he needed to help his mate out, and you needed a project. Perfect setup, I thought. He's always been kind to me when the others haven't, and I wanted that for you. Seeing all the work you do for others...I just wanted to do something nice for you, and it's all blown up in my face."

Progress. Psyche pinches her nose. She has to admit, it does make sense. Of course Zephyr isn't trawling social media at all hours, of course someone recommended her. No wonder Bondi insisted on Psyche going out that night. It had never been a friend who went to one of those parties—it was Bondi herself.

"That's okay. You meant well," Psyche says. "How long have you known about these gods?"

"All my life, it's a very long story. I've got one on my heels, if you'll believe that. Proper weirdo she is. Like a cat that keeps turning up at my door with dead mice. But Zeph said the Court of Flame was always a good time."

Bondi's romancing a god of her own? Or maybe not. That description left a lot unclear. Ugh, there's no time to go into any of this, no matter how many questions Psyche's got.

"We can talk about that 'good time' later," Psyche says. "Can your god get me to the Court?"

"Should do. As long as you use my name when you're summoning her, she should do whatever you like."

Which is it—is this god a weirdo, or does Bondi actually like her? Never mind.

"Great," Psyche says. She sits back up and looks around the apartment. Eros needed something from her Domain to be summoned, so... "What do I need to summon your Oathsworn?"

"Oathsworn?! No, no, she hasn't convinced me to do that

yet. Anyway, her Domains are the Moon and the Wild. It's daytime over there, isn't it?"

"Sure is," Psyche says. "Hmm. Do my cat and houseplants count as 'the wild'?"

"They're about as close as you're going to get in that place," says Bondi. "Take 'em outside, wave around a kitchen knife, and say you're calling on her in my name."

Waving a kitchen knife on a fire escape seems a sure recipe for a trip to Bellevue, but with any luck, she'll be gone by the time the cops get here. Psyche scoops up one of her plants under her arm. She stalks toward the cat tower.

"But I don't know your real name," Psyche says, "let alone hers."

A soft, friendly laugh. "I'm Iphigenia. Iffy, for friends. And she's Artemis, the Queen of the Wild."

The names set a bell ringing in Psyche's mind. She points with her free hand at Latte, who has done nothing to earn this treatment. "Wait a second. You're—Eros told me about the two of you! She said the Queen of the Wild swore off love years ago—"

"I'll tell you about it another day," Bondi says. "From the look of you, you don't have much time to spare."

"Could say that," Psyche says. She picks Latte up. A loud meow and claw are her rewards. Blood's a fine offering, she supposes. Next—a kitchen knife placed in the pocket of her coat opposite the writhing cat. And a question whose answer she dreads. "Bon…Iffy, is it as bad as I thought?"

"Not going to lie to you, you don't look human anymore," Iffy answers. "And that means people aren't going to be able to stand seeing you uncovered. I don't know what's going on, and you probably don't have time to tell me, but I'm sorry, Psy. I really am."

From across oceans and continents, Iffy has struck a stunning blow. Psyche stands swaying in her studio apartment. People can't…they can't stand to see her anymore? How is she supposed to…

"Psy?"

"I have to go," she says. Anything more and she might break down.

Psyche hangs up. With the knife, cat, and plant in tow, she allows herself only a minute to scream. In that scream: her shame, her anger, her guilt and frustration.

It will have to do for now.

Onto the fire escape. She sets Latte and her plant down and raises the knife.

"In the name of Iphigenia of the Court of Australia, I call on the Queen of the Wild. Artemis, I really need your help!"

With Eros there was the flash of fire, the loosening of her limbs.

With Artemis—there is a darkness, the scent of cypress, and the howling of dogs. Latte hisses as the clouds cast a column of shadow upon them. All the rest of the world goes black except the fire escape platform. It's as if they've fallen into the night sky. Hounds pad ever closer, unseen, and soon Psyche hears a growl at her feet.

When she looks, it is not a dog she sees there. A massive rack of antlers crowns a large, queer creature, its limbs long and pale. Too long for anything that belonged to the forest. The figure sniffs at her heels.

Psyche backs up against what used to be the brick siding of her building. "I—I need to talk with the Queen of the Wild," she says. "I need a huge favor—"

The figure stands on its hind legs. How tall it towers over her—taller than Eros! It is then, confronted with the figure's night-cloaked face and glowing, silvery eyes, that Psyche realizes *this* is Artemis.

Beads and feathers sway from Artemis's antlers as she tilts her head. At her heels a spectral dog sniffs at Latte and her plant. Latte, much like her owner, fears no gods—she bats at the dog's nose.

Artemis leans over. With one of her great hands, she holds the top of Psyche's head, as if it were a bowling ball. She turns Psyche's face this way and that. All the while those bright eyes bore into her.

After what feels an eternity, Psyche hears a snarl. She thinks at first that it must come from the dog—but it's still playing with Latte. Better get her back inside before she goes galivanting off to who knows where. But if it's not Latte and it's not the dog, that means…

"You aren't *her*. And you don't share blood with her, either. Ugh."

"I'm sorry, Queen of the Wild, but Iffy—"

Another snarl. "Her name is Iphigenia."

"Iphigenia said that you would help a friend of hers in need," Psyche finishes.

For a long while Artemis stares at her. Those eyes do not blink—they simply watch and watch. This close, Psyche notices that Artemis isn't wearing a mask in the traditional sense. The shadows serve instead, never allowing a glimpse at the features beneath.

"You stink of love and fire."

"I'm Eros's Oathsworn," Psyche says. "Or I was. I'm not sure. I might still be, but to make sure that I am, I need your help."

The scoff that leaves Artemis could make a king beg for forgiveness. She pushes Psyche away. "Strange mortal."

You're one to talk, Psyche thinks. "Please, I really need to get to the Court of Earth. I have to speak to the Blooming Maiden there. Aphrodite sent me on this quest, and if I don't finish it, I'm going to be dead, and divorced."

Another low snarl. The white-eyed god turns away and reaches for her dog. With an arcane gesture, she tugs at its shadowy form and shapes it into a deer. Yet this is no ordinary hind—it stands far taller than Psyche at the withers.

"A favor is a favor. Mount."

In the stories this would be a simple task. Psyche would swing onto the hind's back with little trouble. She would have need of neither saddle nor stirrup to do so—her own leaping determination would see her through.

But this is not the case. Psyche, a jot over five foot two, can't make it all the way. Nor does she have any place to grab.

For five minutes at least she tries to haul herself up, first trying to swing a leg over and next to haul her whole body up to the hind's back.

Artemis watches. She says nothing, which feels worse than if she let loose her obvious disdain. At least then they'd know where they stood with one another.

Asking her for help, beyond just being embarrassing, would probably be useless. How Iffy manages to get a woman like this to do anything at all is beyond Psyche's ken, but she doesn't have the time to worry about that now.

So she turns her attention to the hind instead. Running her hands along its starlit flank, Psyche whispers into its ear.

"I'm so sorry about all the trouble. I don't know anything about riding horses, or...deer. Could you please, noble deer, lean down a little? That way I can get on your back easier, and I don't hurt you trying to jump up."

The hind bobs her head. Then the obsidian planes of her great bulk align, and she kneels down to permit Psyche to mount.

Artemis hums. "Not the worst."

"I'll take it," says Psyche. She carefully mounts the hind. Unsure of where to hold without reins to guide her, she simply hugs tight to the creature's neck.

"Close your eyes," Artemis says. Psyche does so. She hears the bones strung from Artemis's headdress clinking against one another. "No peeking. Might take a while."

"But I need—"

The rest of her sentence is lost in an awful twist of her

stomach. A brightness springs up against her eyelids, one that feels as cool and refreshing as plunging into a forest spring. The scent of pine clears her mind and sticks to her tongue. She is falling, she is turning, she is rolling—and all the while the hind remains steady beneath her. The clatter of bones, the howling of wolves—she cannot hear her own thoughts. All she knows is the dark—and the unshakable feeling that something within it has its eyes upon her. Two piercing white eyes.

It is over as soon as it began. Another violent lurch sends her half swinging from the hind. Psyche's heart hangs in her stomach until she realizes there is at last ground beneath her feet. Then she lets out a gasping breath and squeezes her thumb to keep from vomiting.

But she does not open her eyes. No—she will never again defy that particular order. Even with sweat streaming down the side of her face and her stomach doing backflips, she will not open her eyes.

"Tell me," she rasps, "that we're here."

This time, that most eloquent of goddesses answers her with a grunt. "Open."

Psyche isn't sure what to expect when she looks around. The Court of Flame has its heavy iron gate in a dilapidated alley, Eros's home seems a world all its own, and the Court of Waves she saw only from the inside. Would she find herself in a forest, one whose trees curved every which way? Perhaps a dirt-walled cave...?

No—what she finds is a greenhouse. Or something like one. All around them are exotic flowers and plants—waxy blossoms and needle leaves, delicate petals and rough bark. Overhead a crystal roof shields them from the elements. To her surprise, the sky isn't one of the Court's unnatural hues but New York City's own unnatural blue black. The blocky, gold-spangled shape in the distance must be the Brooklyn Public Library, which makes this…Prospect Park? Or maybe the Brooklyn Botanic Garden?

But she's never seen a door like this on any of her trips to this place. Covered in vines and flowers, it's built straight into the glass of the greenhouse. By it stands a wiry young man in a 1920s bellhop costume scrolling through his social media feeds. If he's noticed the giant shaman woman, night deer, and the girl with molten eyes, he doesn't seem to care.

"Is this…?" Psyche starts.

"You do the rest," Artemis says. She points to the door with her chin. "I hate people."

That…only makes sense, doesn't it? Psyche nods. "All right," she says. "Thank you for helping me. I'll tell Iffy you did great."

"I'll tell her myself," Artemis says. And then she turns away. Her hound follows at her feet, once more a dog.

Psyche takes a breath. The bellhop hasn't looked up from his phone, so she sneaks a look at hers and then has to keep from swearing. Only an hour left on her timer? How the hell had she spent that much time getting here? Prospect Park isn't that far away. She could have taken the train! Didn't Artemis say…

Ugh. She said nothing about getting her here by a particular time, did she? No broken oaths here. Just Psyche messing up again. She's really going to have to work on how she talks to gods. And ask them what they like to be called! It can't just be gods, can it?

No matter; she has even less time to waste than before.

"Excuse me?" she says. "I'm sorry, but is this the door to the Court of Earth?"

"Yeah, please show your invitation or oath—" the young man begins. But then he looks up from his phone and his face brightens with joy...and recognition. "Oh my god. Oh my god, you're Dr. Psy!"

Of all the times! "Y-yes," she says. She tries to flash a smile, though part of her worries what that might do to this young man. Didn't Iffy say her face is dangerous now?

"Whoa, you look so different in person. Have you been going to the Courts a lot? That's probably why. They start to change you after a while. You look *sick*," he says. "Can I get a selfie?"

"Sure, I'd love to. But I have to ask if you'll let me in—I'm sorry, but I'm really in a rush."

"No worries, let's be quick," says the bellhop. He throws an arm around her and holds out his phone. "Three...two... one...Tieflings!!"

Psyche laughs so hard she chokes—which makes for an interesting photo. "You're BigBootyTieflings?"

"You know it, babe," the young man says. He throws up a pair of finger guns. "Normally we're not supposed to let regular people in there, but since we're cool, go on ahead. You know the rules with them, right?"

"Believe me, I got a couple good lessons," Psyche says. She puts a hand on the door. Then, thinking about it, she leans over and gives Tief a kiss on the cheek. "Thanks so much for the help!"

The poor boy looks as though he might die on the spot. She leaves him to his sweet death and heads for the vine-covered door.

If she thought the greenhouse was a wonderland, she's well and truly through the looking glass when she steps beyond the door. Lush clover and verdant grass meet her feet; banyan, dogwood, and gingko alike cover her in colorful shade. Petals are scattered everywhere like the brushstrokes of an eccentric painter. Up above, the sky is the color of new growth. The fields go on as far as the eye can see in every direction, changing here and there but never losing the life that leaps from the earth. To the east there are rice paddies, to the west fields of corn; the south offers barley, and to the north...

To the north there is a house not unlike a hobbit hole—a mound of earth with grass and vines atop it, a stained glass window and a door the only departure from nature. When they first became friends, Psyche and Iffy watched all of the *Lord of the Rings* movies in a daylong marathon. Director's cut, of course. Midway through Psyche asked Iffy what it was like to live in a hole in the ground like that, which earned her a loud groan and lecture about the differences between Kiwis and Australians. Good fun, though, and a memory that brings her comfort in a trying time. Looking at it she feels a sense of relief.

The plants and the hobbit hole aren't the only things around, though. Walking among the flowers and the plants are other gods. Most of them are fully clothed. Nudity must be exclusive to the Court of Flame, then, which only makes sense for them. Here masks take the form of natural growths—moss and leaves that shade the face rather than conceal it entirely.

The first god Psyche spots is a young woman with mossy, coiled hair, tapping a tree for its sap. She's the nearest to the portal and yet does not look up at Psyche when she enters. Indeed, she continues whispering to the tree, her palms flat against it as if soothing a child. Hibiscuses bloom along the curve of her arm. A blooming maiden, surely?

"Excuse me," Psyche starts, "but you wouldn't happen to be the Blooming Maiden would you? I'm looking to find her—"

The woman fixes her with a withering look. A single scoff is all the answer Psyche gets before she picks up her bucket and walks to another tree.

Well. That's no good. But she can't have been the maiden if she was acting like that, could she? Someone else will know. Like that man, over there, trimming a blackberry bush.

"Excuse me—" she starts, but she gets no further. He bares his sharp teeth.

"Can't you see I'm busy? Go bother someone else, hanger-on."

The force of his words slam into her; she flinches. "You don't have to be so rude about it."

"It's rude to bother people at work, wouldn't you say?" he

snaps. "Now go, before your master finds you causing such a terrible ruckus."

He doesn't need to tell her twice. Psyche slinks away, opening and closing her hands as she does. The soothing scents of pine and rose do little to calm her; she resorts to the more mundane processes she learned in school. Focus on the next step, don't catastrophize, try to make it through. Two people hadn't wanted to speak with her, sure, but that doesn't mean everyone will be so recalcitrant.

Maybe the people in the hobbit hole would be more welcoming? Everyone here looks to be busy with their gardening tasks.

She walks straight toward the small home. Should she check the time? No, no, if she does, she's only going to feel more tense, and she has to focus on getting this done. If she checks the time, she's going to imagine Eros still trapped in that cage and it's going to...

Psyche swallows.

She knocks on the door of the hobbit hole harder than she needs to. It swings open at her touch. Inside: soft, orange lantern light, moss coating the walls, and a cadre of gods gathered around tables. Up on a tree-stump and toadstool stage, a woman with petal hair croons into a chrysanthemicrophone. To the left is a living-wood bar, bees flitting from flower to flower along it as the gods sip from their drinks. Behind the counter is...

Zephyr?

Her first godly friend wears a cloak of flowers, but it's most certainly him. That's his pale hair beneath his cap, his mask, and—most importantly of all—his devastatingly charming smile. She watches him juggle no less than five cocktail shakers for a bevy of admirers, male and female, who watch with their heads resting on their hands.

A grin spreads across Psyche's face. This is perfect! She walks straight to the bar, ignoring the looks the others shoot her, and plants her palms on the table. Only when Zephyr pours a tree-woman her glittering violet drink does Psyche try to catch his attention with a wave.

For a moment, when the patrons glare at her, Psyche worries Zephyr holds the fight at the Court of Flame against her—but it is a short-lived fear. He hops with happy surprise and grins, then gives her a big hug.

"Psyche!" he says. "Now what are you doing here, darling? Shouldn't you be charming our resident matchmaker? Your eyes are looking *lovely*, by the way. Will you send Eros my compliments?"

She allows herself a moment of peace in Zephyr's embrace. Iffy planned for the two of them to get together, hadn't she? In a different world, Psyche can imagine it. Being around him makes her feel as if she's fallen into a dream. Hopefully, when all of this is settled, they can spend more time together as friends. Zephyr's far friendlier than any of his fellows.

"I will," she says. In this moment she wants nothing more than to cry into his chest. So much has happened and with so little space to think. Psyche sniffs. "Um..."

"Oh no. Something's wrong, isn't it?" Zephyr says. He

hands her a paper-thin slice of bark to use as a tissue. "Come to the back of the house with me, and we can talk it out."

Before Psyche can protest that he has waiting customers, he gives her two pats on the back and makes his excuses to them. Then he ushers her through another door.

The back of the house, as the case may be, resembles the inside of a mushroom. Gills line the walls, carved away in some places to make space for shelves. The ground springs and squishes with every step. Hard to feel so down when she's walking into a bounce house. Though, then again, don't people break a surprising amount of limbs in those?

The others in the room—a pair of leaf-winged women—turn away as they enter. Perhaps they don't want to bother putting on masks? Or perhaps they, like the others, find something disagreeable with Psyche on principle. Why is it that a den of gods feels so like a high school to her? Back then there were plenty of whispers about the new transfer students—*Outgoing Laura, sporty Cid, and... well. What was her name again...?*

It's beside the point now. Psyche closes her eyes and, as Zephyr guides her to a toadstool seat, pushes the palms of her hands against them.

"It's real bad, huh?" Zephyr says. "Talk to me, Psyche. Whatever it is that's troubling you, you have my word I'll do my best to help."

"You're really okay? Eros told me about the poison, and the fight, and..." Easier to talk about anything other than the obvious first.

"Haven't been better. In fact, some of my colleagues think

it's dashing how close I came to death, and that Passion herself intervened to save me. The whole story's making the rounds. I made sure to throw your name in there, too, of course."

She takes a slow breath. *Focus on the things in front of you, the things you can feel—like the slightly moist but very firm skin of this table.*

"I don't know how much good that's done us," she says. Has she always sounded this pathetic, this small? "Eros is… her mother doesn't like me, because of our oath, and…"

Zephyr's hand covers her. She welcomes the weight. "It *was* a little shocking to see her go through with that. You have to understand she's never shown interest in the long term that way. I can't tell you how many people have asked me if it's true she's off the market. But I've never seen her happier. Every time I see Eros, she asks me about human things to try and understand you better. I had to explain video games to her."

A smile breaks through the gloom. "Teaching her about that stuff is pretty fun. Even if she's uh, not the best at understanding it."

"She's never had to try so hard at it before," says Zephyr. "But for you to look like one of us… Things must have been going well before Her Highness heard?"

All that levity is gone in an instant. Psyche flinches. "I… I broke our oath. I peeked at her face when I swore not to, and that's how… that's why I'm…"

"*Oh.* Oh, Psyche." He squeezes her hand. "It's… Humans are curious, don't hold it against yourself—"

"I'm dead," Psyche blurts. She can't keep it back anymore.

"I died when I saw her, but the parts of our oath that didn't break are keeping me alive. Except that Aphrodite can dissolve what's left of it at any given moment if I don't complete this stupid task she gave me, and—"

"Slow down," Zephyr says. "And don't use Her Majesty's name if you can avoid it. She can hear you when you do that."

Another flinch. Great. Well at least her mother-in-law knows what Psyche really thinks of her now. She shakes her head.

"Her Majesty's always been the jealous sort. It's a sickness of those who reach her rank—almost all of the Court Sovereigns are like that. Except the Queen of the Hearth; I don't think there's a drop of jealousy in that whole Domain." He pauses, takes a breath, squeezes her hand again. "You didn't do anything wrong, Psyche. A girl as charming as you was bound to catch her eye in the worst of ways."

"She wanted to eat me," Psyche whines.

"She eats a lot of girls like you. It's part of how she keeps her beauty. The other part comes in tithes from the other gods. If they fall behind or if they underpay, then she ensures their romantic pursuits go awry, and their personal lives, too. She's like the sun that way—warm from a distance, but all-consuming and merciless the closer you get."

Powerless, all Psyche can do is nod. Who is she to go up against the sun? And yet she can't give up, not now. She opens her eyes, regards her kindhearted friend with determination. "Zephyr, she sent me to get one of those tributes," Psyche says. "Bringing it back to her is my only hope."

He flashes her the sort of smile that makes her forget this

whole thing is a matter of life and death. "Then you're as good as saved. The West Wind has plenty of friends. Who are you looking to see?"

"The Blooming Maiden. Her Majesty said she'd be around here somewhere, but no one wants to talk to me, let alone tell me where she is—"

"The Court of Earth is the Court of Steadiness. They don't like change, and they especially don't like outsiders," Zephyr says. He offers her an arm. "It was cruel of her to send you here knowing that—and fortunate that I happened to be tending bar. Come on, I know just where to find her, and I'll even make the introduction for you."

Psyche takes his arm and sniffles. "Thank you," she says. "We need to be quick."

"Nothing quicker than the wind," he says with a wink. He leads her outside, onto the grass. "Close your eyes and we'll be right there."

He isn't lying. It takes all of a second. In a single rustle of the leaves around them, the air has gone from pine-sap bright to heady and thick with floral tones. Gone is the firmer forest ground, replaced by soft loam. The smell of this place alone is enough to set her at ease—as if she's just imbibed the sweetest of libations.

"Is that the West Wind I see? With a friend, no less!" comes a girl's voice. Hearing her Psyche can't help but smile—she sounds as cheerful as Psyche pretends to be on the internet. "It's so good to see you both!"

"Your Majesty, an honor as always," Zephyr says. "Here

before you is Eros's Oathsworn, Psyche. Though marked by us, she hasn't yet gotten strong enough to view our faces. I therefore kindly request you conceal your beauty, if only for the duration of our conversation. You'll find she comes on important business."

"Passion's Oathsworn! I've heard she's quite the character. Not to worry, I'd never want to hurt her," says the girl. A moment's pause, then: "All is well, Psyche—you can open your eyes now."

When she does, she's greeted by another parade of colors. Flowers everywhere, so far as she can see—a great dome of them overhead, a field of them beneath her feet. The girl before her wears a gown and headdress of the same. Dahlia, echinacea, hibiscus, lily, rose—all find their places somewhere on her raiment. Her hair is the pale pink of first spring, her skin freckled and warm. In place of a mask, she's fashioned a series of small vines that hang before her eyes and nose. Only her mouth remains unconcealed. Like the others, she has sharp teeth, though hers are more like Eros's than Glaucus's.

The Blooming Maiden offers a dazzling smile and a curtsy. "Welcome to my little slice of the Court of Earth! Isn't it lovely?"

"It really is," Psyche says, reverence in her voice. All around there are women in yellow and black with gossamer wings flitting about. Bees, she realizes. "I wish I had more time to look around—you're already being so kind to me, and we've only just met."

"Nonsense, anyone who can cheer up Passion is a friend of mine. You have no idea how sad it is to watch the embodiment of desire sulk at all the gatherings," says the Blooming Maiden. She snaps, and a huge flower opens up into a table right there and then. She plucks a petal from it, rolls it into a cup, and scoops some of the nectar into it. This she offers to Psyche. "Have some ambrosia and be welcome in my home."

It wouldn't be polite to refuse, would it? Psyche tips the petal-bowl to her lips. This must be made from the fruits Eros has been feeding her. Yet this preparation is much sweeter, and much thicker. It slithers down her throat and leaves her feeling fuzzy.

"Thank you," she says. "I'd ask for a tour, but I don't have time. If it pleases Your Majesty—"

"Call me Persephone! Zephyr always does. I don't know why he's being so formal."

"Far be it from me to make presumptions about who can call you by name," says Zephyr with a smirk.

"Persephone," Psyche says. She fetches the box from her coat pocket. "I've been sent here by the Queen of Flames to retrieve her tithe."

"Oh?" says Persephone. She touches a fingertip to her lip. "You know, I thought I'd already given it to her this decade. Isn't she getting a little greedy? I'm sure she could ask the Queen of Queens, but Grandmother is a lot harder to intimidate, isn't she?"

"I'm not sure if that's the case," says Psyche, "but I can tell you it's vitally important to me, and to Eros. If I don't bring this back to her in time, then I'm going to die."

Persephone leans closer to Psyche, staring right into her eyes. The vines sway. Psyche picks a spot on the ground to stare at. Daisies. She's always liked daisies.

"I think I understand now," says Persephone. "That dust I see on you must be the remnants of your Oath, hmm? What a tragedy. Well, I hate to see a girl die before her time, and I'd especially hate for that woman to win. She's just so *demanding*, and she keeps *staring* at me."

Psyche doesn't wait to hear anything else—she holds out the box. "Please, I don't have long to get back."

"Not to worry, I'll be quick. But you and Eros have to come visit me sometime when this is over. We'll have a party!" says Persephone. She takes the box, turns away. Light flashes; a curious rush of air, a plume of smoke. Then the clack of the box closing. When Persephone turns back, she's offering the box to Psyche anew. "There you are."

Psyche takes it, stopping only to check that the lock is firm before tucking it back into her coat pocket. Touching it makes her palms tingle even through the wood. A fraction of godly beauty...

"We'll be by as soon as we can, if everything works out," says Psyche. "I've been telling her she needs more friends."

"Smart girl," says Persephone. "Make sure you stay that way. The Queen of Flames is a tricky one. Zephyr, take her to the gates, will you? I have half a mind to speak to Father about this."

"Your father?" Zephyr says. "Are you... are you certain that's a good idea?"

Persephone shrugs. "Don't you think it's in bad taste for the Queen to be messing with Father's new grandchild?"

Her grandchild? Does that mean Persephone is Eros's aunt? The family tree is already a little confusing—she seems much younger than Aphrodite.

"Your father *will* want to hear about that," Zephyr admits. "All right. Psyche, close your eyes again, I'll get you right back to the gates. And then I've got to join Persephone at the Court of Power. It'll take more than just her word to get through to her father."

"Can't she get there on her own?" Psyche says. She winces. "N-no offense, Persephone. It's just, I don't have much time."

"None taken," Persephone says. "The truth is I'm not powerful enough to leave this Court on my own. Zephyr has to take me. And regardless of whether you make it on time, you're going to need my father's help."

Psyche wraps her arms around Persephone and squeezes her tight. The god makes a surprised sound, but then laughs, and returns the favor.

"You really are unusual, aren't you?" she says. "Not a trace of fear to be seen."

"Oh, I wouldn't say that. But I wanted to thank you, both of you. You've been so kind to me."

Zephyr joins in the embrace. "We're not all awful."

Psyche takes a deep breath. She wants to stay here and have tea with Persephone; she wants to find out more about

Eros from people who know her well; she wants to hide away somewhere there is only beauty.

But she knows she can't.

With one last squeeze, she steps away. Zephyr takes her by the arm, and Psyche closes her eyes.

"Be well, Passion's bride," says Persephone.

And then—the rustle of wind again, the wind whipping through her hair, and it is over. She can hear the car horns outside the botanical garden and feel the air go... flatter.

When Zephyr tells her to open her eyes, she's right back at the gates, with him standing on the supernatural side, and her stuck in the mortal realm.

"Here you go," Zephyr says. "You focus on getting back and keeping Her Majesty occupied. Persephone and I will handle the rest."

"Thank you again," Psyche says. "Hopefully I see you soon."

She turns and glances down at her timer. What she sees almost stops her in her tracks.

Twenty minutes are all that remain.

Anxiety lashes her body to an unseen rack; she feels herself going stiff. No, she can't afford a panic attack. What should she do? What would she tell a client?

Focus on your next step.

All right. Literally and figuratively, then; Psyche walks out of the greenhouse as fast as she can. By the time she's outside it, she breaks out into a run. But to where? What god would help her now?

She makes it out of the gardens themselves and to the

crosswalk. The red light of the Wendy's lends the night an ominous touch. Up ahead, the Prospect Park Zoo, and beyond that, the park itself.

Think, Psyche. There are probably gods of stone, but she doesn't know them; gods of the trees wouldn't want to help her, from what she saw at the Court of Earth. The stars? Do those have gods, too? Could she call out to them? No—they have no cause to help her, either.

The answer comes to her when she bolts across the crosswalk. At the same time, a car peels down the avenue, avoiding her only by skidding to the right. As the lights flash in her eyes and the spray of a splashed puddle coats her fine clothes, she remembers the only other god she knows.

Poseidon.

He wanted to see the Queen of Flames laid low, didn't he? As much as she hates the man, he has good reason to help her. And now she knows well enough to word her request with utmost care.

Standing in the center of the crosswalk, Psyche shouts in frustration, and runs for the park.

How to summon that asshole? Water, probably, though she'll need to find some. Can she make it to the lake from here in twenty minutes? She doesn't have many other alternatives.

The gates are closed—but she climbs onto the stone fence and jumps the iron one.

Never in her life has Psyche been a great runner. No one would ever think her swift or agile, but she *is* determined.

And that certainty will have to carry her.

She's surprised by how little her lungs burn as she sprints through the park. Though when it comes down to it, she shouldn't be—her heart isn't racing anymore, either. Maybe the lack of discomfort is what makes it easier for her to cross the distance without stopping, or maybe it's the single-minded resolve that she will not end this way.

Not that the park patrol is liable to understand.

Their lights flicker on as Psyche crests a hill. The lake is to her right—she can see the bright green algae bloom across it from here. The hill's going to do most of the running for her, but the ranger at the bottom of it will surely try to stop her.

There's nothing for it but to run.

Feet against the pavement, Psyche runs down the hill, momentum threatening to topple her.

It can't. It won't.

First a shout from the ranger: "Ma'am! Stop right there!"

A flash of the car's lights, a shriek of the siren. Still she does not stop.

"Sorry!" she shouts, turning off the path, toward the lake.

"You're gonna be if you don't stop right this second!" returns the ranger. The engine revs.

Still she does not stop. Over the brambles and beneath the trees she runs, hurtling toward the pit of green. God, any other day, the idea of diving into a public body of water in New York City would fill her with unspeakable dread. Tonight she just hopes being mostly dead saves her from whatever's in the water.

High beams flicker on. It's only then that she spots the

second ranger's truck—this one parked by the lake itself. Already the woman has left her vehicle. She stands before the water like a goalkeeper ready to intercept a ball.

Fuck.

In the face of awful odds, in the face of her fear and horror, Psyche lets out a scream.

But she does not stop running—oh no. Instead, she veers *toward* the second van, jumping onto the hood and then onto the roof.

Jumping into the water from here is a foolhardy move. It's too shallow to hold her weight. She's going to break her arm at the very least and probably break more than that. But what other options does she have? And it isn't as if she can die for another five minutes at least.

"Ma'am, get down—"

Fuck, this is going to suck.

Psyche jumps from the roof of the truck. She tries to angle her body toward the water and manages, if only a little. There's about a foot of it where she lands. Not nearly enough to break her fall. She falls straight onto a pile of stones, her shoulder and head alive with pain—but with the water flooding into her mouth, she knows she's already won.

"Poseidon," she says.

Her vision's swimming, her ears are ringing, and the rangers' flashlights tell her she doesn't have long to pull this off.

"Poseidon, you asshole, listen to me," she says. Fuck, the water tastes foul. It takes everything in her not to throw it up. "I'm going to see the Queen of Flame, and I need your help to get there. You told me to…you told me to call on you when I was going to see her. You wanted to see her face. Well, get me there as fast as you can, and you will. Five minutes and you make a fool of her!"

"She's talking to herself. Call the mental services people," says the woman ranger.

Psyche takes a breath and closes her eyes.

"Please," she whispers.

"Ma'am, I don't mean to hurt you—"

The rest is lost in the bubbling of water.

A wave of it rolls over her. As giddy as she is afraid, Psyche shuts her eyes and wraps her arms around herself. Soon the rocks beneath her fall away.

"Bold as ever, I see." Poseidon's voice comes from all around. "What would you do without me, little Psyche?"

"Die," she answers.

"Good that you know the score. I hope you've gotten better at holding your breath."

She doesn't have time to answer. The water sucks her into the depths.

Zephyr's traveling is so gentle as to be unnoticeable. Artemis's is unpleasant, but livable.

Psyche is beginning to think Poseidon can only transport humans in the most horrible, painful ways possible. The water buffets her at every turn. Tentacles coil about her legs only to hurl her in new directions. Salt water burns at her eyes. She feels every twist, every turn.

When at last she's shot out from a geyser beneath the

surface of the Court of Flame, she counts it a welcome release from the pressure. Not even the rough landing upsets her. To have ground beneath her feet at all is so much a blessing that she touches her forehead to it and whispers a thank-you before she bothers opening her eyes.

Poseidon has been true to his oath. The two of them are in the Court of Flame—and better than that, they're in the throne room. Psyche's eyes first find Eros—still trapped within her cage. Her unbeating heart twists at the sight. Yet Eros is reaching out for her the instant they spot one another.

"Psyche! Psyche, you have to get up!"

Easier said than done when she feels this awful—but before she can summon the will to do it herself, a great hand on her back hauls her to her feet. Poseidon stands at her side somewhat smaller than the last time she saw him—a trim eight feet here in place of twenty.

"Go on," he says. "Show me what you came here for."

She doesn't want to look at him, and she doesn't have the time to. Psyche fishes in her pocket for the box. With shaking legs—one of them certainly broken—she limps toward the throne of Love, and holds it aloft.

"Your Majesty," she says. "I've returned... with the box... as you asked."

Aphrodite does not deign to take it herself—her servants lift it to her. She picks it up and studies it, checking the lock.

"I must admit, I am impressed. My brother there is a difficult one to tame. You must have made many interesting friends, hmm?"

"She's done no such taming," Poseidon answers. "All she had to tell me was that I'd get to see your ego take a hit."

Aphrodite's laugh is as painful as it is beautiful. Psyche flinches, but does not falter.

"I didn't open it," she says. "You can check the contents yourself. Please, honor your side of the oath."

"Soooo demanding," Aphrodite says. She rolls her eyes.

And sets the box down on her lap.

"You know, it doesn't matter if I do or not."

"What do you mean?" Psyche shouts. "Open the box! I did it, I did everything you asked of me—"

It is said that the best kind of death is the one you do not see coming. A clean blow to the head can have someone dead before they hit the ground, likewise certain poisons.

Who knew Love to be capable of such a thing?

"You're a minute late, darling."

Chapter Twenty-One

You never forget the way a hospital smells.

It's a strange thing. Not everyone can call it to mind. Many never spend the night in a hospital, nor even enough hours for the smell to be the thing they notice. Yet for those who have spent long nights and hours at the side of their loved ones, or impossible nights of tragedy waiting for news, the smell is one that can never be forgotten.

For months after Psyche's mother died, she could still smell it. No matter how much she washed her clothes, it was there. And it wasn't as if she could just get rid of the clothes—she had spent every single day visiting. It clung like miasma to her entire wardrobe.

Worse—it seemed to spread. First the clothes, then the drawers she kept them in, then finally one day she came home from school and found her bedroom soaked through with it.

That bright, antiseptic smell. The smell of inevitability, and of death.

When she moved to New York for school, Psyche donated

all of her clothes except those she wore on the trip. Rather than buy new ones, she thrifted what she could. The smells that clung to *those* clothes told her of different families and different lives. Cats, cigars, the woods.

Anything but death.

It has been eight years since her mother died, eight years since she last caught a trace of it.

There in the Court of Flame, seated before Aphrodite herself, it is not the splendors of this new world that come to her—but the familiar scent of death.

"No," she whispers. "No, it isn't..."

"You can't be serious. A minute's difference?" says Poseidon.

"I shouldn't expect you to understand, Brother. You'll bend any oath the first chance you get. *Some* of us respect the Law better than that," Aphrodite answers.

They argue. She no longer listens. The rise and fall of their voices is no better than the drone of a doctor and nurse debating how long her mother has to live. She can no more easily forget their tone than she can forget the smell.

No, it is true—she sees it for herself when she checks her phone. A minute too late, one stupid minute. Had she lost it in the ways between? Had she lost it talking to Iffy, or to Zephyr? Had she lost it when she embraced Zephyr and Persephone?

It does not matter. Were she to do the whole thing again, she could not have done it any differently. It would be too contrary to her nature.

Death is coming for her.

There is only one thing that matters now.

She turns from them, the bickering gods, the architects of her destruction. In five steps she has cleared the distance between herself and the great fire of her heart—Eros.

Slumped to her knees in the cage, her love clings to the bars. She pulls with all she has, but the bars do not budge. They cannot budge. There are things in this life that you cannot change, no matter how much you might wish you could. Sometimes it's cancer. Sometimes it's the bars on a cage fashioned by a god to hold his fellows.

"We're all doing the best we can," her mother said.

It seemed facile to Psyche at the time that a woman on her deathbed should say such a thing, but she understands now; she understands.

When all paths lead somewhere grim, you can trudge along with your feet in the mud, or you can march along, watching the sun for as long as you can.

"I'm so sorry," Psyche says. She kneels down before the cage, before Eros, and finds herself smiling. "I wish we had more time together. I wish I got to know you better. There were all these movies I wanted to show you, and books I wanted to tell you about, and places..."

Between the bars, Eros reaches for her bride and holds her tight. Yet even the god's hands are trembling. "I should have protected you."

"You did," says Psyche. "You protected me from so many things. From my own sorrow and awful memories. From a boring, normal life. And from your family, too. You protect so many people and make them all happy, Eros. Please don't blame yourself for this. The last thing I want is to become a sad memory."

Eros sobs—there can be no other word for the awful sound that racks her. Like a drowning woman clinging to driftwood, she holds Psyche. "Psyche..."

Psyche caresses the mask. "He's coming for me, isn't he?"

For there has been a change in the room—a coldness that's swept in like the bitter chill of winter, a wilting of the light. If she looks over her shoulder, she's not sure what she will see. A grim reaper, perhaps? No, nothing so trite as that, she's sure. The gods are nothing if not beautiful.

But it will be death, whatever the form.

"I won't let him take you."

"It's all right," Psyche says. "I...I've been lost before. There were days where I didn't want to die, but if he came for me then, I wouldn't have turned him away. The only thing that kept me going was this...this feeling that I wasn't done yet."

"Psyche—"

"I'll miss my cat. You have to feed her, okay? You have to find someone who'll take care of her. And my sisters, too, you'll have to look after them, even when they don't deserve it. As long as you promise me you'll take care of them, and as long as...as long as you hold me..."

"Psyche, please don't—"

"I think I'll be okay," she finishes. When had she started crying? For her cheeks are slick with tears. "Just keep holding me."

The sobs keep coming, racking Eros's body, each like an arrow finding its mark. Yet all the while she holds as tight as she can. The bars dig into her, calling gold blood from beneath brown skin, and yet she does not notice them.

Psyche cups Eros's face. Then, with a deep breath, she slips the mask away. It falls to the ground with a clatter.

There: the impossible beauty beneath, the face that is a thousand faces, but all with a single fate.

To hold her. To love her.

It doesn't hurt anymore, seeing her like this. Not when she's already dead.

It's time to make this right.

"With love and passion as my witnesses, I swear an oath," Psyche says. How warm Eros's eyes are. "To share our warmth, and our lives, and our love. That my heart will belong to you, all my life and long after it, just as I will look after the heart you've granted me. I swear that I shall be yours as long as you have me, Eros. And I swear that I love you."

As the dawn over the mountains—the light coming into Eros's weeping face.

"I swear," Eros repeats. "I swear that I will love you, and look after you, for the rest of my days. I shall have no other heart but that which you've granted me. I shall share my warmth, my breath, and my life with you—my Oathsworn, my love."

The ground rumbles. Pearls roll across the polished floor as Aphrodite descends from her throne. "Terribly romantic, but it's not going to save you, Psyche," she says. "The terms of our deal were very clear."

"I'm never going to forgive you for this—" Eros roars, but Psyche silences her with a kiss.

"Not now, please not now. Let's just have this moment as long as we can," she whispers.

A moment's hesitation—but the warrior relents, in the end. She presses Psyche's head against her chest.

"Then close your eyes, my love," she says. "He's come."

Oh, Psyche can feel him. Her spine tingles with sorrow, her throat has gone dry. The smell is so thick that it stops up her nose. Yet there is another within that she prefers.

Campfires, laughter, honey.

"Forgiveness will come to you in time, Eros. It's not in Passion's nature to hold a grudge," Aphrodite says. "Dearest Uncle—we've a lovely gift for you today."

Death speaks in the rasp of the dying, in a mournful keen, in a grief so pure that Psyche cannot fathom its words.

Something sharp presses against her back.

"Eros," she whispers. "I love you. You... you really made me happy. Thank you."

Blade meets flesh. Pain like a bolt of lightning shoots through her—her eyes swim with white, her ears ring, her body goes stiff. This is death, is it? This is death...?

No. It must be something else.

For in the wake of lightning there is always thunder—and this time, it is a woman's voice. "Aphrodite."

"My Lord Father!" shouts Aphrodite—so fearful that Psyche does not recognize her at first. "What brings you to the Court of Flame? H-have you come to seek succor and shelter from the weight about your shoulders?"

"Grandfather...?" Eros whispers. Then, pulling Psyche away from Death behind her: "We might yet be saved, Psyche, but you have to keep your eyes closed. Grandfather's splendor is almost too much for *me* to bear."

The pieces fall into place, then, and she cannot resist a smile. "Eros... we will need to thank Zephyr and Persephone, when we next see them."

"They helped with this?" Eros says. She runs her hands along Psyche's back.

Psyche hears the rustling of tableware, footsteps each a storm.

"Quite on the contrary, Aphrodite," says Eros's grandfather. Even hearing her voice sends shivers running down Psyche's body. To her surprise it's a more feminine voice than it is masculine. A rich contralto full of power. Well, gender didn't seem to mean too much to Eros sometimes, so perhaps it's the same here? "My wife and I were having a pleasant dinner when the West Wind brought Persephone to us in a state. Weeping, tugging at my robe, begging me to spare the life of my new grandchild. You can imagine my surprise. And my wife's."

A rich, billowing laugh from Poseidon. "Oh, you're in for it now, aren't you? Sister hates having her dinner interrupted."

"Poseidon remembers well the blow I dealt him when he came crying to me about losing that contest," says Eros's grandfather.

"There's no need to bring my losses up!"

"It keeps you humble," says Grandfather. "Thanatos, old friend—hold back your scythe a moment longer. We must get to the bottom of this matter before we go cutting the girl down."

A rasp, bones in an ice bucket, and the sharpness retreats from Psyche's back. She holds Eros's hand. A sliver of hope so bright it pains her has found its way into her heart.

"Eros!" says Grandfather. "As I cannot trust iridescent Aphrodite, I turn to the aggrieved in this situation. Tell me to the best of your ability why your mother has put you in this and threatened your Oathsworn."

Eros squeezes Psyche's hand. She stands and Psyche follows. If one lets go, will it be breaking some sort of rule? Better to be safe than sorry.

"Honored Grandfather, Lord among the gods, I thank you for your audience," she says. Then: "My Oathsworn's fate was to be my mother's sacrifice. Looking upon her I was struck with a pure love, the likes of which I'd never felt before, and I tricked her into swearing an oath to me to protect her. My mother claims I have been distracted in my duties ever since. When Psyche broke her oath by beholding me, she was left nearly dead."

"Bold for a human, aren't you?" says the newcomer. "I didn't know you liked them so spirited, Eros, or I would have found you a bride sooner. I took you for the soft and gentle type."

"Thank you, Grandfather, but I need no bride other than the one in my arms," Eros says. "Mother placed me in this cage when she found us together so that I could not interfere with her machinations. She sent Psyche on a quest to fetch her tithe from Persephone, expecting her to fail, promising to renew our oath if she returned in time. It was doomed from the start.

"She swore me to silence so that I could not warn her it was useless. All because she disapproved of her. Honored Grandfather, Mother went so far as to incite my siblings against me and attack my Oathsworn. In the mortal plane, no less!"

The fire that enters her when she speaks of this! No one can see her shaking, no one can feel it except Psyche. Psyche's brimming with pride.

"Aphrodite. Have you anything to say in your defense?"

"That girl rejects the fate we laid out for her," Aphrodite says. "She strives for more than she deserves. From the moment she first drew breath, she was meant to be my sacrifice, no more, no less. To ensnare my daughter in this scheming has done Eros a great deal of harm. How am I meant to claim what is mine without hurting her now?"

Poseidon laughs again. "That's the best you can do, really?"

"It isn't a very strong case," agrees the newcomer. "Which makes the solution to all this thankfully very simple. You there, Oathsworn. Psyche, was it? Turn toward me. Mind you do not open your eyes."

Psyche hesitates—but Eros kisses the tip of her ear, and she knows it will be all right.

The newcomer takes four steps. Psyche's skin goes gooseflesh; she feels herself trembling with static energy.

"A fine choice for an Oathsworn. I must commend your taste, Eros."

"Thank you, Grandfather," says Eros. "We will be very happy, if only Mother allows us to be."

"Psyche, I have a question you and only you may answer. In answering it we may settle this business all at once," the newcomer says.

A thousand things flash through Psyche's head—just what is one meant to do when speaking to a god of gods? "Y-yes, Your... Highest... Majesty?"

Laughter, this time from both of the siblings at once.

"Oh, you are precious. For today alone I will permit you to call me Zeus—the name I grant to my family."

"Yes, Lord Zeus," Psyche says. The name alone leaves her tongue tasting of ambition. "What is it you'd like to ask me? I'm eager for us to reach a peaceful solution. We really mean Her Majesty Aphrodite no harm."

"Very well," says Zeus. "Psyche, Thanatos here has a rightful claim to your spirit. If you'd prefer death to an eternity of dealing with Aphrodite's scheming, then you're welcome to it. But if you'd prefer the life you've promised to live with Eros, then answer me this—would you like to be a god?"

Had she any breath left in her lungs, it would surely have left her by now.

"A god...?" she repeats. "I don't understand. What would that mean, to be a god?"

"A fair question," says Zeus. "You would live among us in

these lands forever, free from illness or disease. Only mythic beasts would pose you any threat. We would grant you one of the nascent Domains within the Court of Flame so that you'd remain close to Eros. Now—you would be bound by the Law, and you would be under Aphrodite's sway, but those are the terms of the agreement."

She swallows. A god? She'd never even dreamed of such a thing. Could someone like her really be…?

"The Law," Psyche says. "I, um, I've heard a lot about it, but I don't know…I don't know all of it. No lying, honoring my oaths, and…?"

"If we start listing all its aspects, we're going to be here an eternity," scoffs Poseidon.

"You can only enter the mortal realm when summoned, or when sent there by a higher Domain than your own. And you must heed the orders of the Court to which you belong," Eros says. Then, after a moment's hesitation: "You wouldn't be able to return home. It would be our home, only."

When she searches her thoughts, she already knows the answer.

"My Lord Zeus, I'd like to ask, if I may, for some assurances," she says.

The laugh that comes from Zeus is rather more flirtatious than Psyche expected. "Oh? Very well, bargainer, let's hear it."

"First: I have a cat in the mortal realm, and some plants as well, that I'd like to bring with me. Will you grant them the same as you grant me?"

“A cat! You are bargaining with the Lord of the Gods for a cat!” says Aphrodite. “Do you see what I mean? She is always asking for more than—”

“I happen to like cats. They’re like small lions,” says Zeus. “We’ll grant you your cat as part of your Domain. And I’m certain Persephone can look after your plants. What’s your second request?”

Now she stands straight, for she knows without hesitation that the words she says will break chains.

“That Eros and I be assigned to a different Court,” she says. “It can be a very small one, if you like, one all our own, or one someone else controls, but I think it’s best for everyone if there’s space between us and Aphrodite. You could order her to never interfere with our affairs again, of course, but I don’t think that’s any basis for a relationship, and she could always order us to do something unpleasant. I think it’s safer for everyone if we can meet on equal footing. Besides, Clytie told me Eros’s Domain is nearly big enough to be considered a Court on its own. That’s how this works, isn’t it? Older Domains can become their own Courts?”

Silence throughout the Court of Flame—save a soft gasp of wonder from Eros next to her. Under the pressure of those godly eyes studying her, Psyche neither falters nor sways. If they do not grant her this then they never meant to grant her anything at all.

“People have died asking for less than this, you know,” says Zeus.

“I can imagine,” says Psyche. “But with all due respect,

Lord Zeus, I can't base my decision off what happened to them. I'm not asking for this out of selfishness but out of concern for what is best for everyone here. I can't see a future where placing us in Aphrodite's care leads somewhere other than conflict."

"And if I do not grant you this?"

"Then I will meet my death knowing I did my best," says Psyche.

Another moment's silence—clouds shifting, wind rolling.

"Hmm. I suppose Eros is getting to that age, isn't she..." says Zeus. She sighs. "All right. We'll grant your request. The two of you have leave to form a new Court. Deem it what you like, and consider it my wedding gift."

"Then—yes. I accept. I-I'll...I'll become a god."

Elation, relief—there are a thousand names for the things she feels then, and yet not a one of them seems adequate. As Aphrodite shouts a counterargument and Poseidon breaks down laughing, she finds her way to Eros's arms again.

"Keep hold of your woman," says Zeus. "She's going to be unconscious awhile once we're through."

"I'll never let go of her again," says Eros. She presses a kiss to Psyche's forehead, to her nose, to her lips. "You set us free."

"You did, too," Psyche says. "Hey...you have to help me pick out a mask, okay?"

Eros laughs. "Of course. But the Court's name has to come first."

"That's easy enough," says Psyche. "We'll be the Court of Joy."

She kisses Eros then, as the world goes white.

Epilogue

Some months later, a woman stands on a beach in the middle of the night. On the sand before her she lays a jar full of her own breath, a cat toy, and a copy of *Crystal Dragon Knight XIV*.

"This had better work."

She kneels on the sand. It takes her a few tries to light the candle, but in the end, she manages.

"May the youngest of the gods hear my call and come to my aid. To Love's Bride, to Comfort, I call. Psyche, if you're there…I could really use a friend."

The woman blows the candle out in a single breath.

Then someone takes her hand—a soft hand, and gentle. "You know, I never thought we'd meet up like this."

The woman laughs with her eyes closed. "Neither did I. You really went and did it, didn't you? You absolute madwoman."

"You don't like *Midsommar*, but *I'm* the madwoman?"

"It's a dog-shit movie! Too up its own arse!"

It surprises her how easy it is to argue like this with the god she's summoned.

With her old friend.

"Whatever, Iffy," says Psyche. "I'm really happy to see you."

"Me, too," Iffy admits. She sighs. "I... We have a lot to catch up on, don't we?"

"You can tell me all about it. Listening to people's problems is kind of my thing now. The Soul's a pretty cool Domain, isn't it?" she says. "But... you probably should open your eyes."

"All masked up?" Iffy asks.

There's a touch of sadness then as Psyche hums her assent—but it's gone by the time she speaks. "I think you'll like it."

And, to be fair, she does. The glittering crystals that conceal her old friend's new features are so beautiful they distract from what's happened to her. But there is at least a little of Psyche left. Like the other young gods, she's left the bottom half of her face uncovered.

Iffy swallows. It was always going to hurt, seeing her like this.

Psyche smiles. "It's all right," she says. "Really. I'm happy now, like this. I get to help more people than I ever could before. And, man, you should see the stat spread on this thing. *Prime* drop, I'm telling you. I've got a crazy amount of buffs."

Iffy almost wants to hit her for that, almost, but she shakes it off. Yes—underneath that godly exterior, it's still the same old Psyche.

"All right," she says. "Let's talk."

"How did your talk with Iphigenia go?"

"Hmm. A little intense, but it was good to see her again. And good to help," says Psyche. She pinches Eros's ever-shifting nose, then tosses her ambrosia from their fruit bowl. "She *did* tell me she met you once, though. And, Eri—you just about terrified her."

Eros, newly crowned Queen of Joy, wraps an arm around her Oathsworn's waist and pulls her close. Only with Psyche on her lap does she take a bite of divine fruit. Juice slicks her smiling lips.

"I warned you I was frightening."

"You aren't frightening, stop being dramatic," Psyche says. She leans forward and takes a bite herself—one Eros is happy to offer her. "What you are," she continues, her mouth full, "is *gloomy*. Gloomy Queen of Joy."

But there is nothing gloomy about the way that Eros smiles at her then—nor the tender way she wipes Psyche's lips clean with her thumb. And who would call the kiss that passes between them frightening? For though Passion's teeth are sharp, her kiss is soft as velvet.

Eyes of fire fade to loving cinders. "I've nothing to be 'gloomy' about these days. Not since you joined me here."

And yes, Psyche may now be a god herself—her eyes solid gold, her teeth pointed as Eros's, her blood replaced with something new and inhuman…

But she swears she still feels her heart flutter when Eros looks at her that way. When she says these things.

"You know," she says, smiling, "we got a prayer today addressed to 'Smoldering Joy.' I think it suits you."

Eros hums in thought—then presses a kiss to the curve of Psyche's neck. "It isn't the worst thing I've been called. What was the prayer…?"

"Oh, it's nothing out of the ordinary, but it's from someone who helped me before. I thought maybe we could help out!" she says. "He's a really sweet kid. I used to call him Tief. He wants a date to his sister's wedding, and he was wondering if we could lend him a little extra charm."

A kiss on Psyche's forehead. "Any friend of yours is a friend of mine. We shall lend him my cloak for an evening. But…"

This kiss is far less tender, far less soft—but no less loving.

"Haven't we earned a little time to burn together…?" Eros says.

And who could deny them that?

Look for Bondi's book,
coming in Fall 2025.

Acknowledgments

When I was about seven years old, I wrote a letter to the then-mayor of New York. I begged him to add more books about Greek myth to my little public school's library. I never received a reply, which I found very upsetting, but as a result I started to write my own little stories. So my first thank you must go to the Kafkaesque systems that school librarians must sadly labor against every day. Sometimes all that lack births horny fiction!

More seriously, although writing is a very lonely art form, *publishing* isn't. Any book that you hold in your hands has behind it an entire team of people who have helped it along into existence. This one is no exception. I have a few people in particular I'd like to thank.

First of all, my agent, Sara Megibow—probably the best partner in this business I could have asked for. Sara, thank you for always being on the lookout, always having my back, and always looking ahead.

Leah Hultenschmidt, my editor, put out a call for Greek myth–inspired stories—to which the first version of this story was an ambitious pitch. Imagine my surprise when "what if we did *Eyes Wide Shut*, but Greek, and also threw some fey in there?" actually struck her fancy. Leah, thank you for taking a chance on this frankly wacky concept and coming along for the ride. Your careful attention's made this book way better than I could have imagined.

To my beta readers, Quiel and Rachel Carter, thank you so much for your feedback! Honestly, having your encouragement and flailing throughout kept me going when things got a little difficult at points. Knowing that there were already people who enjoyed this project so much gave me so much confidence. And thank you, as well, for all of the tips about *Final Fantasy XIV*. May your blorbos flourish.

I'd also like to give my tabletop groups a shout-out—Ally, Amy, Iris, Jedi, Joe, and Zee, you guys make getting through the week from a slog into a joy. I always have something to look forward to thanks to our games. Thank you all for being such an incredible, thoughtful group. Please don't kill my meowmeows!

Last, but certainly not least, I'd like to thank my partners. In many ways I would not be here writing this book were it not for their support, thoughtful comments, encouragement, and jokes. To have found such a thing not once but twice is perhaps the luckiest thing in my already very lucky life. Not a day goes by where I'm not grateful for the two of you. I love you both more than words can say. To Charlie and Matt, the reasons I am the person I am.

About the Author

K Arsenault Rivera was born in Mayaguez, Puerto Rico, and has been living in New York since the age of three.

At a compact four foot nine, K is a concentrated dose of geekery. She's incredibly passionate about her interests, including Greek mythology.

You can learn more at:
KArsenaultRivera.com
Instagram @ArsenaultRivera
X @ArsenaultRivera